EQUIVALENT EXCHANGE

NIGHT SHIFT

CHRISTINA C JONES

christina c jones
love, in whatever

AUTHOR'S NOTE

This will be my 50th project.

Fifty.

That's... so much love. So many couples, so many struggles. Weddings and babies and tears and arrangements and friends and businesses, and just... a lot.

Thinking about it brings up a lot of emotions, but mostly, I just feel blessed.

This hasn't been easy. I've loved it plenty, and wouldn't give it up for the world, but mentally, emotionally, even physically, it's been difficult.

But rewarding, still.

Kinda like a relationship. ;)

To my friends and family, thank you for offering six years worth of shoulders to both lean and cry on, for believing in and buoying me, for being the kind of light that refused to let the dark creep in too far.

My betas, present and former, new and old, thank you for lending me your time and your thoughts, preparing me for whatever I'll get from the masses.

My peers, for supporting me, loving on me at these events, sharing me with their readers. Thank you.

Readers... man, some of y'all have been rocking with me a long time. You picked up Love and Other Things and have been on my side ever since, and I appreciate you so, so much for it. That's not to leave those of you I've picked up along the way out! Maybe you read me for the first time this year, or you haven't liked every project, or you only like a few things I've written - I appreciate every purchase or page read, every listen on audible, the likes and comments on posts, retweets and reviews.

I see you.

And you are so, so appreciated.

I've been so blessed to explore my God-given gift for six years. I have no idea what's next on my path, but whatever it is, I'm excited for it!

-Christina C. Jones

ONE

KERIS

I *needed* a drink.

Not like a glass of wine to decompress after work, but like... a *drink*, to dull my overactive senses from the stink of everything that could go wrong, doing exactly that.

It was *all wrong*.

But I ignored the nagging voice of the angel on my shoulder – Natalie – and leaned fully into yet another bad decision.

Letting a glass of whisky make it *all right*.

I ignored my cell phone buzzing in my pocket in favor of a long sip. My eyelids flickered closed as the liquor slid down my throat, simultaneously cool and warm. It was good whisky, oaky and sweet, not that shit that burned your taste buds and got you too loose, too fast. Personally, I preferred a slower buzz.

My phone rang again, and I took another sip.

The timing was too perfect for it to *not* be Natalie, utilizing her annoyingly acute sense of when I was fucking up. From experience, I knew once she started calling, she wasn't going to stop. I knocked back the rest of my glass and slid off the barstool, finding solid footing on my heeled boots before I made my way outside, in search of quiet.

Only then did I go into my pocket for my phone.

I peered up both sides of the streets as I pressed it to my ear, waiting for my friend to answer. It was starting to cool off now, especially at night, driving the bustling crowds that had dominated summer inside for shelter. It wasn't empty, but enough that I had space to pace the sidewalk for the duration of a conversation I didn't want to have.

"*Why aren't you answering your phone,*" Natalie demanded, picking up after the second ring. I knew she'd had her phone in her hand, watching it light up with my name, "punishing" me by making me wait an extra few seconds before she answered.

"I was a little preoccupied." I stared down at the scuffed toe of my designer boots, feeling none of the rage I would've two weeks ago over such a thing.

One week ago.

Maybe the liquor was already kicking in, or maybe the shit didn't really matter.

"You've been drinking."

I frowned, bringing my gaze back up to the neon sign bearing the name of the bar. "And you know this... *how?* Are you watching me?"

Natalie sucked her teeth, so loud and clear that even through the phone, I felt like she was right beside me. "Nobody has time to be *watching* you, though I have considered hiring a babysitter for you. To answer the question – you always refer to your *lush* activities as being "preoccupied," Keris."

"So, I have a tell, and you just weren't gonna say anything?"

"Saying something now, boo."

"Only 'cause I asked. What do you want?" I asked, and I couldn't hear it, but I knew she let out a deep sigh.

"To save you from yourself," she quipped. "But since I know that's not happening, I'd settle for you letting me know you're okay?"

An unladylike snort burst from my throat. "Far from it. You know that."

"I do, I just..." This time, her sigh was loud enough for me to hear. "How are you feeling?"

"Like an atomic bomb went off in my life. You?"

"*Keris.*"

"*What*, Nat?" I laughed, but it felt... hollow. "I don't know what you want me to say."

"I want you to say you're going to go home and get in bed, but not stay there too long without eating, and not keep yourself in a drunken stupor to cope with your current... situation."

"The only thing I can promise is that I'm definitely not doing that."

Nat huffed. "*Duh.* A girl can try though, can't she?"

I scraped my teeth over my bottom lip as I stepped backward, pressing into the rough bricks of the building. "I... I appreciate you trying."

"Send me your location. And text me when you get home."

"Okay," I agreed. As vital as Natalie was in my life, I had to give her *something*, and besides that... a little culpability couldn't hurt. With her on my mind, knowing how worried she'd be, knowing she'd be waiting on that text, knowing how she'd feel if it never came... I'd do right by my friends even when I wouldn't do it for myself.

Once I was off the phone, an almost foreign desire to *just go home* nagged at me. Mostly because *home* wasn't that anymore, and the place I had to call by its name... that place made me want to drink more.

It was the only thing I had though.

The only thing that was still mine, besides piles of material bullshit I'd gladly trade just to have some normalcy back in my grasp. If only...

I laughed to myself, shaking my head as I slid my phone back into the rear pocket of my jeans. There wasn't a damn thing funny except the complete ridiculousness of me wanting "normalcy", as if I hadn't been rejecting it for the last fifteen years of my life.

Every decision colored by a singular focus on not falling victim to the life I'd been prescribed. I wanted to be *different*.

When I laughed this time, it was *at* myself.

Sure, my adult life had gone differently than the struggle I grew up with – a generational struggle I'd been so desperate to escape. Tunnel vision was a bitch though, because I'd simply ended up in a different, deceptively worse reality. The shiny, insidious veneer of a perfect life – the closet, the man, the house, the accounts, the job.

Everything I was told would *never* be mine.

I just *had* to prove her wrong.

"Home" was just a block or so away, which was how I'd ended up at this bar in the first place. *Night Shift* had been the closest spot that was still open, so it won by default. Before, I'd have met my desire for a drink at my fully stocked home bar or visited the exclusive rooftop bar in my building.

Neither of those options were open to me anymore.

Now... I did my drinking at what I'd assumed would be a dive bar but turned out to be much nicer than expected. With everything swirling in my head, I needed another drink now.

The first hadn't done enough to dull my senses.

When I stepped back inside, my barstool of choice was still empty – a little surprising in the loud, crowded bar. The singular bartender from before - a gorgeous Black woman who'd taken one look at my face and immediately poured me a shot – had been joined by a new guy, who was apparently responsible for my side of the bar. The woman was at the other end, grinning and basking in the attention of a group of firefighters who'd gathered at the bar.

"I need another Macallan down here," I called to the male bartender, whose head was down, looking at something on his phone instead of tending to customers. I propped my elbows on the cool polished wood of the bar as he looked up, eyes narrowed, looking for the source of the demand.

I raised my fingers in acknowledgment, and his expression focused into a wolfish grin as he zeroed in on me – a look I was all-too-used to getting. A response I'd carefully cultivated, actually – brows and lashes and professional hair care, a grueling gym schedule, regular appointments with my esthetician, a breast lift. All part of the illusion.

He stopped halfway down the bar to pour my drink, giving me a chance to do a little objectifying of my own. His weathered gray tee-shirt fit close against the contours of his body, with *Night Shift Brewery and Bar* across his broad chest in bold, chipped letters. Thick biceps stretched the arms of his shirt, showing off smooth skin the same color as clover honey, punctuated with occasional deep black tattoos.

Mischievous eyes, a sculpted nose that could've, maybe, been broken a time or two. Full lips, the top one partially bisected with a scar that ran up the side of his face. A light dusting of salt and pepper over a neatly trimmed beard, and a fresh-looking, deep-waved caesar.

Shit.

What a man.

"Macallan, huh?" he asked, sauntering over. When he reached me, he didn't hand over the whisky – he kept the glass in his hand while he waited for a response.

I lifted a shoulder. "Something wrong with that?"

He grinned, scraping his teeth over his bottom lip. "Nah, not at all. Just... a little different for most women."

"I'm not most women."

"Clearly," he agreed. "Why Macallan though?"

"It's smooth."

His eyebrows went up. "Cheaper whiskys that are as smooth."

"I like to feel fancy."

The grin came back. "Oh. Well, in that case..."

He winked at me as he lifted my drink to *his* mouth and downed it, then moved back to the rows of liquor against the lighted back wall of the bar. Glass beer bottles with different names printed on plain stickers where the most prominent things on display, but he didn't reach for any of those. I watched, brow furrowed, as he pulled a bottle from *way* up top.

I recognized the tan label and inky black Japanese symbols that decorated the front.

"I'm not feeling *that* fancy," I warned as he poured the *Yamazaki* into a fresh glass for me, and the other glass too, presumably for himself.

His eyes came back to mine, his marbled irises matching the whiskey as they caught the light. "Don't worry sweetheart – this one's on me."

He slid the glass across the bar to me, then picked up his own, not lifting it to his mouth until I'd lifted mine. I didn't swallow it back like I had with the cheaper whisky – I pulled it into my mouth to savor it like it deserved.

When my gaze drifted back to the bartender, I found him staring, his eyes narrowed like he was trying to solve a puzzle. "You were here last night too, weren't you?"

"You caught me," I answered with a nod, then finished off my drink. "Might be back tomorrow too."

"You really like this bar that much, or are you just drinking something away?"

I pulled in a sigh, pushing it out at the same time I pushed my glass back across the bar. "Let's call it both."

He gave me a nod of ascension and poured another two fingers of *Yamazaki* in my glass. I didn't care if this one was "on him" or not.

Just in case it wasn't though, I sat back and savored it as a gaggle of servers came up, rattling off drink orders they needed to be filled. I watched, enthralled, as he deftly put his share of the orders together – craft beers and long pours and cocktails garnished with fruit. While he worked, the young servers giggled and flirted, which was how I learned his name.

Laken.

I'd never heard it before, but somehow it was fitting, especially with the hint of Louisiana twang I detected when he spoke. *Laken* flirted back, not as aggressively as what they were giving him, but still... enough to kill the possibility brewing in the back of my mind of engaging a *different* vice as an escape from my sad-ass reality.

I went into the inside pocket of my leather jacket for my wallet, pulling out a card to put down on the bar, signifying that I was ready to pay up and go.

Laken retrieved it, once he'd sent the servers off with their orders, taking it with him to the register at the middle of the bar.

I finished off my drink while I was waiting and watched the crowd instead of watching him. The bar patrons were a mixed bag – professionals, students, cops, nurses and doctors, the firefighters up front. There were tables and booths, a loud ass digital jukebox, pool tables and dartboards. Every wood-grain surface was oiled and polished, obvious signs of the care that went into this place.

Not at *all* a dive like I'd expected.

"Ms. Bradford," I heard, and looked up to find Laken back at the bar in front of me. "This was declined," he informed, loud enough for only me to hear. "You got another plan for paying your tab?" he asked, with a sly wink.

Confused, I held my hand out for the card. As soon as I saw the front of it, my face went hot – I knew exactly what had happened.

Walter had happened.

"Sorry," I muttered, my hands shaking with barely suppressed rage as I pulled out my wallet again, making sure this time to retrieve a card attached to an account that bore *only* my name.

Thank *God* I'd been wise enough to get one.

This time, when Laken came back to me, it was with my card and a receipt to sign. It didn't escape my notice that I'd only been charged for the Macallan. Instead of arguing about it, I put an extra-generous tip on the receipt, then opened my wallet to put everything back.

I was so shaken up by the declined card - a card Walter must have canceled – that I ended up spilling half the contents of my wallet on the bar. Laken helped scoop it up to hand to me, but slipped a business card away from the pile.

"*Keris Bradford Design.* You're a graphic designer?" he asked, as I returned my wallet to my jacket.

My eyebrows went up. "Uh... that's what the card says, isn't it?"

"It is," he chuckled. "You mind if I keep this?"

"No, not at all," I shook my head. It was an old card, from before my most recent job and title. I wasn't even sure the contact information was still valid, but... it didn't need to be.

I slid off the barstool, checking my balance before I put my full weight on my feet. Laken's eyes were still on me, instead of him moving on to other, younger pursuits, so I met his gaze, raising my eyebrows.

"What are you about to get into?" he asked, propping his elbows on the bar and leaning across.

"My bed," I told him. "What are *you* about to get into?"

"Your bed. Maybe. Hopefully?"

I laughed, shaking my head. "I think you have other responsibilities right now. Didn't you *just* get to work?"

"Nah – I was filling in a gap," he explained, then pointed behind him to where two new bartenders had joined the area behind the bar. The woman from earlier was gone. "I'm free."

Again, I shook my head.

I wanted to say I wasn't that girl, but I'd been with Walter for over a decade, all the way up until a couple of weeks ago. Had my feelings shifted well before the actual split?

Yes.

But I hadn't dated, hadn't even considered another man since the day I *met* Walter.

I had no idea what I was. What I would or wouldn't do.

A one-night stand had crossed my mind when I first saw Laken, yes. A fleeting thought, one I knew better than to give any energy to.

I needed to go home.

"Home".

I needed to let Natalie know I was safe, and take a hot ass bath, and get some sleep, and finally start trying to figure out how the hell I was going to rebuild my life.

But...

"Not my place," I told him, shoving my own objections away from my mind. Not only would I likely suffer some sort of mental break trying to have sex in my "home", but I also didn't want him knowing where I lived.

I had a black eye.

A very, *very* visible one, and I knew this man wasn't blind. He saw my battered face, knew exactly how much liquor I'd been served, knew I had a credit card get declined... and he still wanted to fuck me.

It didn't exactly set the impression of a standup guy.

But... I didn't *need* a standup guy.

What I *needed* was escape, release. What I *needed* was someone to fuck me until it was blissfully, mercifully, the only thing I felt, the only thing I knew existed.

I wholeheartedly believed he was up to *that* task.

A smile came over Laken's face – wide and white, a little crooked. Panty-wetting perfection that would've convinced me if I wasn't already.

"That's fine – I've got a place right upstairs," he pointed, as if I could see through the ceiling of the bar. "Meet me over by the bathrooms."

He shot me another wink and turned to head off, disappearing in the entryway behind the bar.

This was the perfect time for me to come to my senses, to *not* sleep with a stranger, to *not* engage in risky ass behavior when I knew better.

I *knew* better.

I really did.

With a deep sigh, I started moving, with the exit right in my sights. As I moved along, I passed one of the servers who'd been flirting with Laken. I stopped, getting her attention with a smile.

"Hey... can you point me to the bathroom?"

TWO

KERIS

I expected... a dingy bachelor pad.

Needed it, maybe, to set a mood that went along with what I was feeling.

Rank and run down... a fucking mess, honestly.

So, when I followed him upstairs and found an apartment that rivaled the one I'd banished myself from a few weeks ago, I had to take a second.

I had to take a *few* seconds.

When I asked, he pointed me to a bathroom laced with the natural stone and brushed steel finishings of my dreams, and it made it hard to breathe. *What the hell have I walked into?*

I peered at myself in the mirror, then used a few handfuls of cold water to try to knock the half awake weariness from my face.

It didn't work.

The only thing that *would* work was a tube of concealer and a heavy hand, but I hadn't touched my makeup bag in days. At first, I'd

11

been eager to hide the bruising that told the world *something* had gone massively wrong in my life. I didn't want the stares, the whispers, the quiet inquiries about if I was okay.

No.

I wasn't fucking okay.

I was, however, incredibly tired.

Too tired to pretend I was fine.

Not that Laken gave a shit – I was just some passably-attractive chick he very *easily* picked up in a bar. I was still convinced that where men were concerned, you just had to pass a small test of their five senses. Soft *enough*. Pretty *enough*. Quiet *enough*. Smell good *enough*. Taste good *en*—wait... who the fuck was I kidding?

Most men were too lazy - or selfish, or both - for that one to even matter.

With that in mind, I left the bathroom to find Laken in the open kitchen, pouring glasses of wine.

I cranked an eyebrow. "Seriously? More liquor is the *last* thing I need," I told him.

His response to that was to smirk and hold up both glasses, letting me choose which one, if either, I wanted.

Of course I wanted one.

I accepted the glass and sat down, admiring the beautiful granite counters and impeccably honed cabinets and... *him*. He'd taken off the shirt, revealing a dusting of fine curly hairs across his chest, and sculpted pecs with flat brown nipples I wanted to lick. He was solid, with his jeans riding low enough that the dip leading to his groin was on prominent display.

Laken rounded the counter with his own glass in hand, expertly sipping as he walked. He took the seat beside me, turning on his stool to face me.

"What happened here?" he asked, his brow furrowed as he took my chin in his free hand, angling my face to see the fading bruise.

I shook my head. "Didn't come up here to talk about that, and I'm not about to." I pulled my glass to my lips, draining the contents in one gulp – something I immediately regretted once my tipsy brain caught up to my taste buds. It was *good* wine, the kind that needed to be savored.

"So what did you come for?"

"You *know* what I came for," I countered, watching as he drained his glass too. "You don't have to get me *drunker*. I've already agreed to it."

"Not trying to get you drunk – I just like to treat my guests well."

I smirked. "Don't bother. Just... get more naked."

Laken put his glass down, then ran his chilled fingertips over my collarbone, that simple touch so potent that burned all the way to the pit of my stomach, making me clench. "You first."

I knew when to follow instructions, and this was one of those moments – I pulled my jacket off, baring my shoulders and arms before I tossed it across the counter. Made a big deal of unzipping my boots and pulling them off while still seated. Took off my silk tank top, laying it on top of my jacket.

Laken's heated gaze stayed locked on me the whole time, drinking me in as I removed one item after another. When I stood to unbutton my jeans, he grabbed me by the waistband, dragging me into the space between his open legs. He unbuttoned and unzipped them for me, pushing the tight-fitting fabric over my ass and down my thighs.

"What are your thoughts on... kismet?" he asked, as he bent to push my jeans further down. They fell the rest of the way on their own, and I stepped out, anchored by his big, calloused hands on my hips.

"What?" I asked, too distracted by the growing bulge in his lap to give a shit. He smelled good – *too* good - with the whisky and wine on his breath, and that end-of-day aroma of deodorant and salt and cologne that some men wore so very well.

"Destiny," he explained. "Fate. Is that something you believe in?"

My eyebrow went up as I reached behind me for the clips that held the band of my bra together. "Is this some corny ass way of you claiming you're about to make me see God or something?"

He laughed, and the way the sound rumbled in my chest... the answer didn't matter.

I unclipped it.

"No," he answered, catching my hands before I could pull the garment away. "I'm really asking. Do you believe in it?"

"I don't." I pushed his hands away so I could take off the bra, revealing my breasts – something that would hopefully get this train back on track. "Is that gonna be a problem?" I asked, already knowing the answer from the amazed glint in his eyes as his hands came up to cup my breasts.

His thumbs went immediately to the delicate platinum hoops that pierced my nipples, taking advantage of their hyper-sensitivity to bring them to near-immediate stiffened peaks.

"Not at all," he said, and then his mouth was on me – my whole areola disappeared between his lips, his tongue stiff and perfect against my hard nipple, playing with the ring.

My hands went to his head, the pads of my fingers pressed firm against the soft imprints of his waves, keeping him in place as he tongued me. My head fell back, breath caught in my throat as he tugged both rings at the same time – one with his fingers, the other with his teeth. I shuddered when he let go, overwhelmed by the unexpected abrupt sensation.

He gave me this sexy, mischievous grin as he stood, bringing his size into clear focus for me. I could tell he was tall at the bar, but I was too – it didn't usually impress me. Laken though, still had at least five or six inches of height over me, forcing me to tip my head back to look at him.

"I'd like to taste your pussy," he told me, as he unbuttoned and unzipped his own jeans. I hadn't seen him take his shoes off, but they must be somewhere with his shirt – he was barefoot when he kicked his jeans away. "Is *that* gonna be a problem?"

I gave him a slow shake of my head as he shifted our position so that my back was against the counter, and he lowered himself to his knees in front of me.

Supplication.

That was what this position usually meant.

This felt like something else though.

Even standing above him, *I* was the one in deference, standing completely still except to follow his unspoken commands as he pulled my panties down my legs, taking away my last defense against complete vulnerability. I was completely naked, half-drunk, in a stranger's apartment, utterly stripped of my dignity.

It was *shameful.*

Wholly opposed to the way my grandmother raised me.

I closed my eyes as Laken swept the pads of his fingers up the sides of my thighs, then down the fronts, to my knees. He pushed my knees apart, spreading my legs wide as he brought his face closer to me. He put his nose against the inside of my thigh, inhaling as he traced a path up to my pussy.

I had to grip the edge of the counter to keep myself upright.

I *had* to open my mouth, had to force myself to breathe, had to simply give in to how deliciously *wrong* this was – yielding was the only real option with my clit in Laken's mouth, basking under the careful attention of his tongue. His calloused fingers dug into my flesh as he gripped my ass, holding me in place to acquaint himself with the only part of me that mattered to either of us at the moment.

Every bit of wetness that escaped down my thighs, he chased with his tongue, catching the drip and following the path it had taken back to my center. He wasn't scared to put his whole face in it, wasn't scared to have me all over him. His nose teased at my clit as he licked me, every inhale and exhale of his amplified breathing sending a delightful stream of air over my sensitive flesh.

I arched away from the counter, grabbing his shoulders for reinforcement as he pushed two fingers into me, deliberate and slow.

So delectably slow.

With his mouth on my pussy, and his gaze locked with mine, he investigated and explored until he was able to press those fingers into exactly the right spot, a spot that set off an electric surge of pleasure that hummed through me. He focused on my clit, sucking then licking, sucking then licking, back and forth as he stroked me with his fingers.

Somehow, he pushed in closer, burying his face deeper.

I didn't know or care how he was breathing – only cared that he didn't stop what he was doing with his mouth. My lips parted for some kind of sound, but I didn't have the air to let it out – I'd barely breathed since he touched me, and barely could now. It came in short pants, growing more and more shallow as Laken pulled me toward nirvana.

Pleasure coiled deep in my belly, making my stomach muscles contract and pull as my walls constricted around his fingers. Gripping, trying to keep him near and make sure he didn't stop. I let my head fall back again as he slurped greedily from my pussy, with all the zeal of a man half-starved.

And then he pushed me over that cliff.

Feeling, sight, and sound, all blended together into nothing for that powerless moment of bliss, where I was falling, falling, falling, feeling only satisfaction and release and perfection.

Until reality dashed me against the rocks at the bottom.

He's going to expect me to return the favor.

I hadn't even caught my breath yet and Laken was back on his feet, already grabbing the back of my neck. Muscle memory softened my knees, already prepared to be urged toward the ground for my turn at the altar. His long fingers raked in the hair at my nape, and I stumbled a bit as he yanked me in a direction opposite of what I'd expected.

He pulled me *up*, towards his mouth.

I was hyper-conscious of his hardness against my belly as he covered my mouth with his. He smelled like me, and he smelled like him, and the combination was pungent and intoxicating. So much so that I didn't think twice about opening for him when he probed the seam of my lips with his tongue. I moaned when he lapped into my mouth, tasting like whisky and tasting like wine, and tasting like pussy and tasting like... bliss.

He put his tongue in my mouth and his fingers back in my pussy, ruling both in little flicks and deep plunges. In what felt like seconds, I was coming again while he swallowed my moans, then licked me off his fingers, then went down to lick me clean, again, while my thighs trembled, and my knees threatened to give out underneath me.

He left me standing there while he ambled toward the couch. Once he was there, he turned to look at me and lifted a hand, summoning with one quick motion.

I immediately complied, willing and ready to kneel in front of him.

I *wanted* him in my mouth at this point.

Laken slid those black boxer briefs down his hips, unleashing his dick – thick and beautiful. He caught me by the elbows just as I was about to drop down, pulling me with him to the blanket already draped over the couch.

He sat down and picked up a condom from the side table – I took it from his fingers, opening it and putting it on him before I climbed into his lap. I sank onto his dick without hesitation, relishing the pleasurable discomfort of my pussy stretching to accommodate him. Laken groaned like he was in pain, grabbing the back of my neck again to bring my face to his.

This time, he didn't kiss me.

He just... stared at me like he was looking for something, locking those expressive honey-brown eyes with mine. He didn't say anything, and when I tried to move, tried to relieve some of the pressure of his dick lodged inside me, he dropped his free hand to my hip, gripping and keeping me still.

"*What?*" I asked, in a strangled half-yell half-whisper that I barely recognized as my own voice. I *needed* to move, to ride him.

He smirked. "You're beautiful, Keris. Really fuckin' beautiful."

I snorted, which made my pussy contract around him.

Made both of us let out an audible moan.

"I'm already giving it to you, Laken. You're literally inside me. You already landed the shot."

His gaze roved over my face, landing on my lips before he met my eyes again, and used his grip on my hair to pull me even closer, so close his lips grazed mine when he spoke.

"That's exactly how you can tell I really mean it."

He released his hold on my hip, just enough to let me know I should start moving. So I did. He took my mouth in a bruising, hungry kiss, devouring my initial reaction to the heavenly friction of riding him.

It was *so* delicious.

And *he* was so delicious, not even flinching as I dug my nails into his shoulders as I moved. He'd finally stopped kissing me, finally letting me breathe, choosing instead to watch me as I rode his dick.

He leaned back, arms stretched across the back of the couch like a king. His expression was a heady mix of lust and awe and full-blown reverence. I wanted to deserve being looked at that way, so I rocked, and twisted my hips, and bounced, and swayed, gave his dick the ride of a lifetime.

Every move, even the slightest shift of my hips was tailor-made for his pleasure, but *goddamn* it was good for me too. I was trying my best to not give into the driving urge to just ride him with abandon and cum all over him, but I felt like I had a point to prove.

And maybe he did too.

His thumb and forefinger clamped down on my nipple rings, tugging *hard*. So hard I yelped aloud. I met his gaze with fire in my eyes, but he had nothing for me but a grin as he tugged harder – so hard I felt it between my legs, making my clit ache and throb so intensely that I stopped riding to feel *that*.

"Did I tell you to stop moving?"

No.

He didn't.

So I started again, riding him harder than before, and faster. I watched the expression on his face shift from amused to very, very serious, as he pulled *harder*, twisting the rings and my nipples between his fingers. It hurt like hell, but it hurt *so good*, so I just kept riding, and riding, until finally... he let them go.

The rush of pleasure was too much to bear.

"*Ahhh!*" I gasped, faltering on the steady rhythm I'd created. My nails dug further into his shoulders, pushing dents into his skin as he propped his head back on the couch, watching me with half-lidded eyes.

"*Shit*," he groaned, grabbing a handful of ass and squeezing hard. His other hand went between my legs, pinching my clit just like he'd done with my nipples. "Your pussy is... *fuck*," he growled. He kept a hand between my legs, continuing his sweet torture as he started meeting me with upward strokes of his own, deep and hard.

My nipples were still tingling with the sensation of returned blood flow when he released my clit. As *that* fresh wave of pleasure rushed through me, he used both hands to grab handfuls of my ass as he drove into me, harder, faster, deeper, creating an onslaught of stimulation that brought tears to my eyes. He pulled me down onto his dick, holding me there, making me feel every inch before he pulled back, just to stroke me like that again.

And again.

And *again*.

"*What – are you – trying – to do – to me?*" I managed to get out.

He crushed his mouth over mine for another kiss, then pulled back to answer the question with my lips against his. "I just want you to cum, sweetheart."

Not even five seconds later, I did, as if my body worked at his command. The orgasm crashed into me, snatching away my senses. I couldn't see, couldn't hear, but I could feel Laken's overwhelming presence everywhere, consuming me as my body trembled and quaked. He growled into my neck as his own release came, with another stroke as deep as he could get, which set off another round of tremors for me.

I closed my eyes as he locked his arms around me, urging me to rest against his chest. My heart was still pounding, breath still unsteady, and I could barely feel my limbs – there was nothing I could do to resist.

Just for a few minutes though.

I had to get out of there.

I planned my exit while we caught our breath – taking my moment as soon as he got up to dispose of the condom. As soon as he was out of sight I raced for the kitchen, dressing as fast I could – I didn't even bother with my underwear, just shoved them in the pockets of my jacket.

He'd promised he would be right back.

I wasn't waiting around to see.

THREE

LAKEN.

K *eris Bradford Design.*
Over and over, I sent the luxury stock of the business card through my fingers in an absent-minded flip. I'd stared at it long enough already, as if peering at the neatly printed sans-serif font would make some new information, some new understanding, come floating up from the depths to settle on the surface.

Not so.

Of course not.

Minimalism seemed to be her preferred aesthetic, at least based on the design for her website. Her portfolio was vibrant, and full of color, but the site itself was all soft grays and whites, accented occasionally with inky black.

Her chosen color palette.

As little as I knew about her, I still had the sense that this fit the woman I'd met three nights ago well. The brightness of it all giving the appearance of openness, the gray providing a hint of intrigue, and the black... that was full-blown mystery.

From the time my eyes landed on her at the bar, I'd never gotten the impression that Keris was the type of woman to be interested in laying around to cuddle after. True to that impression, she got what she came for and dipped, which was... far from what I'd become accustomed to.

She was a change of pace.

One that has no plans of ever seeing your ass again, I thought to myself with a chuckle, finally tossing the card onto the polished surface of my desk. I'd forgotten about the card, until it showed up this morning in the tray on my dresser the cleaning service always used to return anything left in my pockets in the laundry.

I knew I'd see her again – that wasn't in question, not in the slightest. I just hadn't known the details. Now though, I had a very clear plan forming in my mind, one that would put – and hopefully keep – Keris Bradford in my orbit until I changed her mind.

She *had* to believe in kismet, if this was going to work.

"Are you still in here mooning over the brawler?" Lark asked, barging unannounced as usual into my office. Her leonine natural hair was pulled up on her head – a style that accentuated the premature grays she was getting more of every day.

I wasn't going to say *that* shit out loud though.

"The brawler?" I asked, lifting an eyebrow as she ambled up to the desk, dressed to tend the bar in ripped up jeans and an equally destroyed *Rookie Red Ale* tee shirt.

"Are you pretending you don't remember the beautiful woman with the black eye that you took upstairs the other night?" she asked, pulling her pretty face into a disbelieving scowl. Her hot-pink glossed lips pursed. "You've been moody and distracted ever since."

"I know who you're talking about." I couldn't deny the "moody and distracted" thing, so I didn't bother. "I'm questioning the nickname."

Lark grinned. "*Oh*. Yeah. I prefer to think she's in a fight club, over the more likely event that some bastard hit her in the face."

Just the mention of that possibility made my jaw twitch. The bruise on Keris' face had obviously aged some, but her light brown skin was fair enough that it was still prominent – especially since she hadn't cared to cover it with makeup. That, at least, made me feel like she wasn't afraid of whoever had done that to her, but her reluctance to speak about it set off red flags.

I didn't care that it wasn't my business – not when as far as I was concerned, Keris was *absolutely* my business now.

"She must have *really* put it on you, big brother," Lark teased, propping her hip against the desk. "You're looking pretty murderous right now."

At the prompting of those words, I released fists I hadn't even realized were clenched, looking up at my younger sister.

She laughed. "*Wow*. Okay seriously... you want to tell me what's up?"

I pushed out a sigh, picking up the business card again. "Phoenix."

Reflexively, Lark's fingers went to her opposite wrist, rubbing the tattoo there. "*Seriously?*" she muttered, even as her lips pulled into a smile. "And you're taking it seriously?"

I shook my head. "Learned my lesson," I told her, pointing at the scars that crisscrossed the left side of my face – healed, but still conspicuous. "When he talks, I listen."

"Hasn't been wrong yet," she agreed, nodding. "What'd his cryptic ass give you in a dream *this* time?"

My fingers brushed the thick paper, lingering over the raised letters of her name. "Not much. Just that... she'd be marked for me."

Lark frowned. "Are you serious, Laken? That woman's face was evidence of a crime not a sign from our dead brother."

"You must not have noticed," I mused, tracing a shape around the card with one finger.

She propped her hands on her hips. "Noticed *what?*"

23

I pulled up my arm, turning *my* wrist to face her – we had the same ink there, a memorial to Phoenix. As she watched, I held it up over my eye, and her lips parted as she understood what I was saying.

"Well I'll be damned," she whispered, crossing her arms in front of her.

I put my wrist down, letting out another sigh as Keris' face came clearly in my mind's eye. Round nose and full lips and high cheekbones, a blonde, layered bob that framed her pretty caramel face. And that fucking bruise, blooming around one big brown eye. Wider on both sides, like wings, with a thin thread of broken capillaries extending from the bottom, like a tail. Above her eye, up into her eyebrow, her thick eyelashes partially obscured another part of the bruise, rounding up and off to the side.

The head.

She may not believe in kismet, or destiny, or whatever.

That didn't mean it wasn't happening.

"Well I'll be damned. Your ass is hellbent on bucking the system, aren't you?"

My biceps strained as I looked up from the boxes of vacuum-sealed hops I was moving into the industrial-grade refrigerator. They were a vital part of the beer-making process, and sensitive to heat, light, and oxygen. Vacuum sealing the bags helped with the oxygen part, but it was still best to not keep them out too long after delivery. It couldn't wait – not even for my father.

"What are you griping about this time, old man?" I asked, returning to my task so I could move on to the next. The work never ended – not if you wanted it to amount to something. And I for damn sure didn't just want this win. I *needed* it.

Failure wasn't an option.

"Just wondering what all this shit is," he groused. When I looked up, he was peering up at the brew kettles that rested beyond the viewing platform.

"*This shit* is going to put *Night Shift* on the map," I explained, as he climbed the stainless-steel steps up to the platform to look around. Nothing was brewing right now – we were clearing house, starting from everything scrubbed clean and sanitized for first brews of a whole new step for us.

Bottling and distribution.

It was a huge – and expensive – undertaking, but would take *Night Shift* from a "brewpub" to a "nano-brewery". If this went well, in a few years I could expand it into the ultimate goal – a microbrewery that could rival my family legacy in size.

There was a *lot* to do in the meantime though.

In a few days, all this machinery would be humming, with fresh batches of our four signature brews – all of which were on tap at the bar already, and hugely popular. Of course, I understood that there was a difference between what people *said* they would buy, and them actually pulling out their wallets. But enough people had asked, enough people traveled here *just* for our brews that I'd been confident in putting the money into it.

I just hoped the shit would work out.

Of course, I wanted to see my brand on shelves around the world, but I put a lot of value on realism – we'd start with bars and retailers in the city first. The relationships already existed to some degree – *Kimble Family Bourbon* had deep roots and long history, extending to Kentucky and Louisiana, predating prohibition. The brand had a reputation for a quality, high-end product that *still* sold well, to this day.

It was the foundation on which I was able to do what I was doing now at all.

"I don't recognize none of this shit," my father groused, turning to me with his bushy eyebrows furrowed. There were a lot of similarities between brewing beer and distilling bourbon, but just as many differences – especially when accounting for the relic copper stills and collectors' item barrels the Kimble Distillery still utilized.

"Welcome to modern spirit production," I told him. "I *have* been meaning to ask you though, what I have to do to get a few empty barrels from you. Wet ones," I clarified, knowing that what I was asking wasn't a simple request. "I'd like to experiment with barrel-aging our stout – see what kind of flavors I can pull from it."

From up on the platform, my father's frown deepened. "Boy, I don't know what the hell you're talking about."

Craft beer was *not* his forte, and he made sure to remind me of it at every turn.

He wasn't fooling anybody though.

Well… maybe his gruff mannerisms and harsh words could fool *some* people, but not me. Beneath that scowl, I could see the pride in his eyes - the unspoken and carefully restrained joy that I was carving my own path in the world instead of simply following his. Of course, Henry Kimble would never actually say that to me.

"Baby girl told me you're about to start bottling. Is that what all that is?" he asked, pointing far across the converted warehouse floor to where the machinery was set up, ready to go with sanitized bottles, plain caps, and basic labels I was hoping to not end up using. I'd made a couple of decisions I'd caution any business owner against – I'd gotten ahead of myself, thinking I could come back to that stuff later.

Now that it was time to actually start, though?

I was regretting being in such a hurry.

"Yep," I answered, wiping my hands on the front of my jeans as I headed to where my father was standing, still up on the viewing platform. From up there he had a perfect line of sight to everything, even though it was really only intended for the actual brewing process.

"You're not doing any cans?" he asked, and I shook my head.

"Not to start," I told him. "I decided to go with one over the other for now, but if it will get you to drink it, I will put it on the agenda, old man."

He let out a hoot of laughter, shaking his head. "I told you, I already talked to my baby girl," he said, in a very *I've got one up on you* tone. "It's already on *her* agenda, young man. You ain't gotta put it on yours."

I shook my head, joining in his laughter. I'd explained to our father more than once that although I'd *gladly* welcomed my little sister in on this venture with me, I'd purposely only offered her a 30% stake. Not because of anything to do with *her* - Lark was smart, she knew beer, and she was a shrewd businesswoman.

But *Night Shift* was *my* baby.

From inception, to finding the space, to the financial documents that carried liability... *I* had put in that work, and the majority of the risk was mine. Even with her in charge of certain facets of the business, when it really came down to it, the final decisions did still – and always would – fall to me.

There was no reason to bring that up right now though.

"Is this the only reason you came by? To rag on me and tell me what to do?" I asked, waiting at the bottom of the steps as he carefully picked his way down. My father was a man of weighty presence – he'd always moved very deliberately, taking his time and yours, because obviously one of those was more valuable than the other.

There was a difference now though.

His painstaking descent was less – *much* less - about being imposing, and more about necessity. Hell, I was only forty and the long days of bringing this brewery to life could have me aching by the end of the day, but it was sobering to see those steps taking such an obvious toll on a man who'd done his level best to appear invincible in his children's sight.

Shit, for the longest, even into my adult years, I halfway believed it.

I... couldn't say I didn't *still* believe it.

The old man might be moving a little slower, but he was still the same Henry Kimble who wouldn't let his family legacy of bourbon be denied by racist detractors from Kentucky to Louisiana and back. His name still held weight in this industry, and still held weight for me.

"Your mama wanted me to come check on you," he claimed, once we were at eye level – another change no one could've prepared me for. He'd *always* stood over me, so the reality that he was *shrinking*...

"Bullshit," I countered, laughing. "She is entirely too busy with her tour planning and all that to be worried about me."

"Marlene is *always* worried about you kids."

Fine.

True.

Mama *was* always worried about me and Lark, especially after what happened with Phoenix. But *definitely* not enough to have sent him a thousand miles away, all the way to Blackwood.

I grinned as something – likely the truth – occurred to me.

"You must have *really* been working her damn nerves, huh?" I asked.

The look on his face said it all. "Listen here lil boy – my woman don't *ever* get tired of me. That's how it goes when you treat 'em right, make sure they're taken care of. But you wouldn't know nothing about that, would you? Since your ol' lady dropped you like a bad habit."

"Well *damn*," I said, clapping a hand to my chest. "You don't think that's a low blow?"

"Don't start none, won't be none, *son*," he told me, clapping a hand on my shoulder. "How is Emil doing, by the way?"

I shook my head. "Fine, as far as I know. I can't say I keep up with what she's doing, since she... isn't my wife anymore."

And hadn't been, for at least five years now, but that didn't stop my father from weaponizing *one of* my worst mistakes against me – the marriage wasn't the mistake, letting it fail was. My family had adored Emil, and rightfully so – smart, funny, gorgeous, whole nine. But we'd been together since college, which lent itself to a certain complacency that I ended up leaning on too heavily. We liked each other fine, but the "love" part... it fizzled.

The cheating didn't help either.

Emil finally got tired of dividing time, me forgetting important dates or not coming home, blowing money I wouldn't spend on gifts for her.

She said my mistress could have me, and I didn't fight her on it.

Night Shift was fledgling at the time and needed my full devotion.

"Marlene still follows her on that social media shit," Pops informed me, stepping away to go peer at my cold storage – where I'd been putting away the hops. "Said she's dating some professional football player – one of the *Kings*."

Damn.

I had to admit, that stung a little.

That was my favorite team.

"Good for her," I responded. "She deserves to be happy."

He turned his curious gaze back to me, staring for a moment before he broke into rumbling laughter, right in my face. "Yeah, right. Shit hurt, don't it?" he asked, and I shook my head.

"Come on." I started in the other direction, motioning for him to follow me. "Let me get you a drink."

Purposely, I took on a much slower stride than usual as I pretended to check my phone, giving him time to catch up to me. Once we were in sync, I led us to the double doors that separated the brewing area from the bar. Right now, it was closed to the public, but eventually I wanted to offer brewery tours and *Night Shift* paraphernalia, similar to what *Kimble Family Bourbon* already had in place down in Louisiana.

It was midday, so the bar was pretty quiet when I let us through the locked doors, securing them behind me.

Calvin, the daytime bartender who usually took advantage of the relative quiet to study, glanced up when he heard us coming. "Boss man," he greeted – not me, but my father – reaching across the bar to shake his hand. That amused the shit out of my Pops, so much so that he looked back to give me a smug grin, even as Cal's face pulled into an apologetic grimace.

"He *was* your boss first," I chuckled, excusing him. I liked to joke that I'd poached the best bartender from the bourbon house back home, but in reality, Cal was the one who'd approached me. He'd met some girl online, thought he was in love, and wanted to move to Blackwood – the only thing holding him back was whether or not he'd have a job.

At least the boy wasn't *completely* stupid.

"What can I get you?" he asked, as we took adjacent seats at the bar.

I turned to my father with a grin, hands up. "What do you say? Have a beer with me?"

"I drink *bourbon*," he declared, his face twisted at the idea of consuming anything else. "But since you're over there looking like somebody kicked your puppy, I guess I can give one a whirl."

I frowned.

Now.

Before, my expression hadn't changed, 'cause I hadn't expected him to agree to one anyway.

Still, I decided to take my wins where I could, clapping my hands together. "Cool. We'll take two of the *Rebirth* stouts," I told Cal, who immediately moved to the fridge for frosted glasses.

"I see you do give bourbon *some* respect around here," my father spoke up, and I followed his gaze to the bottles displayed on the back wall. Of all the liquors we offered, our selection of bourbons was the most extensive, and hand-curated by me and Lark. And of course, the *Kimble Family* varietals took front and center among the top-shelf offerings.

"Just because I chose to do something different, you thought I forgot my roots?" I asked him, brow furrowed. My siblings and I had quite literally grown up at the distillery – bourbon was in my blood. The *main* reason Lark and I weren't at the helm of the family business now was because our cousins were older than us, and as such, had been first in line. We'd gotten lucky, I felt, that our father was the baby of the family. Once he retired as head of the company, it had fallen to the next cousin, who'd been in the business since I was still in college.

The age discrepancy allowed us to take our own paths with minimal resistance, instead of taking the one our ancestors carved. Not that I was turning my nose up at it – not by a long shot. I was deeply proud of my family history, and grateful that working at *Kimble Family Bourbon* would always be an option for me.

I just wanted something different.

"Hell, I can't tell one way or the other, you up here playing with *beer* like one of these white boys," he jibed, making me laugh.

"A good drink is a good drink old man," I replied, as Cal placed the frosted pints on the bar in front of us.

"*I'll* be the judge of that," Pops declared, lifting his glass.

I lifted mine too, raising it for a toast before he took that first sip. "To Phoenix," I said, invoking my brother's name, since he was the inspiration for this particular brew – the first recipe I'd ever perfected. Chocolate malt and cocoa nibs and coffee grounds and the barest hint of dried chiles for a little kick. A wakeup call.

Something shifted in my father's gaze, the mention of my brother bringing on the ghost of a smile. He tapped my glass with his and nodded. "To Phoenix."

I looked away when he raised the glass to his mouth.

I didn't want to be *that* dude – to appear as eager as I felt for my father's approval of this thing I'd built from the ground up. Instead of watching him, watching for the reactions on his face as each of the flavors got comfortable with his taste buds, I cast my gaze behind the bar, taking a quick mental inventory of any bottles that looked low.

Not something I needed to do, at all, but still.

That perusal brought me to the bottle of *Yamazaki* – Ms. Bradford's drink of choice. I'd done so well with keeping her off my mind so I could work, but I was really just putting off the inevitable.

I'd see her again.

Soon.

"Well," my father spoke up, loud and crisp – the voice he used when he was about to speak with authority on something. I gave him my attention, taking a sip myself to soothe my frayed nerves.

"*Well?*" I prompted, when he didn't say anything else, staring into the glass.

He looked up, frowning at me before he took another long drink, and nodded.

"Well... that's a damn good beer, son."

FOUR

KERIS

M s. Bradford, after reviewing your portfolio and past work, we're reaching out to see if you'd be interested in a position with our brand. There would be two major projects, one due within a very tight deadline. The other has more flexibility. In addition to those two projects, your skills would be utilized in an ongoing fashion, as in-house Art Director. You would be responsible for the consistent creation of marketing materials, social media content, packaging and anything else that falls within your purview.

If this strikes your interest, please reply to this email or give us a call to schedule time for an in-person interview to make sure this would be a good fit. Compensation would be discussed at that time, contingent upon a firm offer.

I sat up straight in bed, reading over the email a third, then fourth time.

Then a fifth.

The offer had hit my inbox two days ago, and *of course* it struck my interest. I no longer had a job, and not by my own volition...kinda. Semantics aside, *not* replying to that email didn't feel like a good choice.

I just wished I'd done a little more research before accepting the interview.

In the immediate, I needed to get my name on the schedule. The money I'd set aside during my relationship with Walter wasn't exactly pocket change, but I'd always considered it an emergency fund. I'd get a lawyer to discuss the joint accounts I'd been wrongly cut off from, but I was still busy trying to forget my ex existed to deal with it now.

So... I was living off the emergency fund.

And who knew how long it would take to get my own money from Walter, who would likely drag it into court instead of simply doing the right thing?

Long story short, I needed income, and *Kimble Brewing* was speaking exactly my language. Accepting an interview didn't mean anything – there was no risk involved other than the possible wasting of my time, which I had plenty of.

I got off from scheduling my appointment feeling excited, and *then* I decided to type *Kimble Brewing* into my internet browser's search engine.

Fuck.

Fuck.

Fuck.

I read the email a sixth time, and then got out of bed, typing out a quick text response to Natalie before heading for the bathroom. She'd been all over me, all morning, despite her *own* pressing work responsibilities, making sure I was up and ready to be on time for my interview.

I hadn't yet told her that I'd already slept with the boss.

I'd fucked up well enough over the last few weeks – months, years – the last thing I needed was yet another mistake to deepen the pity and disillusionment in Nat's eyes. Once upon a time, *I'd* been the friend with her shit together, and while I'd never judged her, never viewed her as less than... I couldn't see how Natalie could possibly *not* be disgusted with the way I'd turned out.

She never gave me that energy though.

Sometimes it was *tough* love, but it was always *love* – even the "BITCH YOU BETTER NOT MISS THAT INTERVIEW!!!" that popped up on my phone screen while I was brushing my teeth. I smiled over it, peeking in the mirror at my reflection as I scrubbed, trying to figure out how much makeup I'd have to wear to *not* look like I'd been in a cage match.

Luckily the bruising was almost gone.

Right on schedule.

I'd dealt with more than my fair share through the more unfortunate periods of my life, so I was all too familiar with exactly how long they lasted on me. It wasn't even the pain so much as the angry, purple-splotched reminder that someone reviled you enough for violence to be their chosen communication method. *That* was the part that fucked with me.

And the shame, too.

The message it sent to other people, that you'd been *someone's* punching bag. Of course I'd put on makeup for today, but it wouldn't change the fact that Laken *Kimble* had already seen the dreadful black eye.

Not that it'd kept him from leaving a few bruises of his own.

Those though, I didn't mind – in fact, at least twice a day since our little tryst, I'd found myself replaying it all in my head. I hadn't had an intense sexual experience like that since...well... *ever*. I didn't think I'd only ever had *bad* sex, no, but that night with Laken was... something else. Something on a whole other level.

Something I could very easily get too addicted to, and I was already trying to manage my alcohol intake – I didn't need to be struggling with *two* vices. Both of those reasons had kept me from taking my ass back to *Night Shift* since then, but here I was... heading back to the scene of the crime to ask for a job.

What, exactly, is my life?

Shaking my head, I finished up my oral hygiene and climbed into the shower, where nagging thoughts of Laken and his mouth drew my hand between my legs. No, I couldn't quite replicate the feeling, but my slippery hands and closed eyes were good enough, and vivid memories of that night helped fill in the gaps.

By the time I left the shower, I was somewhat sated and decidedly less anxious. At the very least, I'd taken enough of the edge off my horniness that I wouldn't end up in the man's lap.

I left the bathroom to pick clothes, rifling through the boxes I was still living out of – and likely would until I found a place I could actually feel comfortable in, and call home.

This wasn't *that*.

As it was, deep-rooted guilt lingered over me, from touching myself in the shower. Not even my own, but a feeling imposed upon me from the simple fact that I was present in this house.

My body remembered.

I *knew* the painful consequences of getting caught with my hands between my legs – I was hypervigilant about washing spices and hot sauce from my fingers even now, as an adult. I never wanted to experience that kind of torture again, especially not by accident.

But here I was, having made myself cum, in *this* house, unpunished.

Heh.

Even if anyone else knew, they couldn't do a damn thing about it, 'cause I was a grown-ass woman.

A grown-ass woman who needs a job, I reminded myself, as yet another alarm went off on my phone. It was my final, *"Just put on some damn clothes and GO!"* alarm, my last resort for if I'd somehow overslept. My early rising had given me an opportunity to take my time a bit, but now I needed to make things happen.

I settled on light gray slacks, a white blouse, and a charcoal blazer and booties – a color palette that had never let me down. My sleek blonde bob had reverted back to coils days ago, so I let it stay that way, for timing purposes. A quick toss with some leave-in and oil, and that was done.

Fixing my face took longer.

Instead of my usual "five-minute face", I did ten, taking care with a tube of concealer and that damn bruise. When I was done, there was no sign of it, but I still struggled to look at my face in the mirror.

I looked as good as I was going to.

I grabbed my laptop and portfolio and headed out, not bothering to eat anything. If I did, I had no doubt the food would sit in my stomach like lead, adding digestive discomfort to my already stressed state.

I wasn't worried about getting the job, not exactly. And that wasn't to say I was sure I was going to get it – I simply would or wouldn't. I just... didn't know what I was walking into, not really. I didn't know Laken well enough to say *"he wouldn't make up a job"* to get me back in his presence, but after reading about him – what little there was – and about his family – much more readily available information – I didn't *think* that would be the case.

But still, I didn't *know*.

I was a damn good graphic designer – arguably the best at the firm where I'd spent the last decade and a half of my career. My *entire* career. Chromatic Opulence – CO – was the first design firm to hire me, right out of college. It was also where I met Walter, an intermediate designer at the time, who'd become my assigned mentor. At first, I hadn't paid him much attention on a romantic level, but as time went on – and I spent more and more time working, less focused on a social life... he just made sense.

Later, I realized exactly how fucked up that was – for *both* of us.

I shook my head, clearing Walter from my brain to instead focus on things that mattered – like running through my skillset so I could easily spout it, if asked. Luckily for me, my portfolio spoke for itself – I could potentially navigate the job market in my industry without needing to directly mention CO.

Hopefully.

That whole "call for a reference" thing simply wasn't happening, but again – my work spoke for itself. As I completed the short walk to the building where *Night Shift* was housed, I reminded myself of exactly that, instead of letting my brain flesh out worst case scenarios before I stepped into this interview.

The *Night Shift* building was larger than I realized.

It didn't encompass only the bar, which I was familiar with, but a massive warehouse space behind it as well. I had no idea what was back there but was *great* at minding my own business – I stepped inside the bar.

It was quiet as expected for ten in the morning – not empty, but certainly not packed tight like either of the nights I'd visited. When I walked in, the handsome man behind the bar looked up from what appeared to be a textbook with a grin, putting it aside as I approached the bar.

"What can I get for you, gorgeous?" he asked, giving me a slow perusal that made me feel good about my beauty choices that morning.

"Nothing actually," I told him. "I'm here for professional reasons – an interview with Laken Kimble?"

The bartender nodded, looking a little disappointed as he stepped back, already prepared to return to his book. "That door over there leads to the offices," he explained, pointing at a glass door marked *"private - employees only"* way at the back of the bar. "You'll see an elevator back there – take it up to the second floor. You'll be where you're supposed to be as soon as the doors open."

"Thank you," I told him, then headed for the door he'd pointed out. As I moved, I paid attention for the first time to *Night Shift's* polished décor – lots of glossy hardwood and frosted glass and stainless steel finishings.

Definitely not a dive.

Even the elevator vestibule – which I suspected was usually closed to the public – was nicely decorated, with real plants and a big window allowing plenty of natural light. I took the elevator to the second floor, as instructed, stepping out into an office suite that rivaled any top-floor corporate space – including CO.

I was still locked into that comparison, taking in my surroundings, when the door to one of the offices – the *main* office – opened. In an effort to not be late, I'd actually arrived a little early, potentially ruining any attempt at staggering interviews to avoid interactions between candidates.

Shit, I cursed under my breath, looking around as the door crept open and male voices spilled out. I was relieved when my gaze landed on a communal seating area for the office suite – at *least* I could sit my ass down and pretend to be on my phone instead of looking *completely* awkward.

I had no chance to do that before the door opened completely, and I spotted... them.

The last two men I'd slept with – Laken and Walter, shaking hands and gabbing like old buddies. My palms went instantly sweaty as nightmare scenarios played in my mind.

Was this a setup?

Did Laken tell him about us?

Did Walter put him up to screwing me?

I saw them before they saw me, and I had the wildest urge to turn and run away.

To *escape*.

Before I could do *that* either, something about me must have caught their attention, because they both looked up, seemingly struck by my presence. Likely for very, *very* different reasons.

Laken looked good – a little *too* good – outside of his casual bartending attire, in an impeccably-fit navy blue suit. I wanted, desperately, to keep my gaze there, drinking him in, but my treacherous brain drew me back to Walter.

He looked like he'd seen a ghost.

Maybe that's all I was to him now – an unfortunate specter of a past reality he hoped he could just ignore into non-existence.

I was here though.

I was alive, despite all the wishing and hoping otherwise he'd likely put into the atmosphere in the weeks since we last graced each others' presence.

"Ms. Bradford, I see you have an appreciation for punctuality. I like that," Laken said, grinning at me before he gave his attention back to Walter. "Mr. Edwards – my assistant will be in touch to let you know either way."

"Thank you. *Chromatic Opulence* looks forward to bringing your vision for *Night Shift* to life," Walter replied – presumably his way of telling me the job we were apparently both up for was his. I could've brushed that impression off as simple paranoia if it weren't for the pointed look he shot in my direction as soon as he released Laken's hand from their parting shake.

He wanted to jab.

I, however, did not.

Instead of leaning into the urge to claw his eyes out with my freshly touched-up manicure, I pretended he was a stranger – no, I pretended he wasn't even there. I didn't give him the pleasure of reacting to him at all, knowing that within the week, he'd be hearing from my lawyer about not only our joint account, but the severance package from the job he'd informed me was no longer mine.

I'd missed the window to do anything about the blacked eye, but I refused to let his ass slide on *anything* else.

I walked right past him with my head held high, letting a smile bloom on my face, just for Laken. It was genuine – who *wouldn't* be glad to see his fine ass looking like he was headed to shoot a *Sugar&Spice Man of the Year* cover? – but I would admittedly be much more "professional" if my petty need to put on a show wasn't burning through.

"Thank you for having me, Mr. Kimble," I said, feeling Walter's eyes on me as I approached Laken and shook his hand. Just like before, the man smelled sinfully, impossibly good, and I was grateful for my blazer to hide the immediate hardening of my nipples.

"No," he said, not releasing my hand when the standard part of our professional greeting was over. "Thank *you*, for coming."

My breath caught in my throat as he winked, dropping an obvious – to me, at least – innuendo with his words. I blushed as I accepted his invitation through the office door, hoping like hell that Walter hadn't caught *that* part of the conversation, or at least hadn't picked up the double meaning.

I refused to glance backward to check though.

"Have a seat," Laken told me, closing the door before he moved further into his office – a space that continued the theme of polished high-end hardwood and stainless steel.

I didn't move.

"Was that... planned, or something?" I asked, keeping my voice as even as possible.

Genuine confusion marred Laken's handsome features as he stopped short of taking a seat behind his desk. "Was what planned?"

"That little run-in that just happened with Walter." I swallowed, not wanting to say too much – to appear "crazy". But I *had* to know. "He and I worked together, at *CO*. And... we... dated."

What a fucking understatement.

Laken's thick brows pulled together in a frown. "No," he answered, firmly. "I had no idea." Instead of taking his originally planned seat, he walked back around to the front of the desk, perching against it as he faced me. "Ms. Bradford – Keris – I wasn't even the one who set up these appointments. My assistant did the legwork to find all the potential candidates we've talked to."

I lifted my chin, narrowing my eyes in disbelief. "And she happened to find me?"

"*He*, actually," he corrected. "And no – *I* found you, remember?"

"Is that what we're calling stalking, these days?"

A smirk curved the edges of Laken's full lips, pulling at that *damn* scar. "You let me keep the card. I simply utilized the information. Once I saw your portfolio, I added your name to the list of candidates. You responded to the offer at *your* discretion."

I flexed my shoulders. "True."

"Oh I know," Laken grinned. "So come on, come sit down and let's talk. Something we didn't get to do much of the other night."

His mention of our night together sent a tingle up my spine, but I shook it off to pin him with a serious glare. "Mr. Kimble, I... would prefer we handle this meeting professionally."

"Am I making you uncomfortable?" he asked, giving me back a look that was just as solemn.

I let out a huff. "That's... no, not exactly."

"Are you afraid that our recent sexual experience might preclude you from this job?"

My mouth dropped open at that question, but I quickly recovered, shaking my head. "No, actually... I'm afraid it's the only reason I was asked here. That this isn't *actually* about my talent as a graphic designer at all, but more accurately a ploy to... get me back in your bed. On your *couch*," I amended, but stopped myself from an addendum about the counter.

Laken let out a weighty sigh, lacing his fingers together before he rested his hands in front of him. "Allow me to ease your worries – the job *is* yours, if you accept it, because your resume is the most impressive. *Chromatic Opulence* was the only other candidate that even came close, but between you and me, I found out the designer whose work I was most drawn to from their portfolio is no longer with the firm."

"That designer is *me*," I said, before I could stop myself. One of the firm's stipulations had been exclusivity in after-market display – meaning I couldn't use anything in *my* portfolio that they used in theirs. This left me with plenty of work I could still use to display my skill, so it had never felt like a burden.

I was a little pissed they were still using *my* work to push theirs.

That was irrelevant though – Laken had just informed me the job was mine, if I wanted it, without even taking the time for an actual interview. I was confident in my work, so I absolutely believed the good things he said, but... still.

"You really expect me to believe that you offering me this job has *nothing* to do with your intimate acquaintance with my pussy?" I asked, bluntly.

"Offering you this job has *nothing* to do with that," he assured. "But that's only because you happen to be damn good at what you do, and I happen to be in... *drastic* need. If it wasn't this though... I would've found a different excuse."

My chin lifted in triumph. "So you admit it?"

"Admit *what?*" he asked, with a smooth shrug. "That I think you're a gifted designer who I need on my team to transition my business to the next level, *and* that I found our sexual experience transcendent, and I would like to get lost in you again as deeply as possible, as soon as possible? Yes, Keris. I admit the fuck outta that."

Shit.

I couldn't breathe.

My eyelids fluttered as I struggled to find some words, some line of conversation, that wasn't complete gibberish. "I... this is... this is *completely* inappropriate for a workplace," was the completely lame thing I settled on. I mean... it was true, but I also didn't give a shit about that, at all.

I was in a relationship with my *last* boss, the one I was beating out for this job, for ten damn years.

Laken pushed off the desk, ambling toward me with this unhurried stride that made irrational anger and lust boil together in the pit of my stomach.

"Ms. Bradford," he said, stopping in front of me with barely any space between us. I gripped the hem of my blazer to keep my hands out of the enticing mélange of black and grey hair along his chin. "I understand – but regret – if my approach has made you too uncomfortable to accept a working position. Tell me what I have to do to get inside you again instead."

I inhaled a deep breath with the intention of fortifying myself – a mistake that led my senses being overwhelmed with having him so close. I took a step back – I *had* to.

"Are you *serious* right now?" I asked, and one of his eyebrows perked up.

"Deadass."

"What if I accept the job? *Just* the job?"

He hit me with another of those grins. "Keris... I think we're barely keeping our hands off each right now," he said, with a pointed look at my fingers hanging on to my blazer for dear life. "We both know what it means if you take this job?"

I licked my lips, glad for the *stay in place formula* built into the matte shade I'd chosen for today. "Are you saying that sleeping with you is a requirement of the job?"

"I'm saying it's an inevitability we're both mature enough to recognize."

Frustrated by how *intensely* right he was, I blew out *another* sigh. "Can I think about it?"

"Do you really have to? Or are you hoping a *good* reason to say no will arise?"

"*Oh fuck you,*" I muttered, not really intended for his ears but of course he heard it, and laughed.

"Should I take that as a yes?" he ribbed, closing the space I'd put between us with just one stride of his long legs.

I peered up at him with a scowl, annoyed – with myself – about how... *not* annoyed I was. I hated creeps, and I *especially* hated a creep at work, and this was undoubtedly creep behavior.

Or... it *would've* been, if I wasn't enjoying every second of it.

That was the difference, between being harassed and seduced – both parties enjoying the interaction, and wanting it to go on, and *on*.

"I don't even know anything about the job yet," I reminded him.

"I have a bar, and I make beer. I'm trying to turn that into a brand, and I *need* you to create the visuals. Logo, website, labels, packaging. I need the labels and packaging *yesterday*, actually. I'll top your last salary by fifty percent and give you a full benefits package."

"And your dick, right?"

He flashed a smile. "*That's* not part of the benefits package, but you and I can certainly work something out."

I couldn't help laughing, or the smile that stayed on my face after. "You... you don't even know me, Laken. Why are you doing all of this? *Any* of this?"

"Do you remember that question I asked you?"

I furrowed my brow, confused. "I... can't say I do."

"The fate question. Kismet," he prompted, and I rolled my eyes.

"Honestly... I'd been trying not to," I admitted. "I leave that part out when I replay that night in my head."

He chuckled, bobbing his head as he ran a hand through his beard. "I know, I know. I *get* it. But certain events in my life have caused me to... not immediately discount things I can't necessarily see or understand."

"So... I'm your *one* or something?" I asked, incredulous, and not bothering to hide it. "We were meant to be together, love at first sight?"

I wanted him to say yes.

Needed him to say yes, so I could confirm the ridiculousness of this whole thing and run in the other direction, far away, without being tempted to look back.

"*No*," he said immediately, firmly. "I ain't said shit about *love*," he clarified, igniting simultaneous disappointment and relief in me. Disappointment because... okay, maybe he *wasn't* crazy. Relief because... maybe *I* was, for wanting a real shot at this thing.

This thing being the job opportunity.

He was right, of course – I couldn't realistically imagine a scenario where we *didn't* end up fucking. But beyond that, the job he was offering was essentially my dream.

A large budget – and salary – to bring a brand to life from nothing?

It was downright mouthwatering.

"So... how does this go?" I asked, meeting his waiting gaze. "When do I start? Do I sign the paperwork now, or do you have to break me in first or something?"

I swallowed, hard, as Laken brought his hand to my chin, his thumb hovering over my lips, but not touching. "You'd like that, wouldn't you?" he inquired, wrapping his other arm around my waist to pull me against him. His dick was heavy and hard against my stomach. "If I told you to... get on your knees, open these pretty red lips for me."

God, yes.

My eyes must have answered when my mouth didn't because he grinned before releasing his hold on me.

"I wish I could, Ms. Bradford," he said, moving away from me, all the way to the other side of the desk. "But as it stands, I have another meeting to get to, that can't wait. Forgive me – I'd like that scenario too."

I let out the breath I'd been holding and looked away, uncertain of what was next – or what was expected of me.

"Let me show you your office," Laken said, and when I looked up, he was holding up a key he'd retrieved from the desk.

My eyes went wide. "I get my own office?"

"Sure. And Cal, downstairs at the bar, will get you whatever you need to go with it."

"The bartender?"

"My assistant," he corrected. "He works the bar in the downtime, while he's studying. You get him a list, he'll get the office furnished for you. And he'll also get your paperwork and contract prepared."

I nodded. "Okay."

"That should all be done today," Laken said, leading me out of his office, to one across the suite. It wasn't big, but it was airy, with big windows that looked out to the street. Not exactly a penthouse view, but... it would be mine.

It was perfect.

"This works for you?" he asked, and I nodded my assent. "Good. Then, I'll see you this evening."

My eyebrows went up. "This evening? For what?"

Laken grinned. "So I can introduce you to *Night Shift*."

FIVE

LAKEN.

I was supposed to not be making it about sex.

That was the advice from Lark, days ago, when I first told her about all this.

"*Don't fuck it up before it has a chance to happen 'cause you can't keep your dick to yourself,*" she'd warned. "*Take it slow, get to know her... especially since you don't actually have time for this right now anyway.*"

It went in one ear, and right out the other.

Well, not completely – I *heard* her. I even, rationally, understood she was right. Sex tended to complicate even the best of situations, and I'd already run off the *first* woman I thought was the love of my life because of the demands of my chosen career path. It would be wise to take care when it came to Keris, if I really believed my brother had sent me a sign from beyond.

I *absolutely* believed that, no matter how logically unfounded it was.

My impulse control switch just wouldn't seem to kick in with this woman, which was flat out ridiculous.

I didn't even know her.

Sure, that hadn't kept me from diving face-first into her pussy, but I would've expected reason to kick in by now. Yet, here I was, watching her on the security monitor as she waited for me at the bar – waited for me to give her a tour of my fledging brewhouse, where I'd hired her as Art Director.

That shit was *not* some throwaway job.

Everything was about the internet these days, and our web presence would be vital. As a bar, *Night Shift* had done incredibly well on its own, by simply having a great atmosphere, good food, and most importantly, plentiful, reasonably priced alcohol. We carried the major beer brands, and even had a few on tap. But at *Night Shift*, the signature, house-made brews were the ones that reigned supreme. It was all word of mouth – you didn't *advertise* a bar.

Sales and distribution were a whole other animal.

There was a completely different level of quality control and sanitation, recipes had to be refined and sometimes altered – a beer on tap didn't behave or even *taste* the same as one from a can or bottle. It was a massive, expensive, *stressful* undertaking, with the potential for financial ruin.

And I'd put it in the hands of a woman I barely knew.

Once the beer was made, tasted, cleared and bottled, it needed the final touches. Caps and labels – branding that was distinctive and memorable, that stood out on shelves and stood out on TV screens. It had to be "Instagrammable", had to look good in your hand at the bar, or at a picnic in the park. It had to be modern without alienating the non-millennial demographics. Not too masculine or too feminine, not too colorful or too stark.

There were so many – *too* many – points of balance these designs had to strike, all while being an obviously cohesive product line. On top of that, *Night Shift* had no official logo, which would likely be a necessary part of the website, and a *definite* need for press releases and such.

I was doing this backward.

I'd gotten ahead of myself – all of this should've been settled *before* I purchased bottling equipment and supplies, before I pressed full steam ahead. But in my extensive researching to decide if I wanted to do it or not at all, I'd found a deal here, found a deal there, and found myself with a warehouse full of equipment to take *Night Shift* from brewhouse to nano-brewery.

It was a *lot* of work.

And somehow... I had no real doubt that Keris could do it.

Even with the email I'd received about her from her apparently *wack ass* ex. I couldn't stand a *"forgive me for stepping out of line"* ass motherfucker, and that was exactly what he was, reaching out to "warn" me about her, likely in hopes of securing the job for *his* firm.

He'd leveled accusations of her being hard to work with, oblivious to deadlines, and the one that *really* got under my fucking skin – *"excessively involved with inappropriate socializing with men around the office."* A not-so-subtle implication that she'd been passed around, which even if she had – what the fuck did that have to do with her work?

He said all that shit without bothering to divulge that they'd been romantically involved, which made me write the whole thing off as bullshit. I would've done that either way, 'cause sending the email at all was bitch behavior to the extreme. Even if the job hadn't already been offered to Keris, I would never, *ever* offer it to him.

Keris must've had his ass *completely* twisted up.

I'd be a shady, salty motherfucker if I didn't have her anymore too.

With that in mind, I took my ass downstairs, making my way to where Keris sat at the bar, waiting. She was a little early, again, and had spent her time nursing a glass of something clear – water or soda. I knew it wasn't alcohol – Keris was a brown liquor girl.

"Ms. Bradford," I announced myself as I approached.

Those evocative, clear brown eyes of hers lifted from her phone, their blatant sensuality striking me in the chest as her gaze pinned on me. Keris was an incredibly sexy woman – maybe without even trying, judging from her makeup-free face and comfortable sweater. A marked difference from the professional bombshell from this morning.

Just as fine but appealing in a different way – even from the version of her I first met. This Keris, in an oversized black sweater contrasting the golden skin of her bared shoulder, seemed... shit.

I couldn't identify it.

Maybe... happier.

"Mr. Kimble," she said, returning my greeting as she raked a hand through the soft-looking coils of her hair. "I was starting to wonder whether or not you'd show up."

"You're early." I didn't bother to sit down, since we weren't staying. "Be careful, or I might start thinking you're trying to show me up."

A smile played at her lips, even as she tried to suppress it. "On the *first* day of the job? I'd never."

Ha.

She actually struck me as *exactly* the type to show up on the first day and work effortlessly harder than everyone else, just to prove she could. There was no competition here though – just work to be done.

I motioned for her to follow me, weaving through the steadily growing crowd to get to the back – the more private entrance to the brewery. The elevator was off to the right but keeping straight would put you down in the heart of *Night Shift*.

That's where we were going.

"This is where the magic happens," I explained, leading her past the fermentation tanks to the brewing station. "Mash tun, brew kettle, hot and cold liquid storage tanks," I said, pointing out each piece of equipment as I named it. "The bottling set up is back there, and over here, we have a cold room – that's where the beer is kept in kegs before it goes upstairs, hop storage, all that. It's also where we'll keep our test run of the bottles we make from the beers made over the last few days – they're proofing now, and get bottled tomorrow."

Keris had been quiet, simply taking my words in, but *that* made her lift an eyebrow. "Tomorrow? You... do know I can't have any designs to you by then, right?"

"Of course," I nodded. "Like I said – it's a test run. They'll get plain caps and basic labels with just the name. We'll have customers try them out up in the bar, make sure the taste and everything is right, and let people know they'll be able to purchase for home drinking soon. It just builds buzz."

"Right." She stepped away from me, seemingly admiring the machinery as it hummed along. The distance allowed *me* to admire the fit of the light blue jeans she wore cupping her ass. "And it allows you to do a big reveal at a... launch party?"

I chuckled. "Well, I was just gonna line six-packs up along the bar, but a launch party sounds good too."

"I know an excellent event planner you can use, if you need those services. I can pass her information along."

"Please do," I agreed, not bothering to look away when she glanced back and caught me looking. I met her gaze and didn't waver.

She was a very easy woman to stare at.

Even with that bruise still faintly visible – a bruise I now wondered if her ex, Walter, was responsible for. She hadn't mentioned how long ago they broke up – she hadn't said anything negative about him at all, actually. That, paired with that uncalled for email, made the thought of him putting his hands on her incite even more rage than a situation like that normally would.

"Something wrong?" she asked, crossing her arms.

"What makes you ask?"

"Your eyebrows... they're doing a thing," she said, uncrossing her arms to wiggle a finger in the general direction of my face.

"A... *thing*?" I questioned, not knowing what the hell she was talking about.

"Yeah, like..." she stopped trying to speak, instead using her focus to pull her neatly groomed brows into a deep, exaggerated scowl before she broke into a peal of giggles that made me laugh too.

Okay.

So... she can be goofy.

If she was supposed to be the love of my life or something, that was definitely good to know. Levity was an important quality.

"You haven't been drinking, have you?" I teased her back, and she sucked her teeth.

"I had sparkling water, thank you very much." She pursed her lips, tipping her head to the side for a moment before she looked away from me, to look around. "I have a question for you," she mused, turning to walk up to the stairs that held the viewing platform.

"I probably have an answer."

"Night Shift." She grabbed the stair railing and turned to look at me. "Where did that name come from? If I'm being tasked with... creating this vision for the brand, creating the logo... I kind of need to know the inspiration behind it all."

"Of course," I nodded. "As I believe you already know... spirit making runs in my family – it's no secret. *But,*" I said, approaching where she was standing, with my hands tucked into my pockets, "what isn't quite as well known, or talked about... I come from a family of bootleggers. Down in *Nawlins',*" I told her, letting my persistent accent drip a little heavier than usual, exaggerating it. "Before prohibition, during, after... my folks used to get it done between Kentucky and Louisiana. Exporting *Kimble* bourbon all around the world, through the port down there. Obviously this wasn't exactly...*legal,*" I laughed. "As I said – this is during prohibition. So most times, all their shipping and deliveries, they had to do it by cover of night. So... *Night Shift.* Homage to my ancestors, who said fuck that frail shit, and persevered."

"I love that," Keris nodded. "Not that you were asking my approval, but still. Very solid inspiration I can work from. What about the different beers?" she asked.

"I was *just* getting ready to introduce you to that. I've got a little tasting room around the corner here."

I extended a hand in her direction, and she stared at it for a beat before she accepted. A few moments later, I had her seated in a room I'd commissioned solely for this purpose.

Tasting the beer.

Typically, it was where we tested new flavors, just among the people who made up the staff and a carefully curated number of outsiders. Even with it serving a professional purpose, it wasn't a place that I wanted to feel sterile, like any other test environment.

I wanted it to feel casual and comfortable, just like the rest of the bar. As such, the room was a replica of a section of the booths located just on the other side of the brewhouse wall.

Once I got Keris settled into a seat, I went to the fridge for the samples I'd had pulled for us earlier, and then set about preparing two flights. 4 glasses apiece, filled with *Night Shift's* signature brews.

"This one is the first recipe I developed," I explained, watching as Keris lifted the glass to her lips. Unlike with my father, I fully intended to openly watch her... but she didn't actually take a drink.

"What's wrong?" I asked, and she shuddered a little.

"I... am... *so* not a beer girl," she explained, wearing this sheepish expression. "And I don't want you to be offended if I don't like them."

I shook my head. "No, not at all. I understand. I'm working against the stigma created by that swill that's always plastered across TV, or the cheap shit we all drank too much of back in college. But this is not that, and if you let yourself go into it with an open mind... I think you'll be pleasantly surprised."

Keris raised an eyebrow at me but said nothing. She put the glass back up to her lips and took the tiniest possible sip to test it out, followed shortly by a longer one.

"This one is *Rebirth*," I explained to her.

It was the same one I had given my father a few days ago – the one I created in tribute to my brother.

"It's... it's *really* good," she admitted, not bothering to hide the obvious surprise in her voice. "It's not bitter like I was expecting."

"No," I agreed, letting a broad smile spread across my face. "It's not. Now, there are *some* beers that are specifically sour, as part of the flavor profile. I'm personally not a specific fan of sours though... with some exceptions."

Keris' face wrinkled. "*Sours?* Ew. Well... actually, I don't know. I want to say it sounds awful, but... I drink kombucha every day. And I guess that could qualify as kind of sour?"

"*Wait* a minute," I exclaimed. "Kombucha is literally fermented tea. That's damn near the same thing as beer. A lot of them even have a small alcohol content. If your ass can drink kombucha, you can definitely drink a beer."

She laughed. "Kombucha has like... *flavor* to it though. Fruit and herbs and spices."

"Oh, so you're fronting on me like you didn't taste those hints of cayenne and cocoa bean in the *Rebirth?*"

"No, I'm *not* saying that. I do taste it here, I'm just saying that in general, that has not been my beer experience."

"I guess it's a good thing I'm here to put you on to something new then."

"Well put me on, come on," she urged, reaching into the crossbody bag she was wearing for a little notebook and pen before picking up the next glass. It was brighter than the stout, a red ale we called *The Rookie*.

Lark's favorite.

"Oh, see that's *bomb*," Keris gushed, taking a second, long sip from that glass. Her gaze rolled up to the ceiling as she let the flavors linger on her taste buds, and then pulled the glass up to her nose to inhale. "It's... buttery," she said looking to me for confirmation of her guess. "And kinda sweet. Almost... it puts me in the mind of wine, but not exactly," she mused.

"I could definitely see that," I confirmed.

She took one of the crackers I offered, letting the salty blandness of it mute her taste buds as she jotted down something on that notebook page, in loose, flowery writing. I couldn't read it upside down. She bit her lip a little, giving me a nervous glance before she picked up the next glass. This one was much lighter than the two she'd sampled so far – an ale.

Keris let out a sigh when she tasted that one. "It's subtle, but this one reminds me of... and do *not* laugh at me if I'm pulling this out of my ass. It... kind of reminds me of peach cobbler?" she asked, and I didn't give a single shred of energy to suppressing the grin that crossed my face. It was one thing to taste something you created and feel like you'd done a good job. It was a whole other thing for someone else to appreciate it.

"Yes," I nodded. "Hints of peach and vanilla, ginger, and nutmeg in that one. We actually call it *Auntie's House.*"

"Isn't that just *cozy,*" Keris laughed. "Okay last one. I'm a little scared," she admitted, as she put down her notes for that glass.

I raised an eyebrow. "Why?"

"It just looks so incredibly unassuming and simple, and just like... I feel like it's hiding something, and I don't like that," she said.

I chuckled. "Well... the name of this one is *No Angel.*"

Keris threw her hands up. "Oh my God! *See?*"

"Just give it a chance," I urged. "I'm not going to tell you anything else about it – you just taste it and tell me what you think."

She cringed and hesitated, but still lifted the glass to her lips, letting out a sound of surprise. "*Oh!* This one is a *lot* like a kombucha. Pineapple-y and... oh *shit*. That has a little kick to it or something, what is that?!" she gushed, pulling the glass away to look at it as if the ingredients would appear on the front.

"This beer is my exception to my rule about sours," I explained. "You're right about the pineapple – imported from Hawaii, along with... Hawaiian hot chili peppers. *Just* a hint."

Keris raised an eyebrow and took another sip. "That is *more* than a hint," she said, laughing. "But it's really good. They're all good, actually. *Honestly.*"

"I'm glad you think so. Does this give you what you need to create a visual?"

She held up a finger to me, writing for a longer period before she put the pen down, and tucked it all back in her bag. "*Yes*," she answered, with a triumphant smile. "Not gonna lie – I thought this was a ploy to get back in my panties, but it turned out to be really helpful."

"Keris, I don't have to use *ploys* to get back in your panties. You *want* me there, sweetheart. That's first of all," I said, suppressing a grin over the scowl she shot in my direction. "Second... I wanna know what you're jotting in that little notebook of yours. Let me see."

"*No*," she laughed, clutching the bag to her chest in a protective hold. "My notebook is for my eyes only, sir."

"What, you use it for every project or something?"

She nodded, her face taking on this contented quality I'd never seen before – not on *her*. Childlike, almost. "I do," she confirmed. "And I don't write down anything that special – just words, ideas, concepts, shapes, whatever comes to me in the moment. Flashes that might go into the work. It wouldn't even make any sense if I showed you."

"Try me."

"*No*," she replied, firmly. She still had a hint of a smile on her face, but she wasn't playing, I could tell. "What's next? What else do you need to show me?"

I smirked at her, shaking my head. "Nothing. I'm done. I was hoping you'd be willing to show *me* something though."

"Okay, that's enough of *that*," she said, scooting to remove herself from the seat across from me in the booth. Before she could get far though, I was at the outside edge of the bench seat, catching her by the wrist.

"Hold up," I said, turning her to face me. I moved my hands to her thighs, gripping the backs of them.

She didn't pull away.

"What, Laken?" she asked, crossing her arms. "You said you need these designs ASAP, which means *I* need to get home and get some rest."

"I get that, I do," I told her, moving my hands up to grip her ass, pulling her closer to me. "But... I really think we should celebrate this new collaboration."

"I think you're full of shit."

"*You'd know,*" I countered, continuing my slow perusal, up to her waist. "You're bullshitting like you don't want to be... full of *me.*"

I brought my hands forward, unbuttoning her jeans and pulling down the zipper before I lifted that bulky sweater of hers, holding it out of the way to bare her flat stomach. Her abs constricted and flexed when I brought my lips to her skin, grazing her belly button before I drifted lower. Down to the flimsy fabric of her panties.

"*Laken,*" she hissed, sucking in a breath as she grabbed my head, pulling me away. Her gaze darted around, frantic, even though there was nobody else down here to see us.

"What's wrong?"

I grabbed the waistband of her panties with my teeth, growling as I tugged, and she couldn't help but laugh at that. She thought I was just teasing her, but that animalistic rumble was real as fuck. She was aroused – I could *smell* it. That aroma had me ready to pounce.

"Not here," she said, just above a whisper. It was barely out of her mouth before I stood up.

"Fine," I told her, grabbing the nape of her neck. "We can go upstairs. With the understanding that once we're up there... your ass is mine."

"I'm not into anal."

A deep chuckle rumbled in my throat, and I gripped her a little harder as I dropped my mouth to hers. She opened for me as soon as the tip of my tongue touched the seam of her lips, and I *gladly* took her offer, savoring the flavor of the beers melded together on her tongue.

"*Mmmmm,*" she groaned into my mouth, her hands moving to

grip the front of my shirt. She pressed herself into me as she moaned again, deeper, making me – impossibly – harder than I already was.

"*I'm gonna fuck the shit outta you,*" I told her, muttering it against her lips before I teased her with a nibble that was probably too hard, but I couldn't fucking help it.

She didn't seem to mind.

She grinned. "*Please do.*"

I didn't need *any* further prompting.

I reached underneath her sweater again, refastening her jeans for the trip up to my apartment. Before we moved though, I grabbed her under the chin, lifting her head to meet my eyes.

"Ms. Bradford..."

Her eyelids were low, irises darkened with lust. "Yes?"

"Congratulations on the new job."

SIX

KERIS

I didn't understand what was happening to me.

One moment, I'm sitting in a bar ready to drink myself into a stupor to cope with the wreckage of my life, the next I'm... a personal chew toy for my boss.

Not that I minded anything that had occurred between Laken and I since we met – it had all been rather satisfying. But as I sat waiting for Natalie to arrive for our lunch date, shifting in my seat to accommodate the sore pussy I'd been left with after my latest tryst, it *really* hit me how not-good this was.

I'd always been great at making terrible decisions, but for years the potential damage had been mitigated by a certain level of cushion. My job and finances were solid, I was in a long-term relationship, etc. The bulk of those bad decisions were like... washing down raw sushi with an oversized iced coffee.

Now that everything was in disarray, my shaky decision-making was right back at center stage.

"Hey babes," Natalie gushed as she approached the table, her infectious bubbly energy bringing me an immediate smile. She bent down, planting a kiss on my cheek and then checking to make sure she hadn't left a print on me before she took the seat across from me. "Okay... *you* look amazing."

My eyebrows shot up. "Really? I *did* get back to my esthetician yesterday, so—"

"No." Nat shook her head. "It's not that. I *think* it's because you're no longer carrying the sinking darkness of depression in your eyes."

My tongue caught in my throat as I laughed, almost making me choke.

"*See,*" she added. "Look at you, laughing and stuff, curls poppin', skin skinnin'. You must've heard back about that job!"

Her words had a necessary sobering quality. I'd gotten lucky enough that Nat's catering business had been swamped lately, in preparations for one of their biggest events of the year. As such, the bulk of our communication had been her checking on me to make sure I hadn't done anything to accelerate the downward spiraling of my life.

I hadn't told her yet about Laken.

Any of it.

"I... got the job, actually," I started, setting off an immediate squeal from my best friend. I held up a hand, trying to temper her excitement. "I got the job, because I know the owner of the business. Because I'd slept with him a few nights before, thinking he was the bartender. Oh, and when I showed up at the interview, Walter was there. Oh, and the owner guy thinks we met because of... fate, or something. I haven't asked for details 'cause I don't want to know. The dick is... *flawless* though."

When I finally stopped talking, Natalie was sitting there with her mouth open, not moving. After a few seconds, she gathered a handful of her waist-length box braids, pushing them over her shoulder so they wouldn't cover her ear as she leaned across the table.

"Bitch I need you to repeat *all* that," she said, eyes wide, mouth set in disbelief. "Cause there's no possibility I heard you right."

"You heard me right, Nat." I sat back, chewing at my bottom lip as I waited for her to dig into me, to be my conscience.

She started a few times, brow wrinkled in confusion, shaking her head, frowning, sighing. *Processing* the depth of my stupidity. Finally, she crossed her arms, sitting back in a similar fashion to how I already was.

"You know what... I don't hate it for you."

My eyebrows shot up. "Come again?"

"I *don't* hate this for you," she repeated. "I mean... sure, sleeping with your boss isn't great – you've been down that road before. But good new dick, and a good new job are both good new looks for you. I'm sure you already know the potential of this blowing up in your face, but Keris, baby... after what you've been through, I'm not about to shit on what could potentially be a major win."

My mouth dropped open. "Who the hell are you, and what the *fuck* have you done with my sensible friend?"

Natalie laughed. "Trust, this is still me. I'm assuming you fucked the bartender the night I told you to take your ass home. You should've listened to me, yes. I don't like the risky ass behavior, of course not, but... I know the mindset you were in. And really, if you'd listened to me, would you have a job right now? Wait, it *is* a real job, right?"

"Yeah," I nodded. "It's real. I met some of the other staff this morning, and my office is set up. I've already turned in a logo design."

"And you're definitely getting paid?"

"The employment contract had a signing bonus that's already in my account – one *not* connected to Walter."

Just the mention of his name set off a deep roll of Natalie's eyes. "You said you saw him there, at your interview?"

"Yeah. *CO* wanted to sign Laken as a client for the job, I guess instead of *Night Shift* taking on a full-time employee for it. And... I don't know. I feel like Walter said something to him about me. I don't have any proof or anything though, just this gut feeling."

Nat sucked her teeth. "*Of course* his bitch ass did. *Ugh.*" Nat couldn't stand Walter even before things fell apart between us. He was number one on her shit list now. "Let's talk about something that matters though," she shifted gears. "*Laken.* You're calling him by his first name instead of Mr...."

"Kimble," I filled in for her. "And... yeah, I met him as Laken the bartender, so that's kinda what stuck."

She smirked. "*Laken.* Where are his people from?"

"Louisiana and Kentucky."

"Yeah," she nodded. "That sounds very Southern. Does he have an accent? What does he look like? Is he fine? Does he smell good? What I gotta do to get some details, damn!"

I laughed at her request, pausing to speak to the server and order before I launched into answering her questions. "Yes, he does have a bit of an accent, and it is *very* nice. He is tall and *extra* fine, with this salt and pepper in his beard that is just... it's *so* good."

"Salt and pepper? How old is he?"

"Early forties, I think."

Nat smiled. "So *not* old enough to be your daddy, but old enough for *zaddy*, as the kids say. I like this for youuu."

"First of all – there is nothing to like. I am fucking him – that's all, because I am fresh off a ten-year relationship that ended in violence. I don't need to be doing *anything* else."

Nat pointed a finger at me. "Agreed."

"Second, speaking of Walter – he was *not* old enough to be my father, and I wish you'd quit it," I told her, words met with rolled eyes.

"That sonofabitch is fifty years old."

"*I'm* thirty-six! Thirty-seven *soon.*"

Natalie shrugged. "And? Ten years ago he was a forty-year-old man, and you were a twenty-six-year-old hottie he'd been lusting for five years, just *waiting* for a sniff of your pussy. Fuck him."

"Now *that* we can agree on. I talked to my lawyer this morning – do you know that *bastard* is trying to paint me as some kind of gold-digger, like I don't just want *my* money from the joint accounts? It's resolved easily enough by parsing the transactions and deposits, but I just don't understand why he has to make it hard. I cannot believe I was stupid enough to combine my finances with his."

"Not stupid," Natalie corrected. "Naïve. You trusted him, and he took advantage. Now he's mad you're not under his thumb anymore, and he's doing whatever he can to irritate you. The absolute best thing you can do for yourself is enjoy your cushy job and big-dicked boss as much as you can, as long as you can. And what are you going to do *this* time if you come to a point where you realize the situation no longer serves you?"

I sighed. "I'm going to move on."

"Bingo."

The thing with Walter *never* should've lasted as long as it did. Like, *never*.

I was only "happy" for the first few years, content enough for a few more after that. Marriage wasn't a particular aspiration of mine, so it never bothered me that Walter didn't seek a commitment beyond us living together – thank *God* I never signed a mortgage or anything like that. Around year seven, I started avoiding him. Halfway through eight, I didn't really want him touching me – I was just *over* it.

For our nine-year "anniversary", he insisted we go on a trip together, to reconnect.

I was reluctant, but I agreed.

Midway through the trip, he got completely toasted. We were both drinking, but he was drinking... a *lot*. And we fought – so bad that I refused to spend the night in the bedroom of our hotel suite. I pulled out the sofa bed, passed out... and woke up with my pajamas around my ankles, and Walter on top of me.

When we got back home, he swore he didn't remember anything. He tried his damndest to make me think I was crazy, that I'd made it up. That I was too drunk not to have imagined the whole thing. The soreness between my legs then, the bruising on my thighs?

He didn't know anything about it.

Eight weeks later, *Natalie* was the one holding my hand in a private doctor's office.

I had to seek treatment for a failed pregnancy that damn near killed me.

A pregnancy that wasn't even supposed to be a possibility.

From unprotected sex I didn't – *couldn't have* – agreed to.

It was the final straw for me.

I told Walter I was having trouble with ovarian cysts – not technically a lie, it was something that had always plagued me. Hormonal birth control was supposed to help, but I'd never had a good experience with *those* either. I preferred to take my chances with the natural mechanisms of my body – however flawed they might be.

It was a great excuse to help keep him off me.

I could tolerate him for another year, or even six months, while I stacked up some savings and prepared to exit his life for one of my own. I didn't have a plan, but I was working on one, with Natalie firmly in my corner and ready to step in if necessary.

I hadn't expected him to find out about the pregnancy though. Hadn't expected to be treated as if the loss was my fault, or something I'd done intentionally. Hadn't expected him to admit that he'd been lying about not remembering.

I definitely hadn't expected him to put his hands on me.

If I'd just moved on.

None of this shit would be happening if, when I first felt the urge to stay late at work, locked in my office, just so I wouldn't have to see his face... I'd simply left. I was young, and fine, and talented – I had *everything* going for me.

Why the fuck didn't I just leave?

Whatever the answer to that question was, what was done... was done. It didn't do a single thing for me to dwell on it.

Natalie was right – as convoluted as this situation with Laken was, it really did have the potential to work out well for me. If at any moment that changed... this time, there wouldn't be any hesitation.

R ebirth... reincarnation...reawakening.
I sat back at my desk, letting those words dance around in my mind until they brought forth some type of imagery. It was part of my process, and *always* yielded something good.

My thoughts drifted to the purifying nature of fire. It was... passion, and fuel – a generator. Cleansing, and... transformative.

A phoenix.

"*Yeah,*" I whispered to myself, whipping out a clean sheet of paper and my drafting pencils. I wasn't the best artist in the world, especially not with my hands – I drastically preferred the digital arts. But when it came to something like this, I liked the freedom and flexibility of hand drawing – it allowed my mind to roam a little more freely, with less care for the mistakes.

A while later, I had a concept down – a phoenix that would get intricate detail later, in the digital painting process, with the name of the stout, *Rebirth*, woven into the tail and wings.

This was the last of the four beer label designs, and like all the others, the main subject was set against a dark, swirling starry night sky. The glare from my desk lamp was harsh, casting a stark glow across the pages, but still...

I was *thrilled* with how they'd turned out.

But, since it wasn't actually about what *I* thought, it was about the client – the boss – I tucked my excitement away to wake my computer up. I needed to refer back to the to-do list I'd made myself.

Laken may be in a hurry to get this all done, but I wasn't. Not because I gained any benefit from it taking longer, but because I was picky as hell about the details when it came to work bearing my name. I of course hadn't said anything to *him*, but I was really uncomfortable with how quickly he'd approved the logo sketch, with no revisions or changes.

Design *always* needed revisions and changes.

A slight shift in kerning, a little more color saturation, smoother edges – *something*. Laken was excited though, and for him, this was all about the beer. Sure, he understood the importance of the imagery, and the value in making sure everything met a certain standard in quality.

But it was all about the *beer* for him.

He trusted my talent enough that he would likely approve whatever I put in front of him. And *I* was confident enough that I didn't particularly *need* pushback on my work.

But I preferred it.

Even from people who had no idea what the fuck they were talking about, feedback forced you to either nod and agree, or defend the decisions you made with your work. Even if that defense was only internal. It helped you create with intention, even if the machinations during the creation weren't... intentional. Once it was done, it made sense – it wasn't there just because.

And if it *was* there "just because", well... it shouldn't be.

Creative license was fun, and freeing, but feedback was a necessary checking of the ego. There were things about my style that were just *mine*, that no one would understand, and they didn't have to.

Other things – clashing, ugly, indefensible things – needed to be corrected.

I made a mental note to run the designs by Lark.

She was Laken's younger sister – a year older than me, and so gorgeous and cool-looking with her diamond fangs and nose ring that it made *me* feel frumpy. She was... nice to me. I couldn't complain. There was *nothing* she'd done to make me feel like she had any sort of specific problem with me, but there was... *something*.

I couldn't pinpoint it.

She'd been perfectly polite, and very complimentary of my

portfolio, and she liked my shoes, but... she definitely had some sort of guard up.

Maybe she knew I was sleeping with her brother.

Maybe she *hated* that I was sleeping with her brother.

Yeah.

I would *definitely* take my sketches to her.

She'd tell the truth.

In the meantime, there was a whole list of things I needed to do for the *Night Shift* brand, and I was on my way back to it when a knock sounded at the office door.

Guess the list will have to wait.

I was only a little surprised when Laken peeked into my door, after not waiting for an answer to open it. I hadn't seen him since earlier in the morning, and assumed he'd either left for the day, or was down in the brewhouse.

"I just wanted to check on you," he explained, stepping through the doorway and closing the door behind him. He looked *good.* Dark jeans, and a mustard Henley that stretched across his broad shoulders and biceps.

"I'm fine."

I crossed my legs underneath the desk, trying to quell my body's reaction to him. We'd *just* been together the night before – I was still sore and walking sideways because of him.

"Okay."

That didn't stop him from crossing the span of the office in just a few strides, peering in my face like he didn't believe me. "It's just... you came in here and closed the door after lunch, and you haven't been out since."

"I've gotten up to use the restroom," I defended. "Otherwise, I've... I've been *working*," I said, gesturing at the sketches across the desk. "I didn't think it would be a problem."

He shook his head, pushing his hands into the pockets of his jeans. I pulled my gaze away from the bulge of his dick when he spoke. "It's *not* a problem. It's just... you do realize what time it is, don't you?"

Those words prompted me to look at the time emblazoned in the bottom corner of my computer screen.

"*Oh, shit,*" I whispered, my eyes going wide. "No, I did *not* realize it was after ten at night. I'm sorry, I get... I get really wrapped up sometimes, when I'm working. Am I keeping you from going home?"

He smiled. "Yes and no. I was wrapping up some work anyway, so it was a late day for me too. I *am* waiting on you now though."

"Right," I agreed, closing the screen on my laptop. "I just need a few seconds to pack up, and I can get out of your hair."

"You want to show me what you've been working on before you pack up?"

My eyebrows went up. "Uh... yeah, sure." I picked up the four sketches for the four beers, handing them across the desk as I stood to gather the rest of my things. "I can explain the thought processes if you want, but... I think they're all pretty self-explanatory."

Pineapple cherubs with wings made of chili peppers, castle-like chess pieces on a celestial board, a warm pan of dessert cradled in stout arms. Laken grinned at each one, nodding his approval as he took them in, commenting on the unique ways I worked in the names. When he got to *Rebirth* though, his smile dropped.

"What made you do a phoenix here?" he asked, his voice gruff and his big hands almost wrinkling the paper as he held it up.

I shrugged, nervous. "Um... it just felt like a natural choice, with the name. The phoenix represents change and transformation. New life. Reincarnation... *Rebirth*. I can definitely change it if you don't like it though, it's—"

"No," he interrupted, with a single, curt swipe of his head from one side to the other. "It's perfect like it is."

Really?

From his reaction, you'd think he hated it. He was calling it perfect, but he still hadn't cracked a smile.

"I have a brother. *Had* a brother," he corrected himself, his voice thick with unexpected emotion. "*Rebirth* is a tribute to him. We call it *Rebirth* because his name is Phoenix."

My lips parted as all the air expelled silently from my lungs. "I... I had *no* idea, Laken." I'd read more than one article about the Kimble family – they never mentioned another brother. "If you need me to offer a different concept—"

"It's *perfect*," he said again. "Seriously. I... couldn't have imagined this, so I don't see how anything could be better. These are excellent, Keris."

"I'm really glad you like them," I nodded, suppressing a smile. With all the – internal – shit I'd talked about the relevance of his approval... I was still glad as hell to have it. "Um... these are just preliminary sketches. I'll add the details digitally, and that part will take a little longer than these did. But if there's one you'd like me to prioritize..."

"*Rebirth*," he answered immediately. "That's the one I want first."

I accepted the sketches back from him, stowing them in a folder I'd kept out on the desk for just that purpose. "I will work on that one tomorrow," I promised. "But... I have a question."

He lifted an eyebrow. "Ask it."

I clasped my hands in front of me, letting out a sigh. "Um... I'm sorry if this is a sensitive topic, but... a brother named Phoenix, a sister named Lark... is Laken avian as well?"

Laken's head drew back, mouth curled into a baffled smile – he obviously hadn't expected *that* question. "No, actually. My grandfather's name was Lincoln, but... it was the south, you know? Words get stretched out over the tongue one time, people hear it that way so they keep saying it like that. Now you have to spell it, all that. So... *Lincoln* becomes *Laken* by the time the name got handed down to me. He died just before I was born, so my mother was pressured into naming me after him. With the other two, she got to do what she wanted."

"*Wow*," I gushed. "I... was not expecting that, but it's really interesting," I told him, as I put the last of my things to take home back in my laptop bag.

For a reason I didn't know, Laken busted out laughing, shaking his head. "I cannot believe I told you that shit with a straight face."

"Wait, what?" I asked, slipping the bag onto my shoulder. "I don't get it!"

That just made him laugh harder. "Keris... I made that Lincoln to Laken shit up. I'm not named after my grandfather."

At first, I rolled my eyes, but then I shook my head as laughter bubbled up for me too. "*Why* would you even make up something like that?" I asked.

He shrugged. "I don't know, it's been brewing for a while. I've just been waiting on somebody to use it on."

"So you decided ol' gullible Keris was the one, huh?" I crossed my arms as I stepped around the desk, and he met me on the other side, blocking my path to the door.

"You just happen to be the most recent addition to my life."

"Uh-huh," I said, trying not to breathe in too hard. He smelled good. "So where *does* the name come from?"

"It's a portmanteau." He held a hand to his chest. "I swear. Louisiana, Kentucky – repping the family origins."

"Why on *earth* should I believe you?"

"I don't lie," he said, and my eyes bugged out.

"You lied like... one minute ago."

He shook his head, wrapping an arm around my waist to pull me against him. "I wasn't lying – I was *playing with you*. That's different."

"Sure," I replied. I shifted in his arms, unable to stay still with his penetrating gaze locked on me. "What?"

"You're beautiful."

"Oh, here you go again." I rolled my eyes, twisting out of his hold. I *almost* made it to the door, but he stopped me before I could open it. His hands pressed against the cool surface on either side of me, trapping me between.

"Yeah, here I go again... with the damn truth," he said. "What, you don't believe me?"

"I know exactly how good I look, thanks," I shot back, and he grinned harder.

"So then you understand exactly *why* I'm about to do what I'm about to do to you."

I didn't want to smile.

God, I did *not* want to smile, but I absolutely could not keep my lips from curving upward as he dropped his head, pressing his mouth to my neck. My laptop bag slipped off my arm, hitting the floor with a solid *thump,* but I didn't care.

It was hard to care about anything when Laken's hands were so deftly undoing the ties of my wrap dress.

In seconds, or at least what felt like it, he had my dress wide open, letting out an appreciative groan over the skimpy bra and panties I'd worn underneath.

"Was this for me?" he asked, cupping my breasts in his hands, grazing his thumbs over my pierced nipples.

I met his gaze, nodding as I dropped my hands to the waistband of his jeans. I unbuttoned and unzipped, reaching into his boxers to pull out his dick – already rock hard and heavy in my hands.

He groaned as I closed my fingers over the head, giving it a firm squeeze. "Tell me where you want to put it."

His eyes darkened with lust as he registered my question, and the next thing I knew, he had a fistful of my hair. He used that hold to keep me in place as he covered my mouth with his, kissing me with abandon as I fisted his dick. When he finally pulled back, he lifted his free hand to my face, running his thumb over my bottom lip.

"*Here.*"

I nodded.

And then I dropped to my knees.

I hadn't done this in... a *long,* long time, but that didn't stop me from deciding to do my very fucking best.

I was glad I'd chosen a bra that clasped in the front – made for more of a show when I unclipped it, letting my breasts free from the confines of the lace. I grabbed his dick with one hand, flicking my tongue over the tip as I used the other hand to grab his balls, cupping and squeezing.

A guttural moan slipped from Laken's throat as his hips bucked toward me. I grinned as I grazed his head with my lips - soft, fluttery kisses I hoped would rev him up. I put my tongue out again, licking the mushroomed edge of his head.

Teasing him.

But then I stopped playing.

"*Fuuuuck,*" he groaned, as I covered him with my mouth, taking him as far down my throat as I could. His hand went into my hair, fingers grazing my scalp as I sucked him hard, keeping the suction all the way down to the tip before I released him with a smack of my lips.

He seemed to like that, a lot, so I did it again.

With one hand, I pumped him while I sucked, spreading my saliva to make a perfect, wet mess. The harder I sucked, the louder I slurped, the tighter he gripped my hair. He pressed his free hand to the door for balance as his hips moved, fucking my mouth as I sucked.

I moved the hand that was gripping his dick so he could plunge further, making my eyes water with every stroke. I held onto his hips instead, my nails digging into the firm flesh of his ass as he pumped into me one last time with a loud groan, emptying his seed down my throat.

"*Bring your ass here,*" he demanded, as soon as he'd pulled himself free. I barely had time to wipe my mouth before he was snatching me up, pressing me against the door and urging my legs around his waist as he pushed the seat of my panties aside.

And then he was in me.

Still rock hard, and so deep it took my breath away.

His hand snaked between us so he could press a thumb to my clit, using my wetness as lubrication to send me hurtling towards an orgasm at what seemed like lightning speed.

It was all *so* much.

Him leaning in to kiss me, his tongue quickly picking up the same cadence he was using to fuck me, and his thumb on my clit drumming a secondary beat. I pushed my hands underneath the shirt he was still wearing for some reason, pushing it up and out of the way so I could feel him against me, skin to skin.

I'd barely gotten to savor it when the orgasm hit me.

My pussy constricted around him as he kept moving, kept fucking me harder, faster against the door, keeping me cumming in wave after wave of hypersensitivity until a scream ripped from my throat. My nipples were hard enough to cut glass, pussy throbbing as he suddenly yanked out of me, just in time before another spurt of hot cum came rushing out of *him*.

He managed to catch himself before it got all over me.

"I appreciate that," I panted, catching my breath as he stepped away to get to the box of Kleenex on my desk. My legs were wobbly as hell now, my dress impossibly wrinkled, and I didn't want to know what my hair and makeup looked like now.

But I could at least leave the office without a cum stain.

He grinned at me as he wiped his hand, tossing the used tissue into the trashcan before he set about fixing his clothes. Against the door, I did the same thing.

"So," he said, clearing his throat once we'd both returned to some semblance of decency. "You haven't eaten anything since lunch. You wanna grab a bite?"

He was so cool with it.

So fucking casual, asking me to dinner like he hadn't just face-fucked me.

That grin deepened to a full-blown smile as he waited for my answer, and... as usual, it was infectious.

"Yes," I nodded, bending to retrieve my laptop bag from the floor. "I could eat."

SEVEN

LAKEN.

Just a little further.

Don't you fucking punk out now.

I used my sleeve to wipe sweat from my forehead as I dodged a slow-moving pedestrian on the sidewalk. Just another half mile to go on this run that was kicking my ass.

Once upon a time, five miles wouldn't have been shit – something I'd do on a "day off". In the years since the accident though, it had taken *work* to build back up to even this, and a heavy tolerance for the chronic pain that plagued my left leg. I could only guess my body wasn't a big fan of the metal rod required to put it back together.

As I turned another corner I slowed, but not because of anything physiological. Like a homing beacon, my gaze was drawn to long legs, an ass like an upside-down heart swathed in black-and-white printed leggings, and blonde-tipped natural curls.

Keris.

Her arms were weighed down with reusable grocery bags, and

her stride was slow, like she was struggling. I didn't even need to think about it – I sped up, calling out her name as I approached so I wouldn't catch her off guard.

At least not in *that* context.

She looked back, wearing designer sunglasses, and my first thought was, *It ain't even that damn sunny today.* But once I was closer, right in her face, I could see past the glasses enough to take note of her puffy, red eyes.

That pissed me off.

Instead of asking about it, I took most of the bags from her hands, ignoring her protest.

"Seriously, Laken – I can carry my own groceries. And where the hell did you come from anyway? Are you stalking me now?"

"I live in the neighborhood, remember?" I said, starting in the direction she'd been walking, without actually knowing where I was going. "You wanna tell me which address?"

"Not particularly." She shook her head at me, then contradicted her words by telling me her building – it was close to *Night Shift*, which I already suspected since she always walked to work.

"You do this often?" she asked, once she finally started moving, and caught up to where I was. "Harass women on the street into letting you carry their grocery bags?"

I raised an eyebrow at her. "Do you feel harassed?"

She let out a sigh, then shook her head again as she looked away, trying to hide her smile. "No."

I knew I was coming on strong – I wasn't a man with a medium setting, I was either off or on. Where Keris was concerned, I was definitely *on*, but was trying to temper myself so I didn't scare her off.

For now, it didn't seem as if I'd taken things too far for her sensibilities.

It didn't take any time to make it to the front doors of Keris' building, where I halfway expected her to not let me inside. Instead, she took advantage of me holding most of the bags to dig her keys out, leading me to an apartment that... wasn't what I expected at all.

Just looking at Keris, I would've envisioned an ultra-modern, high-rise condo, in a luxury building. The color palette would be black, white, and varying shades of grey, just like her wardrobe.

This wasn't that.

This was like...

"It was my grandmother's," she explained, as if she'd read my mind. "I don't plan to be here long, so I haven't bothered to decorate, or unpack. Once I move out, I'll sell it exactly as is, be rid of this shit forever."

My eyebrows went up as I lifted the grocery bags to the counter and looked around. There were fake plants everywhere, and yellowing plastic "protecting" a floral-patterned furniture suite. Linoleum on the floor, formica countertops, pastel-yellow appliances... yeah. *Grandmother* sounded about right.

"This is a decent building though," I said, helping myself to a seat at the wood-grained table in the corner of the kitchen. "Good location, easy access to stores and public transportation... you could really transform this place."

"I'll pass. Got no desire to be in this hell hole for an extended period." I watched her as she pulled off the jacket that matched her leggings, baring the sports bra she wore underneath. She tossed it over a chair and set about putting away her groceries in just the bra and leggings – abs on full display, full breasts jiggling with every movement.

Shit.

I focused my gaze higher, on her face, instead of letting it drift to the round contour of her ass as she bent to store her veggies in the bin of that yellow refrigerator.

"Hell hole?"

She stopped what she was doing to shoot a glare in my direction. She was still wearing the sunglasses. "That's what I said, isn't it? And what are you still doing here anyway?" She straightened, propping her hands on her hips. "Thank you, for helping with the bags. But don't you have a run to finish?"

I shrugged, propping my hands behind my head. "I was almost done anyway."

"So you decided to get your disgusting sweat all over my kitchen?"

"*Damn*," I chuckled. "I will wipe down everything I touch, okay?"

"I'll remind you," she sniped, turning back to the groceries. Slamming cabinets, slamming drawers, flinging things into the refrigerator. I watched, split between awe and alarm.

Did putting away groceries always make her this angry?

She stuffed all those reusable bags into one, then stuffed *it* in a cabinet underneath the sink. Once the door slammed closed, it seemed like whatever had been bothering her was done being suppressed. Keris let out a shuddering breath, and quickly turned away from me, covering her face as she stepped further into the kitchen.

Fuck.

There was a basket of clean laundry on the table, so I took a small towel from it, wetting it with cold water at the sink. I pulled Keris out of the corner she'd tucked herself into, turning her to face me as her shoulders trembled with barely repressed sobs. With one hand, I took off those damn glasses that weren't hiding shit. With the other, I lifted the towel to her face, letting the cool temperature help bring her back to a calm state before I pulled her into my arms.

Lark, Emil, and my mother had taught me well – at least on *this*.

Or... so I thought.

"What are you doing?" Keris asked a moment later, as she pushed out of my arms. She was still sniffling, eyes still glossy, puffy, and red, but she was no longer full-blown crying. "This isn't... we don't *do* this."

I lifted a brow at her. "Empathy? Should I have just sat here and watched?"

"I'm not saying that, I just..." she wiped her face with the towel, and then stared at it like it was some foreign object. "I don't know."

"You want to talk about it?"

Her swollen eyes drifted to me; her expression dubious. "With *you*?"

"Why not?" I shrugged. "I've licked your asshole, Keris – talking is nothing."

She laughed, shaking her head as she propped her hip against the counter. "That's a fair point, but um... thanks but no thanks. It's a lot, right now. Mostly ex stuff."

"Is that motherfucker bothering you?" I asked, an instant rush of anger coursing through me, tensing my shoulders.

"Not exactly. Nothing I can't handle."

I heard her words, but her eyes told a different story. Now, more than ever, I was convinced he'd put his hands on her.

"If that changes, you *let me know*," I insisted, and she nodded. "Okay."

"I'm *serious*, Keris."

"I believe you."

I held her gaze for a long moment before she cleared her throat and looked away. "Thank you," she murmured.

"For what?"

She held up the towel in one hand. "This. It helped."

"You're welcome. You need me to wet it for you again?"

Keris' eyes slid to her right – to the sink less than a foot away from her. "I... think I could handle it, if I needed to," she said, with another of those half-stifled smiles.

"You sure?"

"I am."

"If that changes, you *let me know*."

This time, the laugh broke free, completely transforming her face. "Of course," she agreed, quickly regaining the nonchalant demeanor she was trying so hard to hold on to. "So... don't read too much into this, but... I need to make myself breakfast. Do you want something too?"

My head tipped to the side. "Oh, you gone *cook* for a brother, okay!"

"Now *see*," she pursed her lips. "I said *don't* read too much into it. I just figured since you're here anyway, for some reason, it would be... rude not to offer."

I grinned. "I didn't hear anything you just said – I just know you said you'd cook. What's on the menu?"

She rolled her eyes, letting out a deep sigh. "Nothing fancy. Raisin toast and scrambled eggs, some fruit."

"That sounds a whole lot better than my post-run smoothie, so yeah, sign me up."

"Okay. How many eggs for you?"

"Let's say... five?"

"*Five?!*" Keris frowned at me. "*Five?*" she repeated.

"Four?"

She huffed. "There's really no difference," she said, turning to the sink to wash her hands. "That's just a lot of damn eggs."

"I'll clean my plate, *mom*," I teased, as she opened the refrigerator. "*Oh*," I exclaimed, when I saw the carton in her hands. "That's why you're being stingy, you got the extra-organic, cage-free, two-parent home, prenatal massaged eggs."

"*Wow*," she laughed. "They aren't *that* expensive, for your information, but I *don't* appreciate you eating up all my food."

Maybe I could eat up something else to make up for it, I thought, but forced myself not to say. So far, I hadn't managed to abide by Lark's advice to *not* make this thing with Keris solely about sex, but I wanted to honor what I believed my brother was telling me.

"I'll get you more eggs," I offered, and she shook her head.

"I'll settle for you handing me a bowl from the cabinet behind you," she said, pointing before she moved on to get the other dishes she needed. I grabbed the bowl, noting how incredibly neat everything in the kitchen was.

Hell, the entirety of what I'd seen was neat.

It made me wonder about her use of *hell hole* to describe a home that actually appeared quite... *cozy*. I watched her as she cracked seven eggs into the bowl, seasoning them with salt and pepper, whipping them with a fork before she poured them into the buttered skillet waiting on the stove. She stepped away to drop the bread in the toaster, then came back with a silicone spatula to do some actual scrambling. Again she stepped away, grabbing a carton of strawberries that she took to the sink for rinsing before returning to the eggs.

It felt... practiced.

Like this was her standard.

Was I invading her privacy, watching her like this?

I almost wondered if she'd forgotten I was even here, because she was paying me no attention at all, humming some tune I couldn't catch as she cooked. She pulled out two plates to distribute the food though, taking both to the table before she turned to me with raised eyebrows.

"Are you gonna come sit down?"

Yeah.

Of course I was.

The food was good as hell, for something so simple. The silence that came along with it though... that was awkward. Sure, she wasn't crying anymore, but I could feel the dejection radiating off her, and... I didn't know what the fuck to do about it.

Probably because I didn't know a lot about her.

Sex – especially *good* sex – could easily create a false sense of acquaintance. I knew the woman's *body* well, knew exactly where to touch, where to lick. Knew exactly what it took to make her cum.

What I didn't know was what made her *tick*.

"I'm sorry," she spoke up, seemingly out of nowhere. "I'm not very good company right now."

"Well... I invited myself to breakfast," I responded, meeting her misty gaze. "This is *your* home. You can be however you want."

"It's *not* my home," she said. "It's just where I live."

I nodded. "You gonna just keep dropping subtext, or give me some details?"

A dry laugh broke from her throat. "I guess I am being pretty cryptic, huh?"

"Just a little."

She reached for her water, taking a sip before she shrugged. "It's... pretty boring. I got adopted by decent people, and when those decent people died, I was sent to my adoptive grandmother. She didn't want me, but she kept me, 'cause it came with the insurance money from my parents. In return, I got to be her... therapy dog."

I frowned. "Therapy dog?"

"Everything she felt, she took it out on me. In this apartment. And she was, um... troubled, to say the least."

I swallowed the mouthful of eggs I'd been chewing, their fluffy texture suddenly feeling like lead in my stomach. "So... why'd you come back here then? This environment... the memories... I can't imagine any of this feels good for you."

"No," she sighed. "It doesn't. But it's not like I had anywhere else to go. Walter and I lived together, and I *had* to get away from him. I wanted to be careful with my money though. Now that I have the job at *Night Shift*, I've been researching apartments."

Putting my fork down, I sat back. "*Had* to get away from him... because he hit you."

Not a question. A statement, because I knew.

"I don't need you to do anything," Keris said, blinking back a fresh wave of tears.

I shook my head. "I didn't ask you if you did."

"*Don't* do anything." My jaw tightened over the shift in her words. "Seriously, Laken... I just want to put all of this shit behind me. I don't want to keep carrying it, I just want... to be able to move on."

"That implies he's trying to stop you."

She swiped tears from her cheeks with her thumb as another deep sigh pushed from her lips. "It's just petty shit, you know? He'd talked me into joint accounts, then when we broke up... he took my name off the accounts. Canceled my card access."

"When you got declined that night at the bar?" I asked, and she nodded. "So this break up is... fresh?"

Another nod.

"I got a call from my lawyer this morning though – I'll have a check tomorrow. I think he knew he couldn't keep it, he just wanted to fuck with me. Kick me out of our place, fine – I have somewhere else to go. Try to take away my finances, fuck you, I'll hire a lawyer. Fire me from my job... I won't lie... that really messed with me. My work is everything to me, so for him to take that away... that was tough. He couldn't stop me from getting another one though."

Not for lack of trying.

There was no point in me telling her about Walter's failed attempt to edge her out of the *Night Shift* job, since the shit hadn't worked. It would just be adding another negative thing for her to stress about.

It *really* pissed me off though.

In the short time I'd known her, it was incredibly clear to me how much Keris *loved* her work as a designer. The way she spoke about it, how deeply she immersed herself in the fine details of it all, the sheer *quality* of her output... her passion was incredibly attractive.

There was no way that motherfucker hadn't seen exactly the same thing over the time they were together, both in their personal and professional capacities.

And he'd endeavored to take it from her.

Cold bastard.

"I'll have the final drafts for the labels done this coming week," she said, obviously taking advantage of an opportunity to shift the subject. "The detail work is time-consuming, but I promise it'll be worth it."

"I don't doubt that at all," I told her, offering a smile. "I decided on an official launch date, a month out. That should give you plenty of time to get the designs where you want, we can do some packaging runs, take promotional pictures, all that."

"Which I'll be able to use on the site," she suggested. "I'll also need professional pictures of the brewhouse set up, the bar, and the offices. The website should cover all bases. The history of the company, e-commerce, the beer-making process, and... a lot more. Once that's done, then I can work on all the social media branding."

"Sounds like you've got me covered."

"I plan to do my best." Her gaze dropped to my plate, and she grinned. "I see you *hated* breakfast."

I pressed a hand to my full belly as she stood, taking both of our empty plates to the sink. "It was truly terrible," I teased as she turned on the water. I didn't get a chance to say more before my cell started ringing. "Give me a second," I said, not taking the phone from my armband before I pressed the button to answer it. An instant smile crossed my lips when my mother's voice filtered in through my wireless earbuds.

"Laken James Kimble – where the hell is your father?"

My smile dropped, and I frowned. "I... have no idea. I would've assumed he was with you on a Sunday morning, getting ready for church. Good morning to you too, Mama."

"Oh, morning baby, I'm sorry," she said, absently – something I was far from used to from her. Marlene Kimble was, as *she* would say, "*Sharper than a six-inch red-bottom.*" She didn't "do" distracted. Yet here we were. "But last time I saw your father, he was leaving for the airport to come see you, and now that negro isn't answering his phone."

"That was over a week ago," I exclaimed, alarmed. "He was here a couple of days, and then I put him back on a plane to you."

"He was coming back – he insisted. He said you were taking on too much at once, he was worried about you." Her breath hitched in her throat. "Laken, he went to the airport yesterday. Are you telling me you haven't seen him at all?"

"Not since I took him to the airport last week. I *talked* to him yesterday, Mama – he didn't say anything about coming back up here. And everything with the brewhouse is on schedule – he had no reason to be worried about me."

"I'm telling you what he told me, and now no one knows where he is."

I shook my head. "No one, or just me, you, and Lark?"

"Do *not* get smart with me boy!"

"I'm *not*, I'm saying – let's take a step back and not panic quite yet. His assistant handles all his travel arrangements and such, right?"

She huffed. "Right."

"Have you talked to her?"

"No," Mama admitted. "I just thought something was wrong with his phone, so I called you to get to him. I didn't know he was missing until you said you hadn't seen him."

"Then he's not *missing*," I said. "Andrea will have his flight information, and we'll work from there. Maybe he stopped by the distillery first, and his phone is just dead. You know if he got into the barrels with his cousins, they pulled out cards and made it a party. He's probably sleeping it off."

My mother let out a sigh. "Maybe you're right, but... something just feels off. You don't understand how... muddled... he's been lately."

"Muddled?" I repeated back, my eyebrows knitting together in concern. "What do you mean, muddled?"

"Confused. Scattered. I swear, Andrea is the only thing that keeps that man's head on his shoulders some days. I argued against a retired old man needing an assistant at first, but..."

I shook my head. "Mama, why is this the first I'm hearing about this? When he was just up here, he seemed..."

Slower.

Not just physically, either – I'd noticed more than once how he seemed to stumble and hesitate a bit over his words. Noticed his frustration with inconveniences that would've barely fazed him before, repetition of stories he'd *just* told.

I'd attributed it to the normal process of aging, but my mother's level of concern had me wondering if it was something more.

"I'm *not* saying I think he's gone senile, I'm just... I'm worried about him."

The fear in her voice set off an ache deep in my chest. "I know. I understand. I... will see what I can do about getting him to a doctor."

"*Tuh.* Good luck with *that*," my mother fussed. "I'm going to see if I can get in touch with Andrea."

"Okay Mama. Keep me updated."

"I will. I love you."

"I love you too," I told her, and then the call was over.

From the sink area, Keris was looking me right in the face, not bothering to pretend she wasn't listening. "Is everything okay?" she asked, and I nodded, pulling my tired, aching limbs from the kitchen table.

"We just seem to have misplaced my father, but I'm sure it's just some misunderstanding. In case it's not though... I'm going to head out, so I can get washed up and be available to them. What are you about to get into?"

Keris shrugged. "Netflix, a bag of grapes, and... work."

I frowned. "It's the weekend – you should spend it enjoying yourself, not working."

"Ah," she quipped. "But what if I enjoy the work?"

"Fair enough," I nodded. "You won't get any complaints out of me about getting those designs sooner and starting on the website."

She smirked. "Yeah, I thought so."

She'd spent the time I was on the phone cleaning up, so the kitchen was spotless again – I mentally kicked myself for letting her do it on her own.

Next time.

And there would definitely be a next time, as far as I was concerned. I needed a few hours with her that weren't about sex, but I needed them to *also* not be about trauma and family. Hers *or* mine.

She walked me to the front door, and I only took a *moment* to think about it before I leaned in, pressing a light kiss to the corner of her mouth.

I wanted to take it further.

Goddamn I wanted to take it further.

But it wasn't supposed to be about that, so I left it there, securing the visual of her pleased expression in my mind before she closed the door behind me, locking it too.

I was only a few steps down the sidewalk when I got a notification, this time a message from Lark.

"He's in Kentucky – Lisa Turtle"

That was all the message from my sister said, but I understood it to mean I was right – my father had simply gotten together with his cousins and brothers, cracked open some family bourbon, and had a little too much fun.

Somehow... I still didn't feel completely settled though.

My mother's words had really struck a chord with me, especially with my parents getting older, and more fragile now. Sure, this specific situation ended up being okay, but I had every intention of digging into those details to really figure this shit out.

It was necessary.

Knowing my father was okay *did* free me to let my mind drift back to my morning inadvertently spent with Keris. I wanted to know her better, and now it felt like I did, even if it was just a little.

I just had to keep building on it.

EIGHT

KERIS

R*ed or purple?*
   Purple or red?
*Maybe purple **and** red?*

I sat back in my swiveling chair, swinging back and forth at my desk as I ran through color options in my head. I told Laken I would have the final drafts of these label designs to him *this week*, and I really didn't want to renege on that promise.

There was no way I was letting something as silly as choosing the colors for the wording on this last label – *The Rookie* – be the thing that tripped me up. But I *also* didn't want it to be the thing that would send this label back in for another round of edits.

If I got it right the first time, I wouldn't have to worry about that.

Yes, of course I knew that flew in the face of my whole thing about *wanting* feedback. However, the feedback part was for getting the design down. At this point, all the decisions were about... fluff. Since the label design was already dominated by red and black, I went with purple for the words, and hit the save button on the project.

With that, I was done.

I switched screens on my computer, taking myself back to my to-do list. Even though this was done, the abundance of things *Night Shift* needed for this product launch certainly was not. Before I could check "label designs" off my list, a knock sounded at my door.

A knock I expected to be accompanied by an appearance from Laken.

It wasn't.

Instead of Laken's handsome face, I was greeted by a different – but still good looking – man when I yelled, *"come in"*. It was Cal, who I'd first been introduced to as a bartender – a title I was quickly coming to understand could apply to anyone around *Night Shift*, but didn't necessarily correlate to what their *actual* duties around here were.

Laken was a bartender, and he also owned the whole damn thing.

Lark was a bartender, and also Laken's sister, and part-owner of the *Night Shift* brand.

Cal, the first face I saw when I came in for my interview, was apparently not only a bartender but also a student, and Laken's personal assistant. His assistant duties weren't that extensive, which allowed him to do the other two things.

It wasn't that Laken didn't need an assistant – he just had an issue with control and an aversion to delegation, another thing I was coming to understand about the *Night Shift* culture. Luckily for everyone involved, that didn't mean things didn't get done. Unluckily for Laken, it meant he worked himself to the bone.

"Hey Cal," I greeted, not seeing until he'd crossed my office threshold that there was a takeout bag in his hand. Curiosity had me craning my neck to see the restaurant name printed on it.

When he realized what I was doing, he chuckled. "Bossman wanted me to bring you this," he said, carefully placing the bag on my desk. It was from this soul food and Thai fusion spot around the corner from my apartment that was quickly becoming an obsession of mine – I'd had lunch from there two days this week already, and obviously... Laken had noticed.

"He said to ask you if it *"makes up for the eggs"*. I have no idea what that means, but he said *you* would," Cal added.

A big grin spread over my face, and I quickly suppressed it by propping a hand over my mouth as I nodded. "Yes... I know what it means, thank you. I'm guessing he's not around today?"

"Nah, he got on the plane this morning headed to Nola. He had to go see his father."

I knew it wasn't my business, but the mention of that got my attention. I'd heard Laken on the phone that day at my place, very obviously trying to soothe his mother's concerns about something that had happened with his father. He claimed it was nothing when I asked, and I was sure he wanted that to be the truth – was trying to convince himself that it was. But he hadn't been able to hide the concern in his eyes that told the real deal.

I hadn't laid eyes on him since then.

Not that I had any reason to expect I would, since it's not like we were dating, and he was a busy man. Still... after being in this weird hyper-intimate space we'd somehow created with each other... it felt a little off.

Silly girl, you haven't even exchanged phone numbers.

I shook my head, forcing my brain to a more relevant topic. "Oh... is he okay?"

Cal's face wrinkled. "Uh... we actually don't know," he answered, with the level of concern that made me think it was likely something pretty serious. "I don't think you've met Henry yet, but he's a very stubborn, proud man – but he's getting older, and you know how it goes," he said, making a pretty large assumption about my experience with parents. "He's of course not saying if anything is wrong – doesn't want to admit he's not invincible." Cal pushed out a sigh. "I think we're all just hoping for the best at this point. Laken will be back in two days though, before the soft launch with the stand-in labels. And Lark is here, if you need someone to run the official labels by."

Labels.

Right.

Of course he thought that was the reason behind my concern – it *should* be. When it came down to it, I wasn't here for family emergencies, or tender moments with the boss. I was here because I was hired for a *job*.

I really needed to remember that.

It was hard though, with a container of drunken collards in my face.

I didn't open the bag until Cal was gone, but I could already smell them – skipping breakfast had my sense of smell working in overdrive today. I'd finished them in record time, and was considering licking the biodegradable container when another, different knock came at my office door.

This time it was Lark who peeked in, with that voluminous hair of hers tamed into a thick goddess braid that crowned her head.

"Cal said you wanted to see me, about the label designs?"

Damn it, Cal.

"Um, sure," I said, tossing the container back in the bag to dump in the compost bin downstairs later. "I can show them to you now, if you want."

"Man, it smells good in here," she commented, coming through the door at my prompting. She and I were pretty close to the same age, but she felt so much younger – in a good way.

In the *best* way.

I liked my personal aesthetic just fine, but Lark was what I'd want to look like if I were... *cooler.* Comfortable as hell in her skin, flourishing in all her boho-chicness – heavy on the chic. As effortless and laid back as her overall vibe was, I recognized designer when I saw it.

"I just finished lunch," I explained, pointing at the bag on the desk, and she raised her eyebrows.

"Wow, less than two weeks on the job and you're already dedicated enough for lunch at your desk?" She pushed her hands in the pockets of her ripped jeans, and her arms disappeared in the flowy fabric of her bandana-print kimono. "Somebody's trying to get on the boss' good side, huh?"

I blinked. "No, I just... I like the work, and I tend to get caught up. I'm not trying to brown-nose."

"Keris... relax," Lark laughed, taking a seat in the chair across from my desk. "I'm just teasing you – I appreciate that you're as into this as all of us are. And besides... I'm pretty sure you've fully infiltrated my brother's "good side" already."

"I—"

"Close your mouth girl," she giggled. "That is *so* not for you to defend yourself – I know you're sleeping with my brother, and I know it's not really my business. I'm just putting it out there, so it doesn't have to be this whole... elephant in the room situation, you know?"

I nodded, the panic that had gripped my chest a moment ago already dissipating into relief. "I appreciate that. I really like it here, and the last thing I want is friction with you, over anything."

She lifted a pierced eyebrow at me. "Do you know how long I've wanted a sister? Since he ran his *first* wife off. I'm so looking forward to us working together to torture Laken."

First wife?

Sister?

"I can see from the look on your face that I have said *way* too much," Lark mused.

"Yeah, I was just talking about keeping my job, not... becoming part of the family?"

She smirked. "He hasn't told you about the dream, has he?"

"The dream?" I propped my elbows on the desk, leaning in. "That fate shit he's been talking about?"

Lark's head went back, and she let out a cackle of laughter. "Yes, *that* shit. But again... I've said too much."

"*Wait*," I said, holding up a hand. "If you're not going to talk about it, why'd you bring it up?"

"My bad," she apologized. "I shouldn't have. It's just... I know my brother really well, right?"

"Of course."

"And I know... he wants you."

I frowned. "And?"

"Laken always gets what he *really* wants."

I sat back in my chair, crossing my arms over my chest. "I'm not something for him to have."

Lark gave me this smile that was half-admiration, half...skeptic. "Sure, Keris. Let's take a look at those labels now."

W *hat the hell?*
I sat up in the bed, eyes still closed as I tipped my head to confirm I heard what I thought I did before I expended any energy to check the time.

Yeah.

There was someone knocking on my door at two in the morning.

I didn't have any missed calls or anything that would give me a clue as to who the hell it would be, other than pure intuition, which I didn't want to believe. I buried the little spark of excitement that wanted to bloom underneath a healthy dose of reality – even if it *was* Laken, he had no business just showing up here, unannounced. I didn't know him, and I wasn't trying to, beyond being a part of *Night Shift* and the occasional booty call that fell within the usual terms of such things.

Besides... it probably wasn't him anyway.

With my luck, the fucking building was probably on fire.

I grabbed my robe from the chair in the corner, donning and tying it closed as I headed for the door. Whoever was on the other side was still knocking – maybe getting a little louder. I bent a little to get level with the peephole and peered out.

... it was Laken.

Of course it was.

I took a deep breath, then undid the locks, pulling the door open only as much as I *had* to, to look out. "Do you know what time it is?"

His brow knitted together in a frown across that handsome face, and instead of answering my question he put a hand to the door and pushed, testing to see how firm a hold I had on it.

I had none.

The door freely swung open and Laken stepped in, kicking it closed behind him. He was courteous enough – *I guess* – to refasten the locks before he turned to me, sweeping me into his arms.

Trying to, at least.

My eyes went wide as he let me go just as quickly as he'd grabbed me, his expression pained as he pressed a hand to his back and groaned. "Pretend I picked you up and whisked you to your bedroom. Very quixotic."

I laughed, quickly stifling it when that aggrieved look didn't leave his face. "Are you okay?" I asked, putting a hand at his side to shuffle him towards a seat, but he shook his head.

"Flying doesn't agree with me anymore, and I've barely slept the last few days, but I'm good."

I nodded. "Sure, but you realize that *still* doesn't explain what you're doing here?"

"Keris... isn't that obvious?"

This time when he pulled me into his arms, there was no attempt at lifting, but it wasn't any less... romantic. There was no denying how good Laken's arms felt, how incredibly gratifying it was to be pressed close to his warm body or feel his lips against mine.

I'd... *missed* him.

I wasn't sure how it was possible, but it was the only way to comprehend the level of contentment I felt over being back in his presence – even at two in the damn morning. Even with him taking it upon himself to pull off my head wrap so he could sink his fingers into my hair, telling me he'd pay for the trip to the stylist to muffle my complaint.

He had me... all twisted up.

All my reasonings about not really knowing him, about us being virtual strangers, got buried underneath the sheer passion of this kiss, the familiarity of him showing up at my door and me letting him in.

Intimacy I didn't need with *anyone*.

Not after what I'd been through with Walter. Anybody with sense would tell me – I needed time, and distance, and hell, *therapy*.

I needed to be by myself.

My body wasn't trying to hear it though, and... honestly, neither was I. I was aware of what was best, sure, but actually implementing those boundaries with a man like Laken who so clearly, fervently, wanted me?

I wasn't prepared to walk away from it.

"*Bedroom*," he murmured against my lips, and I nodded, turning to lead him in the right direction. He wrapped his arms around me from behind, dropping his mouth to my neck to suck and bite, hard enough that I'd have marks for days, but I didn't give a shit.

I just didn't want him to stop.

As soon as we stepped over the threshold of my bedroom, he unbelted my robe, pulling the sumptuous silk down over my shoulders and letting it drop to the floor. His hands went to my breasts, covered only by my nightgown.

I let out a deep moan, relieved by his touch. My nipples were rock hard, *aching* for him, for the teasing pluck of his forefingers and thumbs through the flimsy fabric. His teeth gripped and tugged at my earlobe, his tongue following the same trail as one hand slipped slower, under my gown. He was hard against my ass, and I pressed into him as his fingers brushed my clit.

"You're really trying to make me lose my mind, aren't you?" he growled against my ear, then not-so-gently pushed me forward, towards the bed. I moved with him, turning to look over my shoulder at him once he'd urged me up onto the mattress, then put a hand to my back, indicating that he wanted me on all fours.

Obviously, I obliged.

I kept the apartment cold for sleeping and felt every bit of that chill as Laken pushed my nightgown over my hips, to bunch at my waist. The bed sank in a bit as he climbed on with me, after I heard the loud thump of his shoes hitting the floor.

In contrast to the frigid air, his big, rough hands were like irons, leaving my skin pleasurably scorched with every touch. His mouth was molten heat on my thighs and ass cheeks, every kiss, every bite, a scald that prickled with blissfully reverberating energy after he'd moved on.

And then he covered my clit with his mouth, sucking and slurping like I was something to be consumed. He used his fingers to tease and spread me apart while he explored me with his tongue, tasting everything he could see before he went back to focus on my clit. He fucked me with his fingers while he tortured me with his mouth and tongue, not letting up on either until I was cumming, hard, with my comforter clenched between my teeth.

I felt him leave the bed, and when I looked back, he was getting undressed, while his eyes stayed trained on me. He stripped down completely, tossing his clothes in the chair before he ambled back to the bed, stroking himself as I watched.

"Can I tell you something?" he asked, as if me saying no were even a remote possibility. He didn't wait for an answer either. "While I was gone, every little bit of sleep I got... I dreamed about your pussy." He slid two fingers into me, and my eyes squeezed closed, reacting to the sudden friction. "I missed her... did she miss me?"

My mouth opened, but I couldn't answer, not with his thumb against my sensitive clit as he stroked me with his fingers. When I didn't reply, he removed his hand.

"I asked..." – I sucked in a quick, harsh breath as he swatted my pussy – "if she missed me. If *you* missed me," he amended.

I swallowed hard then answered truthfully. "*Yes.*"

My whole lower half tensed and released when he slapped my pussy again, harder this time. Wetness dripped down my thighs as I tried my best to breathe normally. He spanked me there again, an even *harder* lick that had my arms giving out, back arching as I fell to my elbows. This time, he soothed the residual stinging with his mouth on my clit, followed by a long, slow lick, all the way up to the small of my back, where he kissed.

"I missed y'all too."

His fingers dug into my hips as he lined up his dick and pushed inside of me, so hard and fast that his balls slapped at my clit.

"*Ah, fuck!*" I screamed, my toes curling as the feeling of *him* reverberated through me. His hands slipped forward, under the gown, cupping my bare breasts as he stroked me, relentlessly, no build-up or preamble.

Exactly like I didn't know I needed.

He grabbed a handful of my hair, tugging to pull me up onto just my knees. The change of position forced a different stroke – slow and profoundly deep, with my hand between my legs and his on top, guiding me. We each took one of my breasts with the other free hand, plucking and pulling my nipple rings. His mouth came back to my neck, sucking and strumming with his tongue.

It was... perfection.

Completely, utterly overwhelming.

I melted into him, my mouth releasing a stream of high-pitched gibberish that ended in me whining his name against the bed as I laid flat on my face, just *my* fingers between my legs, my ankles clutched in his hands as he slammed into me.

I was barely conscious to recognize it when he pulled out, but the hot splatter of his cum across the backs of my thighs and ass was yet another relief.

As was the towel he retrieved to clean us up.

"Oh! You're... okay," I mumbled, a little confused about how comfortable he got in *my* bed after he'd put the towel away. Maybe because we'd always been at his place – or in my office – I'd personally always been in a hurry to get as far as possible away.

Laken wasn't operating in nearly as much haste.

"Damn," he grinned, with his head on my pillow. "I've had a rough last few days, almost put my back out trying to be romantic and shit with you, and I can't even lay here for a second?"

"I *said* okay," I countered. "I haven't put you out... *yet.*" I sat up beside him, making sure my gown wasn't leaving me exposed before I spoke again. "Thank you for lunch the other day. I would've thanked you in person, but you were... in Louisiana, I think?"

He let out a long, deep sigh that reinforced exactly how exhausted he was. "Yeah," he answered, in this fatigued tone that made me feel bad for fishing. "Trying to get my father to see someone about his health."

"Is he sick?"

Laken's gaze went to the ceiling, and he shook his head – but not to answer my question. "We all want to believe he isn't – that it's just normal aging stuff. Forgetfulness, a little confusion, slower body functionality, all that. But... I don't know. I think he's scared. And when my father gets scared, he gets angry, and he's really not trying to hear shit from any of us. So we won't know unless something bad happens. Something worse."

He'd put his boxers back on, so I felt comfortable touching his thigh without it seeming sexual. "Are you... are *you* maybe a little scared too?"

He huffed. "A *little*? I'm fucking terrified," he admitted. "I've lost enough – I'm ready to fucking win. I know everything can't always go my way, but..."

"You don't want to lose him," I supplied. "That's understandable."

Laken was quiet for a long moment. "Can we talk about *anything* else?"

"Sure." I moved onto my stomach, facing him. "I talked to your sister the other day."

He nodded. "Yeah, she approved the label designs. She told me."

"Oh, good. Did she tell you about the *very* strong implication she made that I'd be joining your family?"

"*What now?*" he asked, his accent creeping out as he sat up.

"Yeah, and she mentioned that you were married before too."

"*Goddammit, Lark,*" he muttered, fuming, and... I felt a little bad over how attractive his scowling face was to me. Instead of letting the topic go, as he probably wanted, I sat up too, shifting to a cross-legged position with my gown tucked between my legs.

"So which thing do you want to talk about first?"

His narrowed gaze came to me, annoyed. "Neither."

"Not an option. *Especially* since she brought up that whole "kismet" thing to me too. I think I'm ready to hear that full-blown explanation."

"Somehow, I doubt it."

"Try me."

He raised an eyebrow. "My dead brother comes to me in dreams and tells me things – things that have always come to pass in one way or another. A few days before we met... he told me I was going to meet the person I was meant for. Told me she'd be marked. Then I saw you at that bar, with that bruise over your face... shaped like a bird. Like a phoenix. *You* were the person he was talking about. The one meant for me."

I sat there, lips parted, trying to process the words he'd just offered me. Then I shook my head. "You were right to doubt I was ready to hear that. I would've *never* been ready to hear that," I told him, climbing off the bed.

Was he fucking crazy?

I had no clue.

But I *did* know...

"It's time for you to go," I said, gathering his clothes from the chair so he could put them back on, and leave.

"*Now* you're putting me out?" Laken asked, not moving from where he was sitting. "You asked me for the truth, and I told you."

"And I appreciate your honesty, I do, but... you understand that that's..."

"Atypical," he nodded. "Of course I do. I don't personally subscribe to... the supernatural. I believe in God, and for me, that's about where it stops. But... he's told me to take a road trip for an important meeting instead of getting on a flight – whole airport ends up shut down, and I would've missed it. I had my entire investment portfolio with a company that's being investigated by the FCC now, for fraud and a slew of other shit – if it wasn't for Phoenix, they would've lost my money, like so many others, or have me wrapped up in some legal bullshit. I pulled out because he told me to leave. If it wasn't for that, *Night Shift* wouldn't even be a thing. I get that it sounds ridiculous, but... there have been *so* many other things. I can't even explain."

I huffed. "Those *things* are your common sense, Laken! Your gut, your intuition, warning you about some area where you need to do something different, or make a change. That's all! And if it's not that... it's just coincidence."

"Okay fine... but what if it's not?" he asked, completely serious. "Are you willing to take that chance?"

"I don't have a choice," I insisted. "Less than a month ago, I was still in a nearly decade-long relationship, with a man who... *violated* me. I'm living in a house filled with traumatic memories. I had to pay a lawyer to get the money that was rightfully mine, I'm on probation with a new job... I *can't* do this. Whatever this is. I'm sorry."

"*I'm* sorry," he countered, pulling himself to his feet. "I'm not great at subtlety, or... intrigue. I just want you, Keris, and... I don't know how to couch that in anything other than honesty."

"I'm not asking you to. Just expressing that I... even if I didn't think this whole *destiny* thing was ridiculous... this is a really, *really* bad time for me."

"A bad time for what?" he asked. He took his clothes from my hands, then dropped them to the floor to interlace his fingers with mine. "A bad time for good sex, and breakfast, and... being treated to lunch? A bad time for late-night creeping? Cause I haven't asked you for anything else."

I licked my dry lips as I considered his words.

He... actually hadn't.

"I cannot stress enough," he started, squeezing my hands, "that I know the shit is hard to believe. It makes sense for you to be skeptical – you barely know me, and I barely know you. Which is why I'm not down on one knee right now, with a ring. You're not the only one who was in a long-term relationship. I'm much further removed from mine than you are, but even in the best circumstances, I know breaking up isn't some easy thing. It fucking *hurts*."

I nodded, trying my best to blink back a sudden wave of waterworks that still broke free. Laken reached up, brushing the errant tears from my cheek.

"I won't pressure you into anything, okay? And I swear to you, this personal shit between us? Will have no bearing on your job, because I don't operate that way. With that said... I *am* going to ask you for something. I don't want you to be afraid to say no, but... I really do hope you'll say yes."

"What is it?"

"Just... keep an open mind for me? Please?"

Shit.

The sincerity in his voice, in his eyes, made it hard to even consider the question.

Especially when I didn't really want to pump my brakes anyway. That was simply common sense breaking through – the natural survival mechanisms I'd all but ignored with Walter just begging to be listened to this time around.

And hell... even *they* weren't giving me a red light – more like yellow, to proceed with caution. So with that in mind, along with Natalie's words about enjoying myself until something felt off... I nodded.

"Fine... I'll keep an open mind. But *you* have to agree that if I decide I'm done with... whatever this is – done with you... you won't stop me. You *have* to let it go."

"Okay."

I shook my head. "I *mean* it, Laken. This isn't some sappy movie, where you get to not hear me when I say "no". I will fucking pepper spray you, and my best friend is a registered gun owner."

"*Okay*," he repeated, laughing. "I guess I'll consider myself warned. Are we good?"

"We're good."

"I'm getting older, Keris – my back ain't what it used to be. Can I lay down? Is that okay? You aren't gonna mace me, are you?"

"Oh shut up," I laughed, pushing him back toward the bed, and I followed.

I'd already gotten used to sleeping on the "closer" side of the bed, but Laken wasn't having it. He tucked me on the other side of him, between me and the door – something I understood wasn't to block me in, but was meant for protection.

I didn't need him in that role, but I let it ride, since we were both tired, and it was approaching six in the morning.

And... since I was keeping an open mind and all.

NINE

LAKEN.

I think, maybe, I fucked this up.

Sure, I had Lark's big mouth ass to thank for bringing the topic back up – I would've been waiting a year or two to drop that bomb on Keris.

I didn't blame her for wanting to run away, cause hell... me too.

But when it all came down to it, I'd bought into this thing with my brother, against all laws of nature. I had to see it through.

Only now, Keris would be overanalyzing everything, instead of shit between us just... *happening*.

Which is why a few hours after that conversation, I drug myself from her bed while she was still sleeping and got the fuck out of there – instead of waking her up with my face in her pussy, like I would've preferred.

"Good morning," Lark greeted, when I dragged myself down to the bar to find doing her usual daily checking of the chairs for ripped seats or loose legs. Out of everything she had the option of doing, she seemed to gravitate most natural to a bar manager position, and she was damn good at it too.

"You talked to Keris?" I asked as she moved on from the last chair to take a seat at the bar, where she had her old-school paper schedule laid out. She would plug it all in electronically too, but she always did it by hand first.

Her hand stilled over the paper, pen poised to make a stroke. "Um... yeah, remember?" she asked, keeping her gaze on the schedule to keep from looking at me. "About the labels. She does really beautiful work."

"Cut the bullshit Lark – you *know* what I'm talking about," I scolded, dropping myself onto the stool beside her. "You mentioned her becoming part of the family?"

"I was *trying* to make her comfortable," Lark blurted, dropping the pen to finally turn in my direction. "It seemed like she was freaking a little bit, about me knowing you two are sleeping together. I was trying to convey that... I was cool, that she and I were cool. Maybe my delivery wasn't great though."

My eyebrows shot up. "Wasn't great? You scared the shit out of her!"

"Oh come *on*," she groused, rolling her eyes. "It wasn't even that serious."

We both looked up as the bar door opened, and Keris stepped inside. Immediately, I wondered if the little bun she'd styled her hair into was a direct result of me ruining her carefully wrapped press the night before. I was already sure the collar was about hiding the marks I'd left on her neck.

"Good morning," she murmured, half-frozen, obviously not having expected to see both of us here at this time of day. She didn't wait for a response either, she turned *right* to the employee entrance and tapped in the code, practically sprinting through the door when the indicator light flashed green.

Lark turned to me with a cringe.

"Okay. Maybe it *is* that serious. My bad."

"Yeah, *your* bad," I agreed, laughing. If I believed in the... premonition, or whatever we wanted to call it, I had to also believe things between Keris and I would work out however they were supposed to. Which meant... Lark's inadvertent reveal didn't actually matter.

It just made shit temporarily – hopefully – awkward.

"You don't think she's going to quit, do you?" Lark asked, with this panicked look on her face."

I shook my head. "Absolutely not."

"Oh good." She picked her pen back up, but I shook my head again.

"Nah," I told her. "You may as well put that right back down, 'cause we need to talk about something else."

"What *else* did I do?"

"Not you. Pops."

"Did something new happen?" she asked, alarmed. "I thought you'd told me everything?"

I sighed. "Nah, not everything. You know that trip to Kentucky, that was supposed to go into a trip back up here?"

"Yeah, from a few days ago? Where he forgot to tell Mama he was stopping at the distillery."

"That's not what happened," I told her, propping an elbow on the bar to press my fingers to my temple. "I talked to Andrea – there was never even supposed to be a trip *here*. He'd been talking about it, and she kept reminding him that he'd just been up here, then he'd let it go. That morning, he wouldn't let it go, so she booked his flight. When they got to the airport, he had a full-blown fucking tantrum, insisting he was supposed to go to Kentucky first – like that's what the plan had always been. So Andrea got the flight rebooked, and just canceled the one here completely. He never even mentioned it again."

When I finished speaking, Lark's mouth was hanging open in surprise. "So... what the fuck could this be? Some kind of mental break, or...?"

"To me... I think the signs point to dementia, or maybe Alzheimer's."

"No," Lark denied, shaking her head. "This is too fast, too extreme – I thought both of those happened... slowly?"

"Andrea says it's been happening for months. He's been hiding it as best he can, and she didn't think it was that serious until the thing with the flights. I mean... Pops is pushing up on eighty. She thought it was just old age, which yeah... that's what we're all hoping, but... I don't think it's that, L."

"Daddy has *always* been... irrepressible. Come on. Dementia, Laken? Fuckin' *Alzheimer's*? They wouldn't *dare* fuck with Henry Kimble."

I let out a dry huff of laughter. "I wish it worked like that. I really do."

Lark twirled that pen in her fingers for a long moment, then dropped it onto the open binder. "We've gotta get him to see a doctor," she said. "Like, if we have to drag him ourselves. When he was up here, he was... himself, you know? Slower than usual, sure, but... he was still *Daddy*. So for there to be such a difference, this fast? That's *scary*."

"Yeah," I agreed. "Mama says he's been having headaches too."

"She told me about that. Migraines," Lark corrected. "Like, getting worse and worse, so... maybe that can be our way in?"

I nodded. "We're on exactly the same page. Migraines are no fucking joke, so if it's getting worse... next time he has one, we can force the issue about the doctor, maybe. Assuming he doesn't just hide it from us."

"Stubborn ass," Lark grumbled, and I chuckled.

"Yeah well... neither of us pulled that quality out of the sky."

"I'm not *stubborn*," she insisted.

Lied.

"Yeah sis. Sure. How is the launch planning coming along?" I asked, changing the subject before she started trying to defend herself.

She rolled her narrowed eyes, clocking exactly what I was doing – she didn't argue though. "Everything is cool. Soft launch tonight, official launch in two weeks. That planner Keris recommended is *bomb*. She pulled it all together in no time."

"That's good to know," I told my sister as I stood from my barstool. "I'll make sure to let Keris know her recommendation worked out. *If* I can even talk to her..."

Lark cringed. "Yeah, my bad about that," she said. "I was really just trying to clear the air between us, but you know how I get."

"Yeah, you start talking too much," I teased, bending to give her a quick kiss on the cheek before I headed for the *employees only* door, to follow the same path Keris had a few minutes ago.

Sometimes, it frustrated me that this was the only way to access the office space. It was convenient enough in relation to the brewhouse, but I lived here, with my apartment being on the same floor as the offices but separated in a way that made quick access impossible.

But... that was probably a good thing for me.

That forced separation enabled me to put some necessary distance between myself and the job from time to time. More and more now, as hungry as I was for this thing to be successful, I was starting to feel the toll - mentally *and* physically - of the last seven or eight years of making this business work.

Relatively speaking, *Night Shift* was still a very young business. Not a newborn anymore, and it had strong legs - a toddler. Still open to a lot of wide-eyed exploration, and not a whole lot of fear.

But that was because every risk I'd taken so far had been extremely calculated. In fact, this whole bottling and distribution thing was the *least* well planned out of all the ventures, spurred by a vague sense that I needed to make it happen, and make it happen *soon*.

So I had.

Craft brewing as a business was something Phoenix spoke over me, when he was alive. He sat me down in the corner of his dark little

French Quarter apartment, every surface filled with the figurines and idols that fueled his spiritual beliefs – borne from our ancestors' deep, *deep* roots in the overgrown Spanish moss and bayous of rural Louisiana.

It was eleven or twelve years ago, when I was still working at *Kimble Family Bourbon*, just putting in my years, waiting on my turn amongst the cousins to be the one at the helm. He was... high. Maybe a little bit drunk too, and I pretended not to notice both as he preached to me about how I shouldn't be waiting around to make something happen in the family empire. That I should strike out and do my own thing.

He held up a bottle of what would eventually become *Rebirth*, but back then was something I could barely believe I was willing to drink. A random side project in my basement, to cut some of the overwhelming boredom of the corporate structure of bourbon making. I tolerated it because I *made* it, and that was why Phoenix tolerated it too.

He sowed that into me, now I was finally making it happen.

And he wasn't even here to see it.

He'd never seen the converted warehouse, wasn't here to see the *Night Shift* sign go up over the front doors. Wasn't at my side when I was ordering equipment to build out the brewhouse or traveling the country with me to visit hop and malt farms, sourcing ingredients.

We should've been able to do it all together – the three of us, me, him, and Lark. I appreciated the hell out of my sister, of course, but even she'd admitted before... not being able to do this together was a blow that still smarted.

Instead of going by my old office, I stopped by Keris' first, for no other real reason than seeing her face. When I got back from Louisiana, I had every intention of simply going home, getting in the shower, and getting into bed. To my credit, I *did* do all those things.

Only... once they were done, I was restless.

Even though I was exhausted, even though I was aching, I

couldn't seem to get settled. And the only thing it seemed like it would make it okay... was Keris.

Yet another thing that would sound crazy as fuck if I said it out loud.

I was *not* "in love" with Keris Bradford.

Obviously, I knew that.

But, probably because of the whole Phoenix thing, there was definitely something adjacent to that brewing.

Way too hard, way too fast.

It was why it was so easy for me to assure her I wasn't going to – intentionally, at least – try rushing her into anything.

I was trying to slow this shit down myself.

Sex with Keris was excellent.

Wanting that with her was a no-brainer.

What concerned me though, was that I didn't want to have sex with Keris right now.

I just wanted to *see* her.

"Come in," she called in that sensual, slightly raspy tone of hers. When I opened the door, she didn't seem surprised at all to see me. She turned away from her computer, folding her hands very prim and proper to lay in front of her on the desk. "Laken," she acknowledged. "How can I help you?"

Internally, I laughed at the formality of her greeting, closing the door behind me as I stepped inside. I dropped into the chair across from her, knowing my silence was agitating her.

"Apparently," I said finally speaking up, "The event planner you recommended is working out very well. I wanted to thank you for that."

Keris smiled. "Oh *good*. Natalie went all ultra professional with me when I asked about it, told me the *details were between her and the client*," she laughed. "As if the client and I aren't—" she let herself trail off, giving me the distinct impression those last few words were ones she'd intended to remain in her head. She pressed her lips together, looking toward the window instead of at me.

I started to let her sit with that awkwardness, just to tease her further, but the conversation had reminded me of something I really did want to tell her.

"In any case... since you came through for me, I want to do you a solid right back. If you're really interested in moving to a different place, I'm friends with one of the best realtors in this region. He's not based here, but he's got all the licenses and shit, and knows what he's talking about. He could definitely help you find a place."

Her eyes went wide. "Oh, that would be *great*. With everything else going on, I can feel myself getting lazy about it, and I don't want to get too settled or used to it. I want a place that is completely my own."

"He's coming to the soft launch tonight," I told her, nodding. "So I'll introduce you two then. Well... assuming you're coming, right?"

Her lips parted in surprise. "I assumed it was a mandatory thing, so yeah, I planned to."

"It's not mandatory, but I would definitely like to have you there."

She nodded. "Then I will definitely see you there."

I wasn't sure what I expected the soft launch to look like.

Sure, *Night Shift* was really popular in the neighborhood, had plenty of regular customers and a steady flow of newcomers. Because of the beer, there were different craft enthusiast groups coming to visit us all the time.

We consistently had a crowd, but not... like *this*.

The *Night Shift* social media accounts weren't well-established, simply because it just wasn't my thing. I'd grown up in the thick of a business that didn't rely on the internet to succeed and had concluded that my business didn't need it either. But talking to folks who were smarter than me – something everybody needed at least once in a while – had convinced me of the need for it, *especially* where my distribution goals were concerned.

With the logo Keris created for us, we were able to at least get the pages set up and start doing some light promotion. We'd even been able to get in on the location-based hashtags that our customers had created, getting content from there with the customer's permission.

Well... I say *we*, but really it was all Keris. That wasn't technically part of her job, but it was a role she easily – and seemingly *happily* – took on. Of course, I wasn't going to argue about it since it seemed to be fruitful, without becoming extra work for me or Lark, and was something Cal could take over if Keris grew tired of it.

Between word of mouth, and the hype created from social media, *Night Shift* was totally packed out for the *"soft launch"*. I knew people would come, especially since the beer was free. I had *not* expected *this* turnout, to the point where we had to put someone on the door to make sure we weren't over our legal capacity.

We got people in here every night, never a damn line outside.

It was... *humbling*.

I understood it wasn't really about me, Laken Kimble. These people didn't know *me*. But they knew and loved the *Night Shift* brand, so much that they were out here in a packed crowd, telling people as loud as they could about their favorite beers, from the ones that would be available soon for home purchasing, to the other, a little more obscure flavors that were only available on tap. Even flavors that had been retired or were seasonal.

It was good as hell to hear people so completely passionate about it.

"Damn," Clayton raved, clapping me on the shoulder as he approached me from the side. I was tucked off near the bar, just watching as Lark facilitated a taste test between some of our more serious fans, who claimed they could properly identify *any* beer she gave them. "You *really* did what you said you were going to do, huh?"

When I gave him my attention, I noticed he had a beer in his hand. For now, everything had simple white labels with the name stamped on them. The new labels, the official ones Keris had designed, were coming this week, and would be ready to go for the official launch. For now, they were all top secret.

I nodded at Clayton as he took a sip of his *No Angel*.

"Yeah man," I said, accepting the hand he offered in greeting. "Can't just talk about it forever. Eventually you've got to really be about it."

"I heard that," he said, raising his bottle.

I tapped it with the half-empty *Rookie* I was drinking from. "So what do you think?" I asked him, nodding at the beer. "Not bad from the bottle, huh?"

"Tastes the same to me bro. That's a good thing, right?"

I nodded. "Yeah, the best. We worked hard on the formulation to make sure it kept its integrity through the bottling and storage process. So, *"it tastes the same"* is *exactly* what I want to hear."

"Well, there you go," he said, but I was halfway distracted by blonde tipped curls that had caught my attention.

I watched, curious, as she navigated her way through the crowd, heading towards the bar, where we were standing.

"*Lawd*, that is a fine ass woman," Clayton grunted, and I looked away from Keris to follow his gaze... back to Keris. *Of course* Clayton had spotted her – the man ran through women like it was a secondary profession. It was only because of his lifestyle, constantly moving around selling luxury homes and commercial real estate, that he was able to get away with it without somebody kicking his ass.

Had to be.

This particular woman was off-limits though. And I was getting ready to tell him that, but Keris was already on us, her face spreading into a smile as she looked... *past* me. "Clayton," she greeted warmly, letting him pull her into a too tight, too long hug.

"What, you guys know each other?" I asked, glaring at my friend.

"Yeah," Keris was the one to answer. "I don't know if you've seen his *beautiful* website, but um... I did that. It's still working for you all right?" she asked him.

He nodded. "Impeccably so, thank you." He looked down at her hand, grabbing it and holding it up. "I see ol' boy still hasn't put a ring on it yet, huh?" he asked, and Keris' cheeks flushed with color.

"We're not together anymore actually," she told him.

Clayton's eyes went big, and he stepped in closer to her, pulling both his hand and hers to his chest. "I'm so sorry to hear that," he lied.

"No you're not," I said putting a hand in between them to put a stop to whatever he called himself about to do. "Keris, this is the realtor I was going to introduce you to, but... it appears you're already familiar with him."

"Yes." Keris stepped back and pushed her hands into the pockets of her jeans. "A few years back, Clayton came to CO for some work. I happened to be the designer assigned to his project."

"The designer who wouldn't give me any play or pay any attention to my flirting."

"I was in a committed relationship."

"And now you're not," Clay countered, biting his lip like he'd rather it was her.

"And yet, she's *good*," I interjected, pinning him with a look that, when he met my gaze, he understood *exactly* what the fuck I was saying to him.

"*Ohhh*," he exclaimed as a smirk spread across his lips. "Okay. How do *you two* know each other?" he asked.

"Keris is the newest addition to the *Night Shift* team," I said. "A graphic designer, on staff."

He looked to Keris. "Oh, so you're not at *Chromatic Opulence* anymore?"

"No," Keris answered. "Starting a whole new chapter in my life."

"Which is why you're going to find her a place," I spoke up. "Something that fits her... and still in this neighborhood, of course."

I felt her eyes narrow on me and returned her gaze with a grin.

"Uh-oh – not on the same page?" Clay asked, and Keris shook her head.

"No, it's fine. I do like being close to work, and I... I like the area too. So yes, in this neighborhood," she agreed, after rolling her eyes at me. "I'll get your updated contact info from Laken, and we can talk about my budget. Unless, of course, Laken wants to cover it."

"That wouldn't be a problem," I told her immediately, looking her right in the face as I called her bluff. She definitely didn't mean that shit, but *I* certainly did.

"Absolutely not," she admitted, annoyed, and I laughed.

Clay shook his head, chuckling at our interaction. "Aiight, so... my bottle is empty, so I'm going to go find a couple more of these, and somebody to drink 'em with at my place. Keris – I'll look forward to hearing from you." He held his fist out for me to tap with mine as a parting gesture and shot Keris a little salute before he headed off, leaving she and I alone.

"*I'm good,*" she asked, raising an eyebrow at me as she crossed her arms.

"Yeah," I nodded, not backing down from her gaze. "You are. And you *look* damn good too," I complimented, dropping my attention from her face long enough for a quick sweep of her body, swathed in black, slim-fitting ripped jeans, high-heeled booties, and a long-sleeved *Night Shift* logo crewneck.

"Thanks," she told me, in a dry tone that made me frown. Usually all it took was a little flirting to get at least a grin or *something* out of her, but her mood seemed off.

"You're not seriously upset about me blocking Clay off you?" I asked, frowning.

She cut her eyes up to the ceiling. "*Hell* no. Clayton is a whore, and I'm not interested in him like that at all."

"Okay, so what's up with you then?" I asked. "And don't say nothing, 'cause I know that's not true. Your energy is off."

"It *is* nothing though," she said. "I mean... nothing that matters that much, at least. And certainly nothing *you* can do anything about."

"Are you going to keep being cryptic, or are you just going to tell me what it is?" I asked, prompting yet another roll of her eyes.

She sighed. "I got like... a reminder thingy, late this afternoon. For this wedding next month. It just... the whole thing just has me feeling a little bit off."

I raised my eyebrows. "Were you and Walter engaged?" I asked, that being the first reason that came to mind for why a wedding reminder would put her in a bad mood.

"No," she shook her head. "Even if he'd asked, I would have said no. But the person getting married is one of my old co-workers from CO. I haven't seen anybody from there since Walter stripped me of my job. And, obviously, he and I were supposed to go together."

"Oh," I waved her off. "I'll go with you. I clean up really fucking nice," I told her, and finally got the smile I'd been seeking out.

"Well I appreciate that," she said, "but I'll have to check and see if it's even okay for me to bring a plus one. Walter and I were invited together, as a couple. If we both bring dates, that's two extra people and I just don't know."

I nodded. "That's understandable, but if you're planning to go to this wedding, I need you to find out. Let me know so I can make sure it's on my calendar," I told her. "But in the meantime... you don't have a beer in *either* hand."

Keris grinned. "Well, I was thinking since this is technically a work thing, I probably shouldn't be drinking tonight."

"Nonsense," I told her, shaking my head as I grabbed her hand to pull her up to the bar. "It's a celebration, right?"

TEN

KERIS

I *despised* shopping.

Well... I should amend that.

Because really, I loved shopping in *general*, what I hated was shopping *for* something. Especially when it was *for something* I really didn't want to do.

I wanted to do the wedding itself, it was the whole "being around the people I used to work with" that I could take or leave. And not even because I didn't like them. The whole fucked up situation was just... embarrassing.

Even so, this wedding was something I really didn't want to miss, knowing how good Keisha had been to me when I was still at CO. She and I weren't necessarily friends, but she'd always given me great feedback, was quick to recommend me for projects to get my experience up, and – something I hadn't appreciated at the time, but wish I'd heeded back then – she *really* hadn't liked me with Walter.

Then, you couldn't have convinced me her disapproval of the

relationship wasn't based on some type of jealousy or something. It *had* to be that she just wanted Walter for herself. He was a handsome guy, moving up in the design world and making a name for himself at CO. He was an eligible man, and she was recently divorced.

It *had* to be that.

Age-wise, Keisha was right between me and Walter, and had come to CO when she was about the same age as I was. She'd privately taken me aside to warn me about a predatory culture at the firm, without giving any names. But CO was my dream job, a place I'd fantasized about working when I finished my degree. They were *creme de la creme*.

I thought she was just jaded.

By the time I was forced out, I realized that wasn't it at all.

And she certainly wasn't pining after fucking *Walter*.

I never questioned why she stayed, if things were so dire, because there was already a dearth of black women in our industry. I didn't expect her to be some sort of martyr.

She tried to do her part, by pulling me aside to offer a warning – a conversation she likely had with every young black woman they hired. She was in a management position now, maybe with more power to do something about it than she'd had back when I was just a rookie there, and she first had the conversation with me.

I really, *really* wished I'd listen to her.

All that aside, if she was getting married, I was certainly going to be there to show my support. It did sting that she hadn't reached out to me since the whole thing with Walter, but again... we weren't *friends*.

We were colleagues.

I had no reason to expect that type of camaraderie from her.

I kept reminding myself of that, but as I made my way to the store in search of something appropriate for a fall wedding, I couldn't seem to get it off my mind. It wasn't just her – *none* of my co-workers had reached out to me, not even to just be nosy.

It was strange.

I had hung out with these people, drank with them, been to their baby showers and their adult children's graduation parties. Before I was part of a unit with Walter, I was their co-worker. I worked with them for nearly a decade and a half.

And none of them had even bothered to text me.

Again, it *stung*.

But when it really came down to it, just like Keisha, none of those people were my *friends*, and that was likely my own doing. I wasn't... I'd never been that girl with a big circle. More like a comma – just Natalie. I was quiet by nature, a homebody, honestly.

They were... *co-workers*.

Ones I was lucky enough to get along very well with.

Besides... there was no telling what Walter had said about my sudden absence at the office and company social functions.

I wouldn't let that stop me from showing my support to Keisha by keeping my attendance commitment though.

I just had to find something to wear.

I took myself to my favorite boutique, figuring I could make it a one-and-done thing, without having to run all over town. Luckily, I was right – I was barely through the door before my attention landed on the perfect long-sleeved cocktail dress to take with me to the dressing room.

Great fit.

Great style.

Great color with my skin and hair.

Check, check, and check.

I put the dress back on the hanger and put my own clothes back on, feeling good about the decision as I opened the dressing room door to leave. My gaze fell on a familiar face as soon as I stepped out.

"Keisha!" I chimed, catching her off guard as she stepped into one of the dressing rooms herself.

She stepped back to look around, her eyes going wide as they registered who I was. "Keris! I... I'm surprised to see you! Although I guess I shouldn't be – you always *were* a fan of a good dress."

"Some things never change," I answered back, welcoming the quick hug she offered. "I'm actually here picking out something for the wedding," I told her, and somehow her eyes grew even wider than they'd been before.

"Oh. I... didn't think you still planned to attend."

I shook my head. "You have been *nothing* but kind and accepting to me the entire time we worked together. Of course I want to be there at your big day."

"I appreciate that," Keisha insisted, shifting in her heels. "I just..." She let out an uncomfortable sigh. "With... the thing with Walter... I guess I just assumed you wouldn't be there."

"Oh please, no worries," I waved her off. "I am *perfectly* capable of being civil with my ex."

At those words, Keisha blinked, and for the briefest moment her expression was that of disbelief. But... I'd *never* done anything to give her cause for such a reaction.

"Wow," I said. "Is that really where we are now? Because Walter and I are no longer together, there's suddenly a question of my character?"

"I'm sorry..." She at least gave me the courtesy of looking me in the face. "But Walter told us what happened."

Immediately, I frowned. "If Walter had told you what *really* happened, I am quite sure I wouldn't be the one catching this side-eye right now. What did he say?"

She shook her head. "I'm not about to get between the two of you. That's *your* business."

"Keisha don't give me that. I want to know what he told you guys about me," I insisted. "When I first started at CO, you went out of your way to warn me about the culture there. The manipulation, the lies. And you're really going to stand in my face and tell me that you very likely fell for some of the same bullshit you warned me about? But you can't even tell me what was said?"

She let out a deep sigh. "He said you were pregnant, Keris. That you... hurt yourself, to get rid of the baby, and then flew off the handle when he confronted you about it. Security at CO is under orders that you're not even allowed in the building, because you threatened to hurt *all* of us – not just him."

"And... you *believed* that?" I asked, letting out a dry laugh.

"What *should* we have believed? You disappeared, and you haven't tried to get in contact with any of us since you left. No one has seen you; no one knew where you were, and it's not exactly the kind of thing that you call up a former co-worker and say, *hey so I heard...*"

"Fine," I conceded. "I'll give you that. But are you *really* going to tell me that that sounds anything like me?"

"Keris, I don't know *what* sounds like you, because you keep yourself tucked away. None of us really know you – but *your* design."

I wanted to argue with that.

I *really* really did.

But, the truth in those words made me take a mental step back.

And an actual step too.

"Well... I guess there's really no need for this after all," I said, holding up the dress. "I hope you have a beautiful wedding day, Keisha," I told her sincerely as I turned to walk away.

"Wait!" she called after me.

I stopped, even though I really didn't want to hear it. I just wanted to go home, but I couldn't even do that, 'cause I had work to do.

"For what it's worth," Keisha started, shaking her head. "I figured Walter was full of shit. I figured there was more to the story than what he was saying. But you don't talk to anybody, Keris. You never gave me the impression that I *could* reach out and check on you. And with me being the only woman in Senior Management at CO... as fucked up as it probably sounds... I couldn't stick my neck out to defend you with *nothing* to go on, when you aren't even there anymore. I'm sorry, but that's just the truth."

I pushed out a sigh. "I understand that, Keisha. And I definitely didn't expect you to put your head on the chopping block for something that has nothing to do with you. But he's a fucking liar. Point blank."

"Okay so what *did* happen?" she asked. "Because one day you and I are making plans for after-hours drinks with our normal crew, the next thing I know you just aren't around anymore."

I shook my head, weighing the potential consequences of just telling the flat-out truth versus the more sanitized version. I didn't care to have *any* type of connection to Walter. I didn't want my desire to clear my name to come back and bite me in the ass, but I also didn't want him lying on me to the people who had been my peers.

"I *was* pregnant," I told her. "But I shouldn't have been, because my body..." I trailed off. "My body just isn't equipped for it," I told her, giving her a drastically softened version of my truth. "I lost the pregnancy before I even knew I was pregnant, and I never even told Walter about it. I'm *still* not sure how he knew. But to say I purposely did something to end the pregnancy? That's a lie. And when Walter found out about it, he hit me. *That's* why we broke up. *Part* of why we broke up. Nobody saw my face, because I couldn't show it, because of what he did to me. *That's* the truth."

"Keris," Keisha whispered. "I'm so, so sorry."

I shrugged it off. "It's whatever," I told her. "I'm moving past it now, with no intention of dwelling on it, and no intention of reliving it – but it's not okay for him to lie about me, not after what he did."

"Did you go to the police?" Keisha asked, and I rolled my eyes.

"And say *what* Keisha? I accomplished more, with less hassle by just moving out."

"So he just gets to put his hands on you with impunity?"

"No." I shook my head. "*I* get to move on with my life without court dates and further embarrassment. Really, all I want is to put it behind me. I didn't even want to talk about it now, but knowing that he said that shit to you guys... it really..."

"It pisses you off," Keisha finished for me, wearing a scowl. "And it pisses *me* off too. You're right – I fell for some of the exact shit I warn other women about at this place. Again, I'm so sorry. Honestly, I had no idea you were going through that."

I shook my head. "It's not your fault. I *do* keep things close to the vest, so other than Walter telling the truth there's no way you *would* have known about it."

"*Still*," Keisha said, her tone holding a bite of anger as she shook her head. "I really should cuss his ass out."

"Please don't do that," I immediately chimed. "I'm trying to move on, remember?"

Keisha sighed. "Okay. But only if you *don't* put that dress back and have your ass front and center for the Cha-Cha Slide at my wedding. You look amazing, and I need Walter's tired ass to see you in that dress."

I thought about it for a second as I laughed, then nodded. "Sure Keisha," I agreed. "I'll be there."

She reached out her arms for another hug, and I obliged. When she stepped back, she gave me another once over. "Seriously... are you using a new moisturizer or something? What is it, 'cause even when you were telling me what was going on, you looked happier than I've seen you look in years."

I shrugged. "Just getting out of that situation that didn't serve me anymore?" I guessed.

Keisha twisted her lips. "Nah," she said. "It's more than that. Are you going to yoga, you seeing somebody, what is it?"

"I did find a new job," I said, offering another guess. "And it makes me happy, making the labels and packaging, running social media, all of that for a beer brand. I get a ton of creative license and it's been amazing."

"It sounds like it. I'm *really* happy for you Keris," Keisha said. "You always were one of the brightest talents at CO and working at a corporate firm like that can be kind of... stifling," she finished after a pause. "What you described sounds like a better fit for you anyway."

"Yeah," I agreed. "It is."

"So, none of this nonsense about not attending the wedding. I

2

will see you there, and I will talk to my coordinator about making sure you are *not* seated next to Walter."

"Thank you," I said. "And would it be okay if I brought someone?" I asked, and Keisha's eyebrows perked.

"Bring someone... as in a date?" she asked, and I nodded.

"Yeah. Like a date."

Keisha smirked. "You, in *that* dress. With *this* glow, and a *date*?" She wrapped an arm around my shoulder. "Oh, sweet Keris. I'm imagining Walter's face, and I just... thank you so much for this wedding gift."

"Hey, is Laken here?" I asked Cal, as soon as I saw him behind the bar at *Night Shift*.

"Yeah," he nodded. "He just went down to the brewhouse," he said, tipping his head in that direction.

"Thanks," I told him and then headed that way, forcing myself to slow my steps so I wouldn't seem... overeager.

Even though... overeager was a fairly accurate representation.

I really, really wanted to talk to Laken.

It wasn't so bad for me to admit that... was it?

I made my way down to the brewhouse, a path I'd only ever traveled before in Laken's company, when he'd taken me to taste the beers that first night. When I stepped through the doors this time, I was surprised to see that there was a bustle of activity going on, a whole staff of people down here going through the process of beer making.

Which... made a whole lot more sense than Laken doing every single little thing for *Night Shift* himself.

Duh, Keris.

Of course there was a team, for this level of production.

Laken spotted me before I could get very far, and before I could spot him.

2

"Keris!" he called, and I followed the sound of his voice up to the stainless-steel platform that abutted the huge vats of what would eventually become drinkable beer. "Let me introduce you to the team."

Even though I wasn't really in the headspace for that, I followed his prompting. Aside from the people running the bottling equipment and unloading a truck from rolling doors I hadn't noticed before, there were a couple of guys on the platform with Laken.

All of their eyes stayed on me as I approached, all appreciative in different ways.

Laken was the only one, however, who took the liberty of staring like I was his next meal. I shot a scowl in his direction, hoping he'd take the hint to stop it as I ascended the steps.

He just grinned harder.

"Guys, this is Keris Bradford – she's our graphic designer, the one who put together the labels and packaging for us."

"Oh, word?" the guy closest to Laken quipped. "It's really good work," he complimented. "You really did your thing with those."

"Thank you," I told him, just before Laken moved on. "Keris, this is Keith, Jeremy, and Ellis. These are the guys who bring the recipes and all of that to life," he said. "The brewing team. They help me develop new recipes and bring recipes of their own. Keep the equipment running from day to day. And... they just love the fuck out of beer," Laken said, and they all broke into laughter as the guys approached me with hands outstretched.

"You're not going to tell her our crew name?" Jeremy said, grinning as Laken and Ellis groaned.

"We call ourselves the BBC," Keith said, and my eyes went big.

"Brothas Brewing Club," Jeremy laughed. "Get your mind out the gutter Ms. Bradford," he teased me.

I laughed too. "No, *you* get your mind out of the gutter," I told him. "Because *I* was thinking... British Broadcasting Company."

"No you *weren't*," Laken chuckled.

"Billionaire Boys Club?" I attempted something different, and they all laughed again.

"You're going to get along just fine around here," Ellis told me as he shook my hand.

Once we were done with those introductions, Laken took me around to introduce me to more of the brewhouse staff. Once *that* was done, he took me back out to the elevator bank.

"Okay," he said... "You ready to tell me what's up with you?"

I frowned. "What do you mean what's up with me? There's nothing up with me."

Laken raised an eyebrow. "Oh, so you came down to the brewhouse, something you've never done before in nearly three weeks of working here, for no reason? Keris, come on."

I shook my head. "Fine.... I *did* have something I wanted to talk to you about. But I've decided it's nothing and I—"

"Nope," Laken insisted, shaking his head at me. "You can talk to me. How many different times, in different ways, do I have to say that for you to believe it?"

"It's not about how many different ways or times or whatever you say it," I said. "It's about me not really knowing you. *Why* did I have such a strong urge to come and talk to you?"

"Don't fight it – just go with the flow," Laken urged. "Now come on, you had something talk to me about. What was it?"

"Well... I went shopping for the wedding today, and I ran into an old co-worker. The co-worker whose wedding it is actually."

Laken crossed his arms. "Okay. How did that go?"

"Well... it ended up well enough, but in the process of our conversation, I found out that Walter lied to all my colleagues there at CO. And if he lied to my colleagues, I have no reason to believe that he wouldn't have taken it to past clients as well. And I swear, it's not like I'm trying to make it a big deal. I'm not *trying* to hold on to it... I just want to move on, but," I let out a big sigh, barely believing what was about to come out of my mouth. "He told those people that I killed his child. And then had some sort of mental break or something where I threatened to... shoot up my job or something, I guess. It's just a mess. A complete mess."

He shrugged. "And?"

My eyebrows shot up. "What do you mean, *and*?"

"I mean... who gives a fuck? I mean, I know *you* give a fuck, but at the same time... obsessing about it isn't doing anything for you. You can't change the shit he did, but you can decide not to let it mess your head up."

I huffed, shaking my head. "It's really not that easy though."

"But it could be. You just need the right distraction."

I bit down on my lip as I met his gaze. "Um... is that your way of offering?"

Laken glanced at his watch, then nodded. "That could definitely be arranged.

ELEVEN

KERIS

"Stop playing and just show it to me."

Laken grabbed me around the ankle to keep me from moving my foot away and I cringed. And *giggled*.

Apparently, with him, I was a woman who *giggled*.

"It's gross," I protested. "How did we get on this anyway?"

Still holding my ankle, Laken raised my foot to his face, like he was examining it. "Well, it started with you grabbing the covers with your damn toes to move them, and I'm still trying to figure out what the fuck is going on. It *looks* like a regular foot."

"My feet are definitely not regular," I countered. "I could make money."

Laken pressed his lips to the arch of my foot. "Are you offering to jack me off with your feet?"

"*Ew, No!*" I shouted as he laughed. "Is *that* the type of thing you're into?!"

"I could *get* into it," he said, his eyes going big a second later

126

when I curled my toes around his nose and pulled. "*See*," he exclaimed. "We could monetize this. I'll be the masked model you seduce with these... monkey ass toes," he teased, and I had to cover my mouth to stifle the shriek of laughter I let out.

"Give me my damn feet," I said, snatching away from him.

He had a big grin on his face as he climbed up to the bed to get his face level with mine. "Don't be like that. Just *show* me."

"I'm not showing you *nothing*."

"*Please?*" he begged, pinning me with those marbled brown eyes that were so damn hard to look away from.

I'd told myself – *tried* to tell myself – I was much too used to Laken for his charm to have any more effect on me than it already had, but that was far from true. In reality, every second I spent with him pulled me further into the dark and deep, but I... wasn't afraid.

I just knew that I *should* be.

We were barely a week past his admission of believing we'd been brought together by some sort of fate, which was...crazy. I should've *really* kicked him out after that, should've been figuring out my resume. Definitely *shouldn't* have accepted his help with finding a new place.

All the "shoulds" and "should nots" were laid completely bare for me. I saw each and every one and understood them too. It was a *bad* fucking idea, and every new part of this thing with Walter perfectly uncovered why I had no business getting involved with yet *another* boss.

Nothing about the logic changed how I felt though.

And Laken nuzzling the soft coils of his beard against my neck only served to melt even more of my tenuous hold on common sense away.

"*Please?*" he asked again, this time following the word with his tongue along the rim of my ear. His arm circled my waist, pulling me in close to him, and... *fuck me,* I couldn't think of a single other thing that felt as down-to-the-bone peaceful as this.

"Fine," I conceded, turning my head to look at him as I stretched out my foot. He was *so* interested, his gaze focused down my leg as, with him watching... I cracked my toes.

"*Goddamn*," he muttered, alarmed, as he brought his eyes to my face. "That doesn't hurt?"

I shook my head. "No, it feels *great* actually. You turned off now?" I asked.

A little smirk came over his lips as he pulled me tighter. "Nope. I'm thinking about how much you're going to make when we monetize this."

"*Stop*," I giggled, giving him a playful shove that didn't move him at all. "I'll tell you what – if *Night Shift* ever needs some extra cash, I will fuck you with my feet on camera, and we can split the profit. Cool?"

"*Cool*," Laken agreed, holding out a hand. "Shake on it."

"I'm *not* shaking on it," I told him, flopping back on the bed. "You have my word though." I reached up a hand, raking my fingers through the salt and pepper of his beard – much more pronounced now that he'd let it grow out some.

"You keep doing that," he said, and my eyes widened.

"Do I?"

He grinned, letting his eyes close as I kept rubbing. "Yeah. You like it?"

"I do. Tell me you're keeping it."

Instead of answering, he laid down beside me. Once his head touched his pillow, he dared a peek in my direction.

"I'm guessing that's a *no*," I groaned, tugging playfully at it. "But it looks so *good*."

"It's a damn *hassle*," he complained. "It's only here because we've been so busy preparing for the launch."

"You've just gotta get used to it."

I sucked in a subtle breath as he trailed his fingers over my collarbone, down between my breasts, to my ribs. Speaking of being used to things, I expected his manual perusal to continue all the way to the parting of my thighs. Instead, he stopped at my belly, covering it with the flat of his hand.

His gaze came up to mine, wondering, and I lifted an eyebrow. "What?"

He propped himself up on his elbow and wet his lips with his tongue. "I'm about to ask you to talk to me again."

"Is that not what we've been doing?"

"You know what I mean."

I looked down at his hand, still resting on my stomach. "Yeah. Fine. What is it?"

Laken sighed. "What Walter told your coworkers..."

Oh.

Oh.

I pulled myself back into a seated position, and his hand slipped away.

"If it's too private, you don't have to—"

"No," I interrupted. "It's fine, of course it's something you'd want to know. Yes, I was pregnant. No, I didn't end the pregnancy on purpose."

A shadow of something passed over Laken's face. "You miscarried."

"Um... kinda? It was an ectopic pregnancy, so it never would've succeeded in doing anything except killing me anyway. That's almost what happened, actually – I was bleeding to death, and I had to have laparoscopic surgery to remove the pregnancy." I pointed to the tiny stylized computer mouse tattoo that covered the tiny scar on my abdomen. "It wasn't the first time it happened – it happened before a long time ago, but they just gave me drugs that made me sick as hell that time."

"Damn." Laken shook his head. "I'm sorry to make you talk about it – I know it was probably traumatic."

"It's fine." A mirthless laugh bubbled from my throat. "With the kind of luck I've had in this life, I honestly think it would be *more* surprising if my story were any different. It just wasn't meant to be."

Laken thought about it for a moment, then put a hand against the base of my spine, swirling his fingers in a circular pattern against my skin. "So... we haven't been using protection lately. Does that mean you're on some type of birth control? I'm asking because I don't... I don't want us to be caught off guard by something like that."

"Don't worry about it," I told him, looking down at my hands. "I've already employed a permanent method. Just... to not have to worry about it again."

His fingers stopped. "So... you're saying that you... *can't* get pregnant now?"

I nodded, even though I doubted he could really see it with our positioning. "Does that make you reconsider your belief that I'm... *meant for you?*" I asked, turning to face him.

His eyes were intense, eyelids low as he tilted his head from one side to the other. "I was married. In the early years, we struggled with fertility, a lot. Not just getting pregnant but staying that way. It fucked us up," he admitted. "So, we decided to stop trying. Came to terms that it wasn't the path for us."

"Is that why you two got divorced?"

"No." His fingers started moving again, tracing circles on my back. "We were good for a while after that, but then my brother died, and I poured myself into the business. Grief mechanism I guess."

"Makes sense."

"Makes sense but fucked my marriage up."

"You think it was just that, or that neither of you really got past the losses?"

He nodded. "Yeah... it was that too. I think we pretended for each other, but every moment was a reminder. I don't ever want to go through that again. So to answer your question... no. You not being able to get pregnant doesn't make me reconsider anything. It makes me even more certain."

"That's terrifying."

"Yeah," he smirked. "It really is, huh?"

I moved away from his touch, scowling as I met his eyes. "*We don't even know each other,*" I reminded him, words that had become a constant refrain in my head and from my lips, for the past few weeks.

"I know that little tat is to hide a laparoscopy scar. I know you *hate* being lied on or misunderstood. I know you're more than just a graphic designer – you're a team player and would likely excel at *any* role I handed you. I know you shrink away and put up a wall rather than allowing yourself to be vulnerable. I know *that* comes from the abuse you endured as a child – you refuse to be at anyone else's mercy again. That's why you left when Walter put his hands on you. You refused to accept being a punching bag again. I know you can scramble the hell out of some organic eggs. And you like that weird-ass soul Thai food. And you can crack your toes. And you only wear black, white, and gray. And—"

"*I get it,*" I interrupted him. My face was already hot, and probably flushed a deep red. I couldn't hear anymore.

"Does it bother you, knowing I've been paying attention? To know that I've noticed *every* little thing about you?" he asked, sitting up.

I swallowed, hard. "Yes," I admitted.

"I'm sorry." He reached forward, brushing messy straightened strands away from my face. "I can't help it. You're a very interesting woman."

"No." I didn't want to, but I gave in to the urge to nuzzle my face into his hand. "Not interesting. Tragic."

"Is that what you see? That's not what *I* see."

I blinked. "Tell me what you see."

"I see... an incredibly talented, beautiful woman, with an abundance of potential and opportunity at her fingertips. The past happened... it's done. You don't have to let that define who you are. I see *you*. Just you. Not any of that other shit you think makes you "tragic". I just see Keris."

"Don't do that," I told him, shaking my head.

"Do what? Tell you the truth?"

"It's not that, it's… your ability to *always* say exactly the right thing… it's petrifying, Laken. I don't think you understand the position I'm in."

"I don't think *you* understand the position you're in," he countered. "Am I about to sit up here and act like I'm perfect, like I can promise to only ever make you happy, like there will never be friction, all that? *Hell no.* It's not realistic. But I *can* tell you that I'm not the motherfucker you left."

I huffed. "It's not like you'd say so if you were."

"True," he admitted. "And I get it – you don't know me well enough to take me at my word. Which is why this back and forth you seem to keep pulling us into… it's pointless. You don't trust me yet – you *shouldn't*. I haven't earned that, because it requires some combination of… time, proximity, and evidence that three weeks of work and sex haven't gotten us to yet. I'm good with that, and I'm not trying to rush you."

"You keep saying that, and *yet*…"

He frowned. "Don't put that on me. You're feeling the pressure because you're having trouble reconciling your head and your heart. Which I *also* get, because I'm going through the same damn thing."

"Fair enough."

It honestly made me feel a little better, knowing I wasn't alone in this conflicted feeling. I didn't want to be stupid – didn't want to be so desperate for companionship and some poor imitation of love that I ended up right back in a situation like the one I'd left. But the way I *felt* with Laken… it was undeniable.

"You're not going to scare me off," he said, and I looked up from staring at my hands to meet his eyes. "You can unravel yourself in whatever layers feel comfortable for you, but there's not shit you can show me that will change what I know as the truth."

"And what is that truth?"

"That you were marked just for me."

"Why does it make you so uncomfortable when he says the "right" things to you?" Dr. Alexander asked, staring at me from her thick teal frames.

I hadn't been to her in years – a decade or so, actually. I was surprised she even remembered me, surprised I'd been allowed to snag a last-minute appointment, through the good luck – and good graces – of a cancellation.

Not even Natalie knew I was making an appointment with a therapist, but God knows it was necessary. Had *been* necessary for years actually, but was something I kept putting off under the guise of being "okay"

I was *not* okay.

Not now, and not when I stopped going to her all those years ago. Things weren't peachy before – had *never* been, not for me, which was why I needed the therapy in the first place.

But after that... that was where I made the real wrong turn.

"Because...there *has* to be some sort of catch. Right?" I answered her question, then leveled one of my own, which made her give me the same kind smile that had me spilling my heart left and right.

"No." She swept a handful of sandy-brown locs over her shoulder. "Sometimes people are just... good people. Perfect? No, of course not. But *good?* I believe most are."

I threw my hands up. "How do I know which I'm dealing with though?"

Dr. Alexander nodded. "Yes, that is the tricky part, isn't it? And unfortunately, I don't have an answer that would offer any immediate discernment. You can pray for revelation, but sometimes God is using that person to cultivate our minds, to develop. You can judge by actions, but some people are great actors. We can consider words, but the right orator might talk you into believing anything. There's the trusting of the "gut", but what does one do when that trust has only ever led them astray?"

"Yes, to all that," I insisted, and she laughed.

"Tell me the truth, Keris." She fixed me with her heavy-lidded hazel eyes like she was staring straight into my soul. "The relationship with Walter... do you *really* feel as though you followed your intuition with that?"

I cast my gaze down to the intricate pattern woven into the rug underneath my chair. "Honestly... no."

"Explain."

Groaning, I pressed myself back into the plush padding of the chair. "I... I don't know. There were just... there were times when I knew the relationship wasn't it for me. Even before we moved in together, before the joint bank accounts, all of that. I knew better. But... it was something solid. It was comfortable. And it's not like I was being mistreated, or abused, so..."

Dr. Alexander nodded. *"That. That right there.* "It's not like I was being mistreated or abused." That was your threshold for whether or not you would avail yourself to this man – this significantly older man – who did nothing for you. Because on an interpersonal level, that was imprinted on you – the mistreatment and abuse you were dealt at your grandmother's hands, and maybe even before that, *before* you were placed with the couple who became your parents. That trauma was with you when you came to me as a very young woman, and it is *still* with you now."

"How do I get rid of that?"

She shook her head. "You don't. I know that's not what you want to hear, but that's not how this works, unfortunately. Your experience with your grandmother, it happened. Your experience with Walter... it happened. You can't erase or undo it, and you can't rid yourself of the scars that came along with it. What you do is you keep your eyes *forward.* When you find that your mind wants to drift back to that place, the instinct is to let it happen, to let it connect – for what? How does that serve you, or advance your progress?"

"So I'm supposed to pretend it didn't happen?"

"You can acknowledge, even internally, that it happened, without letting yourself dwell on it. It's *hard.* Some times will be harder than others, sometimes you won't succeed – be gentle with yourself in those times. And celebrate when you overcome it. But every time you feel it, every time that negativity creeps up... you at least have to *try*. The brain is too powerful for you to win every battle, Keris, but you can at least give your enemy – your negative self-perception, past missteps, traumatic memories

- the fight of your life. Because really... that's what this is. You are *fighting for your life*. Are you going to lose without even picking up a sword?"

I sat back in the chair, turning her words over in my mind.

"I'm sorry to say that our time is almost up for today," Dr. Alexander spoke up again, after giving me a few minutes to think. "But... you're familiar with Newton's third law of motion, correct?"

I frowned. "Um... I think so? Forces acting against each other, something like that?"

"Yes," she confirmed. *"For every action, there is an equal, and opposite, reaction."*

"...okay. What does that have to do with me?"

"Everything. A few moments ago, you insinuated that there had to be some *"catch"* involved, with this dreamboat of a man who has turned his attentions on you. You believe this negative statement because your life has been inundated with negative interpersonal experiences – even *very* recently. Besides your relationship with your friend, Natalie, you don't believe anything – *anyone* – good can happen for you."

I pushed out a sigh. "It sounds so bleak when you say it out loud."

"Because it *is* bleak," Dr. Alexander agreed. "But... I'd like you to consider it this way. You've had these deeply traumatic experiences – a force going in one direction. But in accordance with Newton's law, there has to be an equal, opposite force pushing back. I am *not* telling you what you should or shouldn't do with this man who believes you're his soulmate. I *am* asking you to consider... what if this time now, these *good* things... are your equal, opposite reaction?"

I left Dr. Alexander's office with my head swimming, and my cell phone notifications full of missed calls, all from one unfamiliar number. I put the phone to my ear as I headed for the lobby, listening while it connected to my voicemail box.

I snatched it away as soon as I heard Walter's voice.

Calling on the fortification I'd just received from the therapy appointment, I pressed the button that would delete the message, without listening to it. I did the same thing with the other three messages he'd sent, not caring to hear a word he had to say about anything.

There was *nothing* for us to talk about.

I relayed that same conclusion to my lawyer in a quick email, asking her to pass it along to Walter's lawyer, to pass it to his client. I had no desire to be roped into bullshit.

Instead of going back to the *Night Shift* office as planned, for last minute touches on the website before the official distribution launch, I decided home was a better option. I could change into soft pajamas and work from my bed without judgment.

And without Laken's presence clouding my thoughts.

I'd been purposely avoiding him for days, and to his credit, he'd taken the hint. He'd surprised me with lunch a time or two, and I'd found flowers waiting on my desk more than once, but the man himself had kept his distance. It probably helped that he was busy with the preparation for the launch.

In my head, I ran over my own to-do list for when I settled at home. I let that distract me for the few blocks it took to get there, with a quick mental detour to fantasize about the dreamy loft Clayton had one of his partner agents show me, a block over.

As soon as I turned onto my own street, a prickle of awareness cleared all the distractions from my mind.

Walter was in front of my building.

Pacing back and forth, waiting for me, occasionally peering up the street. It was busy enough that he hadn't spotted me yet, and before he could, I turned to walk the other way.

What the fuck does he want?

I didn't have to wonder how he knew – or maybe just guessed – where I would be. He'd been with me at the reading of my grandmother's will, had insisted it was "financially prudent" to hold on to the apartment I hadn't wanted to keep. An apartment she likely purchased with life insurance money meant for *me*.

I had a thing about hotels, and an allergy to cats that meant I couldn't stay with Natalie. It was no big shocker that he'd know where I was, but still... what the hell did he want from me?

Now, I wished I hadn't deleted those messages, maybe then I'd at least have some sort of heads up for whatever bullshit was about to land at my feet.

I'd been walking with no aim other than getting away from my place before Walter saw me – not because I was afraid of him, but because I just didn't want to interact with him. When I stopped though, it was in front of *Night Shift*.

My heart didn't stop racing until I stepped in.

I *fully* intended to go hide in my office, and stay there all night if I had to, but voices from the other side of the bar drew my attention before I could start in that direction. It was Laken and Lark, accompanied by an older couple they bore too much resemblance to for them *not* to be related.

To be their *parents*.

And they'd already spotted me.

"Keris!" Lark called, waving me over. "Come here for a second, we want to introduce you!"

Just like last week, with the brewing staff, I wasn't remotely in the right headspace to make a good impression, but I forced it aside in favor of cementing myself as part of the team. I compelled my feet to move and a smile to my face, pulling all the warmth I could muster as I extended my hand, to the woman first.

"Oh please," she said, sidestepping my hand to pull me into a tight hug. "I'm Marlene Kimble honey – I saw that beautiful work you did on those labels. *Thank you* for honoring my baby that way. I told Kenny I want that artwork on a canvas for my office."

My eyebrows went up. "Kenny?"

"That would be me," Laken spoke up, in an exasperated tone that only made his mother laugh.

"*Kenny*," she said, pointedly, just before cupping my face in her hands. "You said she was a great artist. But he didn't say not a word about how *gorgeous* you are."

"Let that girl alone," a gruff voice sounded – Laken and Lark's father. He eased Marlene back, sticking out his hand in greeting. "Henry Kimble. *Kimble Family Bourbon*, you may have heard of us?"

"I have," I laughed, accepting his firm greeting. "Very smooth."

That made Henry grin – the same big smile as Laken, only with a lot more salt than pepper. "Ahhh, you're a fan?"

"I'm more of a whiskey girl myself," I admitted. "But I've never turned down a *Kimble & Coke*."

Henry winked at me. "Don't worry – before you know it, I'll have you converted."

"I look forward to it," I teased right back, not missing the "look" exchanged between the siblings and their mother as I interacted with him.

"You've already heard Lark and I talk about her, obviously, but just for the record – she's Keris Bradford, our graphic designer," Laken said, rounding out the introduction. "They just got here from the airport – we were about to go down to the brewhouse to see the finished bottles all set up in the four-packs. You want to join us?"

"I shouldn't," I shook my head. "You're with your family, and I—"

"I *insist*," Marlene said, taking me by the hand. "Laken, take that heavy bag from her shoulder so she doesn't have to carry it around."

Laken shot me a smirk as he followed his mother's directive, taking my bag and leaving it with Cal behind the bar for safekeeping.

And just like that... I was on my way to the brewhouse with the Kimble family.

Once I was there, I was glad to have been roped in – it was my first time seeing the packaging all complete. Labels, caps, and the specialty four-pack carrier, not in a mockup on my screen, but all brought to life.

It was my first time doing this type of thing.

At *CO*, projects at this level were reserved for senior designers – I'd done countless websites, logos, tee shirts, business cards, all manner of things.

But *this*?

This was a first.

I took a few steps back, putting some distance between myself and Laken's family as they admired the culmination of years of work. With a bottle of *No Angel* clasped in my hands, I tried my very best not to allow the tears forming in my eyes to break free, but to no avail.

"You really put your heart into this, didn't you?"

I looked up to find Henry in front of me, peering into my face. He was holding a bottle of *Rebirth*.

I answered his question with a nod. "I try to with every project, but... some mean a little more than others."

"They certainly do," he agreed, holding up the bottle in his hands. "I was already proud of my boy, but this – seeing *this*?" he turned it so that the phoenix design wasn't covered by his hand. "This is the gravy. I thank you, for this."

"That's all Laken," I told him, shaking my head. "He gave me the name, had me taste it, explained the flavor profile and all that. I just went where his words about it led me."

Henry's eyebrows went up. "He didn't tell you this was in honor of his brother?"

"No, not until after. When he saw the design."

Henry's head bowed, and he turned to face in the same direction I was, looking to where Laken was still standing with Lark and Marlene. "I'm not surprised. He told you how he died?"

"No. It's never... no, we've never discussed it."

"Phoenix was always... troubled," Henry started, and I raised my hands to stop him, thinking I'd unwittingly suggested I wanted him to tell the story.

He ignored me.

"That boy was born marked, and me and Marlene... we always knew we wouldn't have too long with him. Those demons... they were on his back *tough*. We did anything and everything we could, but it was too much for him. So he ah... self-medicated." He paused there, shaking his head. "Laken found him. Tried to rush him to the hospital, but it was already too late. That's how he got those scars," Henry revealed, pointing vaguely towards his own face.

"I... I don't understand," I admitted, when he didn't elaborate.

"He ran off the road," Henry explained, as if it were obvious. "With his dead brother strapped in the passenger seat. Almost died himself trying to save his brother."

I put a hand to my chest as those words sank in. Laken had mentioned his brother to me, and I'd just assumed the scars were from some kind of accident. I hadn't expected something so... *heartbreaking*.

"I see him a lot, now," Henry told me. "It was just Laken at first, and I thought it was just grief. Thought the boy was out his mind, which I guess wouldn't be that surprising. He's spoken to all of us, over the years. But now... it's like he's all I see."

My gaze drifted to the bottle in Henry's hand, the neck of it disappearing in the tight clutch of his fist. "You're talking about Phoenix? That's who you're seeing?"

Henry didn't blink, didn't budge, didn't give any indication he'd heard me as he stared at the bottle. After several seconds passed like that, I put a hand to his shoulder, pulling his attention back to me.

His eyes closed tight, and then he smiled at me – giving me another glimpse at Laken in thirty years. "You really put your heart into this, didn't you?" he asked, holding up the bottle.

My smile slipped. "We... we talked about that already, remember?"

"Now how could we have talked about something that just came to mind, young lady?" he asked. "Do you know who you're speaking to?"

"I... of course. You're Henry Kimble, *Kimble Family Bourbon*."

"That's my name," he grinned. "And who might you be?" he asked, extending a hand for me to shake.

"I'm... I'm Keris, Mr. Kimble. Keris Bradford. Graphic designer for *Night Shift*... remember?"

He shook his head, frowning like I'd lost my mind. "Of course I remember you – you put your heart into this bottle design, didn't you, young lady?"

Before I had a chance to respond to that, we were joined by the rest of the family. The conversation went on, but ever-perceptive Laken pulled me off to the side while the others continued chatting.

"You okay?" he asked, putting a hand at my waist. "Pops didn't offend you, did he?"

I shook my head. "No. It's just... it's nothing we can't talk about another time. You should be enjoying your family. And I've got work to do, so I'll see you later."

"You sure?"

"I'm *positive*," I insisted, stepping away, in the direction of the exit.

Laken didn't look convinced, but he accepted it – likely because his family was there. I said quick goodbyes and then retrieved my laptop bag from Cal and headed for my office.

I had *way* too much swirling in my head.

TWELVE

LAKEN.

*P*eaceful.
 That was the first word that came to mind when I returned to my bedroom from the shower to find Keris still passed out asleep. She'd shown up at my door last night, still wearing her same clothes from work, which let me know she'd been putting in extra time on the website.

And then, instead of going home, she'd come to *me*.

There was something she wasn't saying, but that wasn't unusual with Keris.

Showing up at my door, *was*.

So instead of harping on the unspoken details, I let her inside, and reveled in the benefits of whatever she was trying to get her mind off of.

Reveled in the fact that she'd, without a single word of prompting, spent the night.

I had a full day ahead of me, with my parents being here, and all the last-minute managing involved with the official product launch in two days. I didn't have time to sit down, still mostly undressed, coffee in hand, to watch Keris sleep. But I took it anyway.

This shit was weird, man.

I wasn't one of those dudes who fucked off his whole twenties and thirties and then suddenly wanted to settle down – I wasn't even thinking about it.

At all.

After Emil left, I was laser-focused on *Night Shift* – it encompassed my work, my social life, the people who helped bring it to fruition had become my friends, damn near family. Any time I had left, was quickly consumed by being a Kimble. And every once in a while, yeah, I'd engage in a quick fling.

Never serious.

Keris Bradford had thrown me off-kilter.

My eyebrows lifted as she stirred, and I watched her come awake. Her eyelashes parted just enough for her dark, coppery irises to come into view as she frowned.

Probably wondering where the hell she was.

"Good morning," I spoke, offering a hint that made her flinch, and her eyes opened further. Her gaze wasn't pointed at me before, but she shifted in my direction at the sound of my voice.

And smiled.

A blow to the fucking chest.

One of my first impressions of Keris had been that she didn't smile much, and it worried me before I realized why, at the time, they were so hard to come by. Now, I saw it often enough that if one didn't easily appear, I knew something was up.

This, though, was a new experience.

Keris, in my bed, first thing in the morning, after spending a good portion of the night buried deep inside her. Her hair was a disheveled mess, her face puffy and swollen with sleep, nude body twisted haphazardly in my sheets.

Beautiful.

"What time is it?" she asked, scrubbing a hand over her face. Her fingers went to her hair, immediately hitting a roadblock of tangled strands. "*Shit.*"

"It's just after seven," I told her, putting my coffee down on the windowsill. "I've got something for you."

Her eyes went wide as she sat up, wrapping herself in the sheet – unnecessary modesty when I'd seen, touched, tasted every part of her. "Something for *me?*"

I grinned, making a point of looking around. "You're the only other person here, aren't you?"

I stepped into the closet, walking to the back shelves for a box that had been there at least a week. As soon as I came back into view, Keris started shaking her head.

"Laken, no. I don't need gifts—"

"Hush, woman," I told her, putting the box down on the bed in front of her. It was big enough that I'd brought it in with two hands, so I could understand why it might be a bit intimidating. "Just open it."

She shot me a stubborn glare, but innate curiosity won over obstinate nature. She pulled the top from the box and peeked inside, then instantly sat back and looked away, her expression indecipherable.

"Really, Laken?"

I crossed my arms over my bare chest and frowned. "What? Did I do something wrong?"

"No," she answered quickly, shaking her head. "The opposite. It's just... it's... it's *really* thoughtful." She gave her attention back to the box, lifting out a pouch containing a brush and wide-toothed comb, and various hair products curated for me by Lark.

"Well... last time I asked you to spend the night, your excuse was that you didn't have any toiletries or clothes to be ready for the next day. I rectified that *immediately*, but... this is your first time overnight since then. I noticed you didn't try to sneak out this time anyway though."

Her happy demeanor deflated a little, and she sighed. "Well...
that's a bit of a double-edged sword, if I can be honest."

"You can *always* be honest with me, Keris."

She pulled her full bottom lip between her teeth, worrying it for a
moment before she spoke again. "Walter was at my place yesterday,"
she admitted. "I had an appointment that I went to, and then I was
walking home, I spotted him. He was in front of the building, waiting
for me. So I came here instead."

"That's what was bothering you yesterday," I realized, and she
nodded.

"I have no idea what he wanted. He'd called and left some
messages, but I deleted without listening – I just didn't need the
drama. But then he was in front of my place, and I just... I needed to
feel safe, so I came to *Night Shift*."

"You came to *me*."

She raised her eyebrows at my assessment but didn't – *couldn't* –
deny it. "You were busy with your family, so I got some work done.
Got a *lot* of work done. But then it was late, and I was *so* tired,
and I—"

"Didn't feel safe, so you came to me."

"*Why* are you harping on that?" she asked, in a huff.

I shrugged. "I'm just making sure I have the lay of the land. For
the record, you can *always* come to me, always talk to me. And I'll
make sure Walter is taken care of as well."

"I don't need you to get involved," she insisted. "My lawyer is
contacting his, and we'll handle it like that. You have enough on your
plate."

"I don't have *shit* precluding me from making that motherfucker
leave you alone."

She raised an eyebrow. "You have me asking you to leave it
alone."

"I'm not even going to pretend to consider that," I admitted. "Ask
me something else."

"*Laken.*"

"Neither of us has time to argue about this," I told her. "Look in the rest of the box."

Rolling her eyes, Keris picked up the box and turned it over, dumping the contents onto the bed. "There. I looked."

I met the challenge of her gaze with a stern expression of my own, forcing away the smile that wanted to break free.

"You wanna act like a badass child, daddy will absolutely spank your ass," I growled, taking a step toward the bed. "Or your pussy. Just... wherever it lands, sweetheart."

She flipped the covers away from her, baring her naked breasts and bare pussy as she spread her legs. "Thought you didn't have time?"

Fuck.

I glanced at my watch – I was already late for breakfast with Lark and my parents.

"I don't. Get dressed, you're coming with me."

I pointed to the bed, where she'd dumped the box. The new underwear, jeans, and distressed gray sweater were piled in a heap.

"You picked this for me?" she asked, distracted from our almost-mad sex by the clothes.

"I did. Do you like it?"

She held up the pretty lace bra and panties, then the sweater, giving all the items a drawn-out inspection before finally meeting my eyes. "They're fine."

"*Just* fine?"

"They're perfect," she conceded. "You know that. Somehow."

"Not *somehow*. Paying attention. Get dressed – *please*."

"Dressed for *what*?" she called after me, as I headed into the closet to grab something for myself.

"Breakfast with my family."

"Oh I'm not doing that."

When I turned around, she was in the closet doorway, holding the toiletry bags – one for hair, one for everything else.

"I figured that," I admitted, pulling a sweater from one of the hangers. "Turn the lock behind you when you leave – I've gotta get out of here."

I tugged the sweater over my head, surprised to find Keris still standing in the doorway when I looked again.

"Your father... no diagnosis yet?"

I frowned as I pulled a pair of socks from the dressing-table drawer. "No. He insists nothing is wrong, and there hasn't been another incident, so it's been tough to force the issue of seeing a doctor with him."

"What exactly qualifies as an *incident*?" she asked, "Because yesterday, down in the brewhouse... there was this moment, where it was like he completely forgot who I was, even though we'd just been introduced. He was repeating himself, and... I don't know. It just didn't feel right."

Damn.

"Okay," I nodded, grabbing shoes. "Thank you, for telling me. I'm going to talk to him about it again today, because... it *doesn't* feel right. We can't let it go just because he wants us to."

"I hope I'm not adding unnecessary worry, I just knew you were all concerned about him," Keris started, but I interrupted her with a kiss before moving past her in the doorway.

"You absolutely did the right thing," I told her, sitting on the edge of the bed to put my shoes on. "If I can help it, we're getting this thing resolved, *today*."

———

"So Lark says the young lady you introduced us to yesterday is the love of your life," my mother said, hitting me with that verbal sucker punch not even ten minutes after I'd joined them at *HoneyBee*.

I shot a scowl at Lark, then bought myself some time from responding with a long sip of water.

Across the table, my mother stared at me, not letting up.

"That really wasn't Lark's place to talk about," I said, with a pointed look at my sister, who apparently didn't know how to keep her mouth shut about this. "It's more complicated than that."

"Do you think I'm stupid?" my mother asked, raising an eyebrow. "Because I'm quite sure I'm capable of understanding a *complicated* concept. So *it's complicated* is only a viable excuse for not answering my question if you don't believe that about me."

"Could you *not*, woman?" I urged, not at all comfortable with the way this conversation was going.

"I most certainly *will*," she countered. "Henry, make him tell me."

Seated beside her, my father shook his head. "See that's the problem," he said, nursing a glass of orange juice, I heavily suspected was spiked with *Kimble* bourbon. "You always want to tell a grown-ass man what to do."

My mother rolled her eyes. "Oh *God*, are you really starting with this again?"

"I ain't never stopped, and when I *do*, I'll start again as many times as it takes to get you to leave me the hell alone about it."

"You're right – I'm the most terrible wife ever, for wanting your stubborn half-senile ass to go see a doctor. Please, everybody, forgive me."

Ah, hell.

I couldn't think of a better model of #Blacklove than my parents. They've been married a long ass time and had always gotten along well. Of course, growing up, we'd seen the occasional, normal argument between the two, but they never subjected us to any type of excessive fighting or anything like that. They exemplified mutual love and respect.

Until my mother tried to get my father's stubborn ass to the doctor.

I guess that was just his breaking point.

"Phoenix told me it was her," I spoke up, offering my personal business as the sacrificial lamb for them to cut their arguing.

"Whether or not it's going to work out that way, I don't know. I'm just telling you what he told me."

"But you know he's never been wrong before," my mother said. "We really should feel blessed to still have his spirit with us in such a way."

"Blessed, haunted, same difference I guess," I countered, causing my mother to shoot me a scowl.

"You shouldn't speak about him that way," she scolded me, and I shrugged.

"If I don't know anything about my brother, I know he *definitely* wouldn't have been offended by that," I said. "You know I take him seriously."

That reminder seemed to satisfy my mother enough. She nodded, then sat back again, still wearing that same expectant look.

She was waiting on the rest.

"There's nothing to tell Mama," I said. "At least... nothing to tell that's any of your business," I teased, but in a serious enough tone for her to understand I meant it.

She huffed. "*Fine*, I'll let you be. She *is* a pretty little thing though," she added, which was high praise from a woman who had never been shy with her hyper-criticisms of anybody her children dated. In fact, Emil was the only other woman to ever get a compliment like that from her.

"I just have one question," she said, "And then I'm going to leave it alone..."

"Babies are absolutely off the table," I told her, already knowing her *one question*. "I'm too damn old to be trying to have babies anyway."

"Who said anything about *you* having a baby," my mother countered. "How old is Keris?"

"Thirty-six."

My mother frowned. "Oh, I guess that is kind of up there, isn't it?"

"Well *damn*," Lark objected. "I'll have you know, thirty-six is *not*

149

old, and plenty of women my age – and older – are having perfectly healthy pregnancies, and perfectly healthy babies. *Excuse you.*"

"That doesn't mean you're not on the tail end, sweetheart," my mother said, propping her chin in her hand as she focused on my sister. "And with no marriage prospects on the horizon, well... I should probably focus my grandchild-getting efforts on your brother."

Lark sucked her teeth, shoving her chair away from the table. "Yeah, 'cause that's worked out so well for everybody so far?!"

"Damn, low blow!" I called after Lark's retreating back, trying to figure out how the hell this conversation – which wouldn't be happening if she'd kept her mouth shut anyway – ended up with *me* catching a verbal bullet between her and Mama.

Mama dabbed at her mouth with her napkin, shaking her head as she prepared to get up and go after Lark. "That girl...," she muttered, gathering her purse.

"Is *just* like you," my father and I both said, nearly in unison.

She shot a glare at both of us in turn, then moved off to follow her daughter.

And hopefully apologize.

"I swear that woman gets bossier with every year she ages," my father said, pulling my attention to him. Before he could pick it up, I snagged his glass, bringing it to my nose for evidence of what I already suspected.

I was right.

"I know people do mimosas with breakfast all the time, but you don't think *that* is a bit excessive?" I asked, earning myself a glare.

"Here *you* go with the bullshit too," he groused. "An old man can't even have a drink in peace?"

I threw up my hands, after I'd given it back. "You can have your drink, definitely. I'm just saying... you never used to drink before noon, so I'm wondering what's different now."

"I told you a second ago – I'm an old man now. Between these old bones and that old woman, I need a lil' something to take the edge off."

"You sure it's just that?" I asked, not believing a word that had just left his mouth.

He frowned. "What else would it be?"

"Headaches, forgetfulness, confusion… I feel like there's no way the liquor is actually *helping* with any of that."

"I'm about sick of you. *All* of you," Pops grunted, raising his voice. "I've told you, more than once – there ain't a goddamn thing for any of you to be worried about with me. The next person says something, I'm whooping their ass."

I chuckled. "Well, I guess you better go ahead and square up old man, cause I'm not letting this shit go."

"Why the hell *not*?" He'd just taken a drink, and when he slammed the glass down, juice splashed all over his hand and the white tablecloth, but he didn't seem to notice. "I've been hustling since I was fifteen damn years old, working the family business and expanding and growing, putting in my time to build this family's legacy. I get a little confused, and you motherfuckers are treating me like I'm drooling and shitting myself. I may be old, but I'm still sharp as a tack. You won't railroad me – *I* run this company, and that won't change without a damn fight."

I pushed out a deep sigh. "Pops… you retired from *KFB* two years ago. You're on the board of directors, yes, but… you're not in charge anymore. And this is *exactly* what we're so concerned about."

"It was a slip-up, boy," he countered. "Ya ass wasn't reminding me I wasn't in charge when you were asking about those bourbon barrels for this beer shit, were you? You know how much those damn barrels are worth?"

I sucked my teeth. "Man, don't change the subject. But since you brought it up, just so we're clear – yes, I *do* know how much the barrels are worth, and I've got no problem just contacting my cousins about them, *along with* paying market value. I was trying to include you."

"You ain't gotta do me no favors."

"It's not about what I *gotta* do," I snapped. "It's about what I *want* to do, and what I'm *going* to do – and that's not let this shit ride, no matter how many deflections you want to bring up, or fights you want to pick. You want me to leave you alone? Fine – I have better shit to do than babysit your cantankerous ass. But I'm not letting a goddamn thing go until you see a doctor. You want to hate me for it? That's fine."

"You've got a lot of nerve boy, talking to me like I won't whip your ass!"

I shrugged. "Like I said – square up whenever you're ready. The perfect excuse to drag you to a doctor."

"You think I'm playing, don't you?" he pressed on, picking up his glass to swallow the last of the contents. "Your leg ain't been the same since you fucked it up trying to play savior to your brother – just like you're trying to do with me. Well you couldn't make him do shit, you won't make me do shit either!"

I picked up my own glass, sipping from my water in an attempt to quell my growing irritation. "You should know this tantrum doesn't mean shit to me."

"He told me, he told you not to come. If you'd been with your wife instead of down in Louisiana running after him, your leg wouldn't be fucked up, would it? Should've listened to him."

"What the fuck did you just say to me?" I asked, putting the water down to fix my father with the kind of glare I usually would reserve for... shit, a mortal enemy. There was plenty I could take on the chin and keep it moving, but *that*? Fucking *taunting* me about Phoenix's death, and the subsequent car accident that had almost claimed *my* life too?

Nah, we weren't doing that.

My sudden shift in tone had rendered my father quiet, his nostrils flared as he eyed his empty glass.

"You're my father... and I'm trying to respect that. Trying to do right by you, *just* like I tried to do right by my brother. And you wanna throw it in my fuckin' face?"

152

"I'm *trying* to teach you a lesson," he snapped back. "To not be out here expecting any damn favors!"

I frowned. "Man, *what*? What favors?"

"The *barrels*," he growled at me, like I was being purposefully dense. "Your cousins might want to ship them up here to you for nothing, but I say if you wanna be in business, then you conduct yourself like a business. You should *buy* them, just like anybody else would have to."

My head tipped to the side, eyes narrowed as I realized his mind had completely disconnected from the conversation. Either that, or he was shifting because he realized how massively out of line he'd been with that comment about Phoenix.

But... Henry Kimble had *never* been one to back down from a confrontation. Even when he was wrong, he dug the fuck in, which is why we were in this situation now. Besides that, I doubted he would play on his supposed mental degradation, when he was in denial that it was even happening, and desperate to dispel any doubts.

The evidence was right here in my face though.

Of course I believed the stories I'd been hearing, but seeing it firsthand was a whole other thing. There was no anger in his eyes, no sign of the contentious energy we'd been building before – just his usual austerity when it came to "teaching me the business."

It was massively unsettling.

"So, your sister decided to leave," my mother fussed as she approached the table, without Lark in tow. "And I know you've got a lot of other things to do, Laken, so we won't hold you."

I raised my eyebrows. "I... haven't even eaten yet."

"Oh, don't worry about that. I flagged down the server and had her pack your breakfast to go. Henry and I are going to go do some exploring around the city, then meet up for lunch with friends of ours."

"Friends of *yours*," my father corrected, as he stood from his chair. "I'm going to hit the head," he told us, walking off. As soon as he was gone, I turned to my mother.

"About getting him to a doctor? Set the appointment, for as *soon* as y'all get back home. I'll fly down and drag him in myself if I have to."

I *really need this to be a less shitty day,* I thought, as I headed back to the bar from the brewhouse. From my slight friction this morning with Keris, to the shit with my father, to getting back to *Night Shift* to find out the labeling machinery had malfunctioned, it really seemed like nothing was going my way.

As long as it's cool for launch day.

As long as it's cool for launch day.

I repeated that in my head, reminding myself that most likely, everything would be perfectly fine for the launch. My parents showing up two days earlier than their planned arrival had definitely thrown me off, when I had what felt like a million final details to attend to. It would all work out though.

It *had* to.

After the work I'd put in, the things I'd sacrificed, I wasn't accepting anything else. A huge part of this thing had been making my family proud – showing my father that his lessons hadn't been in vain, that I'd developed into a man capable of building something.

I just hoped he'd be able to remember and appreciate it.

There was a lot weighing heavily on my mind as I walked into the bar to check in with Cal about my schedule for the rest of the day. Of course I had it available on my phone too, but it was different having it relayed to me – easier to absorb the information.

I didn't get the chance to ask though.

As soon as I stepped into the bar, my gaze landed on Walter Edwards, and my eyes narrowed.

To my credit, I hesitated, remembering the request Keris had made for me to leave that situation alone. My reluctance to address him only lasted as long as it took for her bruised face to enter my mind, and all the other little bullshit he'd been on since then came rushing back with it.

My feet started moving before my mind could even catch up, and before I knew it, I was right up on him, clapping a hand on his shoulder with enough force to make him wobble on his barstool, then gripping with enough force to make him cringe.

"*Walter*," I greeted, taking the empty seat next to him. "Just the man I wanted to see. How the fuck are you?"

He smiled uncomfortably, clearly taken aback by my affable energy. "I... I'm good. Thank you for asking."

"You're welcome. What are you doing here?"

He picked up a half-full glass of beer from the bar, tipping it in my direction a bit before taking a sip. "Heard a lot of buzz about the craft beers. Thought I'd come check them out."

I nodded, balling my hands into fists to keep me from smacking the glass from his hand. "Nice story, but... why are you *really* here, Walter? I'm a busy man, so save the bullshit."

He scratched his head, blinking owlishly behind frameless glasses. "Well... uh, you never replied to my email, about Keris Bradford. I guess I was worried about how that worked out. I'm sure she used our company's name on her resume, so... just protecting the brand."

"Protecting the brand?" I grinned, then leaned in toward him a bit. "I thought I told you to save the bullshit?"

"It's *not* bullshit, it's—"

"*Don't* fuckin' lie to me, man. You're sitting at my bar in the middle of the day because you were hoping to run into Keris, weren't you? Because you don't understand how to let shit go, do you?" I asked, scrubbing a hand over my chin. "You see how easy that was to say? And yet, you chose to lie to my face."

"No more than she has, I'm sure," Walter sniped. "Did she tell how she manipulated and stole from the company?"

"It's none of your business what Keris has told me, because *she* is not your business anymore. I get it – I'd be hurt too, if I lost a woman like her. But this shit you're doing now? It's got you out here looking like a bitch, when you could easily just let it go."

He smirked. "Let me guess – she's fucking you now too?"

I smiled.

I smiled long enough for that smirk to melt right off his face, and then I looked around, gauging the distance between where we were at the end of the bar, and where the entrance to the back room was. I took a quick accounting of how many customers were in the bar, and how much attention they were paying to what was happening with me over here.

I decided the reaction I *wanted* to have, was too great a risk, so close to such an important day.

And then I snatched Walter up by his collar anyway.

I moved quickly, and with purpose, ignoring the spilled beer as he helplessly flailed against my hold. Before anyone except Cal could really take notice, I had Walter in the back, where I shoved his punk ass against the wall.

"Not *too*," I said, right in his face as he whimpered. "*Only*. She's *only* fucking me now, and that's why you're goddamn bothered, isn't it, Walter? *Isn't it?!*" I growled, making him flinch. "You had a *decade* to present yourself as somebody worthy of having a life with, but you're a fuckin' failure, aren't you? And you can't just let her move on. *Why?*"

"I—"

"*I don't actually give a fuck*," I asserted, moving my grip to his throat. "Tell it to God, your mama, your therapist, your dog, whoever in this world gives a shit about you, my man, 'cause me? I don't," I whispered, giving him a smirk. "Don't show your face around here again. Don't show up at Keris' place. Don't eat at her favorite restaurants, don't shop at her favorite grocery stores. Order your shit, Walter, okay?"

"That's ridi—"

"I'm *not* fucking around with you," I told him, deadly serious as I tightened my grip. "Don't call her. Don't bother her. Not even a little. If somebody brings her up to you, you don't even know who the fuck she is, Walter. Do you?"

I waited on him to shake his head, then let him go and stepped back, ready to knock his fucking head off if he decided to take his chances and swing.

Instead, he bent at the waist, gasping and choking for air. "You just attacked me!" he claimed, glaring at me as he caught his breath.

"Get the fuck over it. And get your drunk ass out of my establishment."

"I'm not drunk!"

"My bartender and I recall differently," I told him, shrugging. "And I'm sure the police will love to hear your story of coming to *this* bar to drink, after being turned down for a job that I ultimately hired the ex you're harassing for. As a matter of fact – *do* call them. It'll be good for the restraining order, along with your harassing phone calls, and the pictures of you hanging around outside her apartment."

I was bluffing, sure, but he didn't know that – something he made clear with his mouth dropped open and eyes wide.

"I just—she won't answer the damn phone, after the way she... she just *left*," he complained, damn near on the verge of tears. "And she told our colleagues I hit her, letting them believe I was abusing her or something the whole time. And now, there was an accounting error in splitting our bank accounts. *She owes me money.*"

"*Consider it severance pay*," I barked at his pathetic ass, sorely tempted to throw a blow.

Frantically, he shook his head. "She already got severance pay from *CO*, but I bet she's not telling that part, is she?!"

"I'm talking about severance from *you*." My face pulled into a sneer I couldn't help. "You don't need that money – you just want her to give you some attention. Well – you caught mine instead. Get the fuck out of here."

He didn't waste any time scrambling out, just like the weak-ass insect he was. I followed as far as the bar, watching as he damn near tripped over his own feet leaving.

"Yo – what was *that* about?" Cal asked. "I didn't overserve him, did I?"

I shook my head. "Nah. But if you see him again, don't serve him at all. Put his ass out of here and call me."

THIRTEEN

KERIS

"No, no, *no*, you're doing it wrong," Natalie scolded, taking away the *Night Shift* branded products I had in my hand. "It's tissue, t-shirt, another layer of tissue, bottle opener inside the glass, *then* you put that in, and lay another layer of tissue on top," she explained, showing me for about the fifth time what the finished product should look like.

Not that I didn't already know.

I was just incredibly distracted, from Laken's surprise gift box of all the things I needed, to his low key attempt to get me to breakfast with his parents, and then, most of all, the report I'd gotten from Cal about Laken hemming up "some old dude" in the bar yesterday.

I just had a little feeling about that.

Especially since according to my neighbor, Walter had abruptly ended his attempts to stake out my apartment. Laken hadn't said anything though, and I wasn't about to ask. Not when he had much bigger things to be concerned about.

Tomorrow was set to be one of the biggest days of his life. There was nothing on this planet that could make me ask that man if he'd talked to my ex.

"Are you even paying attention?" Natalie asked, taking yet another wrongly prepared swag bag from my hands. "Is the dick really *that* good that you can't even focus, girl?"

"I'm not even thinking about that right now, for your information," I shot back, and Natalie smirked.

"*Right now*. Right."

"Okay let me go find something *else* to do to help prep for launch," I threatened, and started to walk off, only to have Natalie drag me right back to the conference room table where we'd set up.

"Oh no you *won't*," she said. "This is the most time I've gotten to spend with you in weeks. You're not going anywhere."

"You say that like *you're* not the one who has been all booked and busy," I reminded her.

"So that's supposed to make me miss you less?"

"Of course not, but it sure does soften the blow, doesn't it?"

"You sure are right about that. How is the apartment hunting coming along?"

"I'm already settled on a place, I just need you to come look at it with me before I make a final decision."

Nat raised an eyebrow. "You're waiting for me? Why don't you just get Laken to look at it with you?"

I sucked my teeth. "Because I don't know what the hell I'm doing with Laken, or how the hell that's going to work out. I don't want him helping me choose that place to be... imprinted on me, you know? It's bad enough that he put me in contact with the realtor. At least I already knew Clayton so that makes it not quite as bad. But whatever this is that we're doing, if it doesn't work out, I want this place to be something I did on my own. Sanctuary."

"But *my* imprint is fine?"

"Duh," I answered. "Your ass is stuck with me forever."

"Wow, another thing you're right about today," Natalie teased.

"And I see you're admitting that there *is* a thing now, between the two of you?"

I shrugged. "At this point, it would just be silly not to. I mean, don't get me wrong – I *do* still have my concerns. He doesn't exactly act like it, but it's not lost on me that Laken is my boss, and we see how that turned out last time."

"Oh girl," Natalie shook her head. "You go through another situation like last time, I can tell you now – I'm going to jail. I'm just gonna shoot his ass."

I opened my mouth to tease her about that, but then I shut it because... Natalie honestly might. Her family owned *Forty Acres*, one of the largest black-owned hunting gear companies in the country. She, like every member of their family, had learned how to shoot young, and she still regularly went to a nearby gun range to "decompress".

It was really about a 50/50 chance.

"I don't think you're going to *have* to shoot anybody," I told her, laughing. "Even with all my reservations... Laken makes me feel good. And after talking with Dr. Alexander, I'm really trying to lean into it. Learning to trust myself again."

"That's good," Natalie smiled. "Really, *really* good."

"I agree. And now... didn't you have a date a few days ago? I never heard anything else about that."

Natalie put down everything in her hands, slapping her palms against the table. "Girl. Let me tell you about *this* motherfucker!"

I t made sense to shut the bar down leading into the launch. Everything needed to be perfect, so we needed the place empty so we could employ deep cleaning and decorating, set up the displays, all of that. I knew those things were happening, but what I *hadn't* expected was the opening and decorating of the patio, for a special dinner and pre-launch party for all the *Night Shift* staff and their families.

I... didn't have anyone to invite.

Natalie had likely communicated that to Laken, and neither of them said anything to me about it, taking away the chance for me to feel bad about the very insular nature of my life.

I appreciated that.

Because now that I was here – now that the party was going on, and I was surrounded by faces that were becoming more and more familiar – I didn't feel bad at all.

I felt at home.

Even among Laken's family, I didn't feel a shred of the loneliness I'd briefly expected when I realized what was happening.

It was beautiful.

I found myself tucked away in a corner to take a quiet moment away from everything, and to just absorb it all. I'd never been out here before, because it was really too chilly for the patio at night, but now space heaters had been installed, making it feel cozy. String lights lined the huge wooden beams that comprised the ceiling, and special shades put something of a barrier between us and whatever was outside. Music pumped through the speakers.

It felt... *good.*

Like I was finally somewhere I really belonged.

"Why are you off in the cut over here?" Laken asked, offering me one of the *Rookies* in his hand – one with official labeling.

"Just taking it all in," I told him, accepting the beer. "This is gorgeous. Everybody seems happy."

The corners of his mouth curved up as he took a seat. "Everybody?"

"Including me," I assured. "Seeing everybody with their families, friends... it doesn't make me feel melancholy. It gives me hope. Reinforces that there *is* good in the world."

I looked away to take a long drink from my beer, and to get a break from the intensity of his gaze. Even without looking at him, I could feel Laken's careful scrutiny, could feel him looking straight through to my soul, seeking out the veracity of my words.

"Come here," he said, drawing my gaze back in his direction. I'd been standing, anchored against one of the varnished wood beams of the pergola. I'd found the position perfect for my quiet observation, but now, Laken was patting his lap, beckoning for me, and I... I hated how enticing it was.

"In front of all these people?"

Laken shrugged. "Why not?"

"Well... I didn't realize we were ready to "go public", I guess."

He nodded. "We probably aren't. But if you come here and let me tell you why I want you to, you'll understand. You probably won't like it though."

My eyes widened, alarmed. "It's not like... the IRS or something?"

"What? *Hell no*," Laken chuckled. "I give the government whatever my former IRS auditor accountant says to give them – I don't want or need those kinda problems. So, *no*, I'm not about to... ask you to testify on my behalf, or whatever just went through your head."

"*Duh*." I took a deep breath, pushing through my – likely unnecessary – hesitation to take the few steps to get to where Laken had settled.

He grinned big, putting an arm around my hips to pull me down to his leg. "Now... this isn't so bad, is it?"

"I never thought it would be."

I knew *exactly* how good it would feel, and that was kinda the problem. As much as I was trying to take Dr. Alexander's words to heart, as much as I *wanted* this to be the "equal, opposite reaction" she'd spoken about... there was some part of me that still didn't believe it was possible.

Didn't believe I *deserved* it.

"I have to tell you something," Laken said, pulling me away from that defeatist mindset I was supposed to be avoiding. His words were... tentative, which was alarming. I couldn't recall ever hearing anything but absolute certainty from him.

"Okay..."

"My ex-wife is coming tonight." He paused there, presumably giving me time to absorb that before he moved on. "My mother invited her, before she knew about anything between you and I, and I wasn't informed until a few minutes ago. I can *assure* you – Emil doesn't want me. At all. If anything, she's coming to rub in my face how happy she is."

When he finished speaking, I nodded, taking in his words. "So... knowing that your ex – an ex that all these people know and love – was on the way here... you came and asked me to sit in your lap. Seemingly to signal to everybody that you're not lonely, and pining over her?"

His face wrinkled into a frown, then slowly morphed to a sheepish grin. "... Yes?"

"So you're outing us to save face in front of your ex? *Purely* to cushion your ego?"

He ran his tongue over his scarred lip, nodding. "Yeah... it sounds pretty bad when you say it out loud, huh?"

My eyes narrowed at him for a long moment, but then... I laughed.

"Oh thank *God*," I gushed as I relaxed into him, shoulders sinking in relief. "You have *no* idea how happy this makes me."

Laken's eyebrows pulled together in confusion. "*Huh?*"

"Oh man, you don't understand. I... you... you understand that you've been absolutely too good to be true, right?" I asked, and the furrow in his brow deepened.

"... okay."

"*Well*, it's really been freaking me out. But *this?* This selfish, egotistical move? *Finally,* a damn flaw with you," I giggled, cupping his face in my hands. "Thank you, for proving that you are, indeed, human."

164

Laken shook his head, laughing as I kissed his face. "Sweetheart, trust me – I've got *plenty* of these flaws you seem so thrilled to see."

"Bring 'em on. Bring them *all* to me, full disclosure."

He tipped his head back, meeting my eyes. "And give you more reason to try to run off?"

"Nope," I denied. "I've never needed perfect. Never expected it. Knowing that you're not somehow impervious to the shit the rest of us mortals struggle with? Makes me *less* afraid."

His eyebrows went up. "This is... *so* far from the reaction I expected."

I laughed, taking a sip from my beer. "Well get ready, because this next thing is about to *really* blow your mind."

He took a sip too – a much longer one than I had. "Okay..."

I leaned in, looking him right in the face. "I... *really* don't give a shit about your ex-wife."

His eyebrows went higher as his hand slipped lower, cupping my ass. "Is that right?"

"Yup. *You* believe I'm your... destiny. Correct?"

He smiled. "Correct."

"And you're not a stupid man, are you?"

"I... like to believe otherwise."

"Okay. So, if you believe I'm your soulmate, and you're not stupid enough to jeopardize that by being inappropriate with your ex... why should I be worried about her?"

He scoffed. "The same human nature you were just so impressed with me for displaying."

"So... jealousy, then?" I asked. "This woman must *really* be something if you believe I should be jealous of her."

"*Should* be? No. You look good as fuck."

"I know."

He raised his eyebrows at me. "Wow, conceited much?"

"Not at all," I countered. "Just very confident in the appearance I put in effort to maintain, and *very* prepared to walk away from whatever this is between us, if it starts looking like it's not going my way. Do you know how vindicating it would be to tell my *therapist* "I told you so"?" I asked, laughing. "So... like I said – not worried about the ex. If anything, her presence will reveal some things one way or another, and I'm in a space where I can move forward accordingly, with whatever that is."

Laken nodded. "I appreciate the maturity. Because when I see *your* ex, I want to put his head through a fuckin' wall," he admitted, in a way that – embarrassingly – turned me on. I was getting ready to dig into that particular thought, when the door leading to the bar opened, and in walked the subject of our last few minutes of conversation.

I could just *tell*.

Smooth, deep brown skin, perfectly coiffed pixie, impeccably dressed.

Big-ass engagement ring.

Bigger baby bump.

Laken didn't know.

It was clear in the shock on his face.

And hell, maybe *no one* had known, based on the way the women flocked around her with a lot of squealing and excited babbling.

I lowered my head, resting it against his. "So it looks like it's not *my* feelings you should've been worried about," I mused, and he nodded.

"I think you might be right."

I pulled myself from his lap so he could stand, and wrapped my arms around his waist. "Nobody cares about me and you. I don't think they even noticed."

"Nope."

"When you introduce me to her... just say graphic designer, okay?"

"You're probably right."

"I definitely am," I told him. "Are you okay?"

He nodded. "Yeah."

"It kinda stings though, doesn't it?"

"Yeah."

I smiled and lifted a hand to pat his face. "There you go again, with that damn humanity. Stop it."

Laken chuckled, then grabbed me by the hand, leading me to where Emil still hadn't been able to get very far into the party. Instead of waiting, he cut the line, walking right up and interrupting her with some of the brewing team to pull her into a hug.

I hung back.

Observing.

I could definitely, *definitely* see why my potential jealousy had been a concern for him. Emil was beautiful, and they had deep, deep history.

She'd been his *wife*.

I was beautiful too, so that part didn't faze me. I realized now though, I'd been a little cavalier with my declaration of *not giving a shit about his ex-wife*.

He gave a shit about her, so obvious in his eyes as they interacted, and if her body language and lingering hand on his arm was any indication, she gave a shit right back.

I wasn't *jealous* though.

I didn't know how to designate what I felt as I watched them, but it wasn't *that*.

Then, Laken must have said something about her obvious pregnant state, because she put a hand to her stomach as she smiled and replied to his words. His face was smiling, genuinely enough that it reached his eyes. But... there was something else too.

Compunction.

He was happy she was having a baby, but still feeling the pain of their lost relationship, even now. Yet again, I found myself experiencing the thing opposite of what I likely should – I was *glad* to see it so plainly in his face, that he still felt something for her. That was normal, that was human, that was... *undesirable*.

It lent itself to creating a necessary balance, putting a nice-sized chink in the pedestal his actions so far had built. Not that I suddenly

CHRISTINA C JONES

thought he was "bad" now, it was just... so much easier to trust the imperfections.

"Keris," Laken called, motioning for me to come to where he was. I plastered a smile on my face to match the one Emil wore, then watched hers fade ever-so-slightly as Laken draped an arm around my shoulders. "This is Emil, former first lady of *Night Shift*. Emil, this is Keris –" Laken hesitated, and I shot him as subtle of a *don't-you-fucking-dare* look as I possibly could. "She's our new graphic designer. That's all she wants me to say right now."

"You just can't help yourself, can you?" I scolded, pushing out a sigh before I gave Emil my attention, offering her my hand in greeting. "Nice to meet you. You look *beautiful*," I told her, vaguely indicating her belly.

"Thank you," she said, putting a hand to her stomach. "My fiancé and I kept it under wraps as long as we could... just in case. But it's kinda hard to hide now," she explained, speaking not just to me, but to Laken too.

"I thought you were looking a little fuller," Marlene gushed, dipping into the conversation. "But of course I wasn't saying anything. I'm just *so* happy for you!"

"Thank you," Emil offered, graciously, even as her gaze skipped uncomfortably between me and Laken. "And I... didn't mean to crash the party like this and snatch all the attention. I thought you knew I was coming."

Laken grinned at her, shaking his head. "The second part, I believe. The first..."

Emil's nose wrinkled. "Yeah... you're right," she laughed.

At least she was honest about it.

And really, she seemed nice – she was sweet to me for the rest of the time she was there, complimenting my work on the *Night Shift* branding, and intimating she might have a freelance project to potentially hire me for.

And, surprisingly, pulling me – *just* me – aside before she left, to ask if I would be okay with her presence at the launch the next day.

168

Her marriage had been one of the required sacrifices to make it happen, so... why the hell not?

"The last thing I want is to make you uncomfortable," she told me, as we stood alone in the bar, the sounds of the party muted by the closed doors. "I swear, I didn't even know there *was* a... *you* ... when I told Laken's mother I would come."

I nodded. "Yeah. I... kinda have a *look where I am without you* moment planned myself, so... I get it. It ruins it a little if they're seeing somebody already though."

She laughed, shaking her head. "Yeah well... hopefully your "moment" isn't five years in the making, like mine."

"No, just a few months for me," I chuckled. "But I won't have a big gorgeous ring and much-wanted pregnancy. Just... a really great dress, and Laken's big ass."

"Hey, a great dress is *not* to be downplayed." She sighed, pushing her hands into the pockets of her jeans. "And... honestly... neither is Laken."

"But you divorced him."

Emil nodded. "I did. But not because he was a bad guy, it just... it wasn't our time. I believe it all worked out the way it should though. Good and bad, it always does."

Neither of us said anything for a long moment, but then finally, I cleared my throat.

"Wow. This is... a really awkward conversation."

"Yeah, it is," Emil laughed. "So I'm gonna..." she pointed toward the exit, and I nodded.

"Yeah. Um... see you tomorrow, I guess."

She blinked. "Right. And um... thank you, for that. For not being mean about it. But... I saw this place come to life... from the ground up, really. I'll only stay for a few minutes."

"Don't rush yourself on my account," I told her, shaking my head. "The Kimbles were your family... probably still are, if their reaction to you means anything. And all the staff, the brewing team... I can see how much you mean to them, and vice versa. I have no interest in taking that from you."

Not after the things I'd been through, with my lack of connection and family. It was difficult for me, and at the same time a deep, unfulfilled craving. I wouldn't dare block her access to that, especially when – if I was trusting my gut – this woman was no threat to me.

She thanked me again and then saw herself out, leaving me in the bar alone. I toyed with the idea of stepping behind the counter to pour myself a drink, and then enjoy it in the relative silence.

But that natural proclivity for isolation was exactly what I was trying to get away from.

When I turned to head back out to the party, Laken's face was the first thing I saw – pressed against the glass, peering through the door to spy on my conversation with Emil. I flipped him off, making him laugh as he stepped back to open it for me.

"You good?" he asked, and I nodded.

"You?"

He nodded, and I believed him.

So... the night moved on.

Laken's parents were next to leave, after a bit of an outburst from his father. Henry didn't *want* to go, but it was late, and obvious that the crowd was starting to wear on him. Launch day would be long, and busy, and he needed rest – we *all* did.

Helping his parents into their Town Car marked the unofficial end to the party.

An hour later, Laken and I were upstairs, switching our drinks of choice from beer to something a little harder.

"So..." he asked, dropping to a seat beside me on the couch, and putting a hand on my leg. "You want to tell me what you and Emil talked about?"

"Sure. Right after you tell me what you and Walter talked about."

He shrugged, taking a sip from his bourbon. "I told his ass he wasn't allowed at his favorite grocery store anymore, in case you were there. You?"

I blinked. "I... told Emil I didn't mind her being present at the launch tomorrow."

"She asked you?"

I nodded. "Yeah. I think she didn't want her being there to make me feel bad."

"But... what if her being there made *me* feel bad?"

"You're her ex-husband, Laken. I... I don't think she cares if you feel bad."

Laken's head tipped to the side as he thought about it, then nodded and took another sip of his drink. "Fair enough."

I laughed, easing myself into a position where I could rest my head on his shoulder. "Tonight was interesting. And good. Really good."

"It was," he agreed. "And hopefully, tomorrow will be even better.

"It will be. *Definitely.* The work has been put in, and everything is in order."

"So you're saying... you and I could just stay in bed all day, let it run on autopilot if we needed to?"

I smirked, turning and putting my legs over his lap. "Maybe. If we needed to."

With one arm stretched across the back of the couch, the other raising his bourbon to his lips again, Laken peered at me, without saying anything.

"What?" I finally asked, when I couldn't take any more of his quiet, concentrated inspection. "Why are you staring at me?"

"You want the answer you'll like, or the answer you won't? Both are true."

I wrinkled my nose at him. "The one I won't like."

"As expected," he grinned. "I'm staring because I'm... trying to figure out what shifted, with me and you. And when the shift happened."

"There was a shift?"

"Yes." He reached out, brushing my hair back. "You've accepted that you were meant for me."

My eyebrows shot up. "I *have*?"

"You have," he nodded. "Or am I misreading you?"

I shook my head. "I... I think it's more that I've accepted what will be, will be. And I've resolved not to run away from it. What was the answer I *would* like?"

"That I was staring because I was trying to figure out where I wanted to lick you first." He drained the rest of his bourbon and then pounced, making me giggle as I melted into his hands at my waist, and his mouth on my neck.

I squirmed as he slipped his hand into the waist of my leggings, then panties, groaning over the fact that I was already wet. I'd been that way since he pulled the bourbon out – sex with him was always good, but with a little bourbon in his system... I knew what to look forward to, and I was ready for it.

Until his phone rang.

"*Fuuuuck,*" he muttered, reluctantly dragging himself off me to get to the kitchen, where he'd left the phone. Usually, such an interruption would have gotten ignored, but the night before launch... couldn't take the chance.

I didn't see the screen before he answered, but from the look on his face, I immediately knew something was wrong.

"*What*?!" he barked into the phone, his face a mask of solid, scarred stone as he listened to whoever was on the other end of the line give an answer. "When?" He ran a hand through his beard, tugging at the soft coils. "Okay. Okay. I'm... I'm on my way."

"What happened?" I asked, as soon as he hung up the phone, letting it clatter onto the counter before he smacked the smooth natural stone surface with his hands. "Is something wrong in the brewhouse? The labeling machine malfunctioned again?"

He shook his head, complete bewilderment in his eyes as he lifted his gaze to meet mine. "No. It's not that, it's... my father. He had some type of seizure or something in his sleep, at the hotel. It woke my mother up, and she called an ambulance. They're on their way to the hospital now." He pushed himself up, still looking lost as he glanced around. "Keys. I... I gotta go, I gotta—"

"I'll take you," I offered, immediately.

"No, it's late, and you—"

"Laken – *hey*," I urged, grabbing his hands in an effort to get him to stop moving. He was dazed from the news, and likely a little drunk. "You've been drinking. *I* will take you. I never did touch mine, see," I told him, pointing to my full glass of bourbon still on the coffee table. "We'll find the keys, and I'll drive you. Okay?"

He nodded but was honestly in too much of a stupor for me to be certain he was even clear on what was happening. I knew it wasn't the liquor, not really – Laken was no lightweight.

He was in disbelief.

We were both still dressed, and just had to throw on shoes once we found the keys. I hated driving, and didn't do it much by design, but I was good enough to get us there, with some urgency.

We were minutes away when his phone rang again, but I forced my attention to the streets. I pulled up to the emergency room entrance on damn near two wheels, putting the vehicle into park before I turned to Laken, who hadn't moved.

"We're here," I prompted, thinking he was just afraid to go in – afraid of what he'd find.

But he shook his head, staring straight in front of him as he dropped the phone from his ear, and spoke words that sent a stab of pain through my chest.

"It's too late."

It wasn't fair.

It was really, *really* unfair.

After everything he'd been through to finally get to this day –

launching *Night Shift* into the retail market – only to not have his father there to see it. To get this close, and have it snatched away...

Of course he wasn't there.

None of the family was.

It was only because of a quick phone call with Lark, with her insisting that the launch not be canceled, that we went forward with it.

Me, Natalie, Cal, Emil, and the BBC.

It didn't feel quite right, but we made it happen.

There was no shortage of people there to speak Henry Kimble's name, no shortage of drinks dedicated to him. We recorded the storytelling and toasts, and of course the first tastes and reactions to the beers, everything.

When all was said and done, there was a business to come back to, still.

That was what we told ourselves, to get through the day, to get through the "party" atmosphere of the launch. We smiled, and laughed, and put on the necessary happy faces, but really, we were all just... *shocked.*

It was no secret to any of us, that Henry wasn't well, but we hadn't expected it to come to *this*. Or at least... not so suddenly.

I'd taken that long, horrible walk into the hospital with Laken, had felt Marlene's heart-wracking sobs in my chest. Lark was only barely holding herself together, just enough to explain the limited information they had about Henry's sudden death – heart failure, related to the seizure that had woken Marlene from her sleep in enough time to try to save him.

But... there was no history of epilepsy.

What we knew now, that we hadn't last night, was that a tumor had been growing in Henry's brain. It was responsible for his rapid decline, memory loss, the mood swings... everything.

Not that knowing made the absence any less potent.

Honestly... the knowing probably made it worse, for Laken.

I hadn't seen him since I stepped away from the hospital,

intending to grab breakfast for the grieving family. I was walking into *Urban Grind* when I got the call from Lark, that the family wanted us to make the launch still happen, in Henry's honor, by any means necessary.

So... I put all my energy into making the launch happen, by any means necessary.

My tank was completely empty – down into the negatives – by the time the last patron left. I dropped myself onto a barstool, my everything aching, head propped on my hand as I watched the service staff run through their nightly cleaning routine.

"Hey... have you heard from Laken at all?" Emil asked, her hand pressed to her belly as she approached. Her fiancé was with her today and had honestly been a great help to pulling this all off.

Thank God for good people.

I shook my head. "No. His phone is going straight to voicemail, and I didn't want to bother Lark. I was going to shoot a text, then try to get a couple of hours of sleep before I went to the hotel, to try to check on them. I think they're all in pretty bad shape." I let out a sigh. "You can't be in great shape yourself."

She gave me a sad smile. "No, not really. I did talk to Lark earlier, but just verbal condolences. I don't want to be a bother, like you said. But... yeah. It hurts."

"I'll make sure they hear how much you came through today, when you *really* didn't have to. Go home – I know you're exhausted."

Her big ass – fine ass – fiancé put his hands on her shoulders and squeezed. She sank into him a little as she nodded. "Yeah, I should probably get off my feet. It was good to meet you though, Keris. You've got good energy."

"Eh, I'm a work in progress," I told her, accepting the hand she offered with a grin. "I'm sure we'll see each other at the homegoing service."

She nodded. "Yeah."

Soon after Emil left, Cal approached me with a four-pack of the just-launched beers in his hand. They were mixed up – a bottle of each variety.

"You look like you're about to pass out," he said, eyebrows lifted, as he put the beer down on the counter beside me. "If you don't already know it, I'll give you the code to get into Laken's place. Go upstairs and get some sleep. Take this with you, so it doesn't get mixed up with anything else. We wanted to make sure he had bottles from tonight, specifically."

"But there's still—"

"*Go*," a different voice chimed, from behind me. I looked over my shoulder to find Natalie approaching, hands propped on her hips. "You got no sleep last night, after running all day, and now you've run yourself in the ground *again*. We've got this. Go. *Rest*."

I didn't have the energy to argue, not really.

I already knew the keypad code for Laken's apartment, so I didn't need Cal to relay it. I dragged myself up there, and through the front door, and... stopped in my tracks, when I saw Laken.

I had no idea how he'd snuck past everyone to get up here, when we all thought he was at the hotel with his mother and sister. But... there he was, seated at his kitchen counter, blanketed in darkness that was only softened by the moonlight streaming in through the window.

The bottle of bourbon he'd just opened for us last night was half-empty, as was the glass dangling from his fingers. His eyes were the only thing that moved when I stepped into his view, glossy and dejected and... ravaged with grief.

And I... I had no idea what to fucking do.

"I didn't know you were up here," I said, quietly, as I approached the counter, and deposited the contents of my hands. "We thought you were at the hotel."

He still didn't move. His gaze left me, drifting to his glass to stare long and deep, like he wanted to drown himself in the contents. "I needed a moment alone."

"Understandable." I closed the last of the distance between us, hesitating for a long moment before I touched his shoulder. Just my fingertips at first, and then a full, comforting hand on his back, and then... my arms were around him. "If you want me to go... I will. Just tell me."

He didn't say anything.

For a long time.

And I took that as my cue to let him go, just long enough to pull up a seat right beside him, as close as I could get. And then I sat there, quiet, until he finally turned to me.

"I could've saved him," he declared, his voice cracking over the words. I put a hand to my mouth to choke back my own urge to start sobbing. But... he was so clearly heartbroken that it was going to break mine too.

"You're not a doctor, Laken. You're not a surgeon. You didn't know."

He shook his head, tossing his half-filled glass onto the counter. I flinched as it crashed to the floor. "I *should've* known. I *should've* insisted. If I'd just... he was suffering, and none of us knew. I was so fucking focused on this goddamn beer, when I should've... I failed him. Just like I failed my brother."

"You *cannot* blame yourself for that."

Laken scoffed, picking up the bottle to drink straight from there. "Watch me."

"*I won't*," I told him, pulling the bottle from his grasp, and putting it behind me on the counter. "Hey – listen!" I grabbed his face in my hands, making him look at me. "If you wanna self-medicate, I get that, okay? I swear I do. You're *hurting*, and I understand. But I won't watch you self-destruct."

He stared at me for a long time.

And then... he crumbled.

Tears sprang to my eyes as I pulled him into me, for his head to rest against my chest. My fingers trailed along his back, trying to offer *any* kind of relief to his devastation, even though I knew it was... pointless.

"It's gonna be okay," I whispered, wishing I had anything more than a meaningless platitude to offer as anguish ran through him. I didn't bother wiping my own tears – I let them fall free, mingling with his as they soaked the *Rebirth* crewneck sweatshirt I'd worn for the launch.

I put my hand to his head, cradling him against my breasts as he mourned his fresh loss. This night should've beautiful for him – should've been the mark of a new era... a point of pride.

Not this.

I closed my eyes, trying to find some composure of my own, to no avail. Instead of wracking my tired brain, I let it go – I just kept my hand going in that hopefully soothing motion and said the only thing I really could.

"I am so, *so* sorry."

FOURTEEN

LAKEN.

Delivery *just arrived in the warehouse. Dock two. – Cal.*

I frowned at the text – at the lack of information it held – wondering if a lack of sleep was finally catching up to me. We were in surplus with our brewing supplies, to handle the influx of orders associated with our distribution endeavors, so I couldn't think of what the hell could be getting delivered.

Instead of mulling it over too long, I got my ass up to go see for myself. I'd been sitting at the desk too long anyway, and could use the opportunity to stretch my legs, and check in on the brewhouse.

To conduct business as usual.

It was the only way I knew how to not... fall apart.

I couldn't do it.

I didn't allow my gaze to linger on the office door across from mine, purposely angling my head anywhere else until I was out of the office suite. I got by the bar staff with as abbreviated of a greeting as I could pull off, then made my way through the brewhouse to the warehouse area, where the delivery guys were unloading a truck.

Bourbon barrels, with the *Kimble Family Brewing* branded on the sides.

I didn't know if this was something my father had arranged, or if my cousins had taken it upon themselves. Either way, the sight of those barrels turned my stomach inside out as that breakfast conversation – one of our *last* conversations – played in my head.

I didn't want any fucking favors.

I couldn't accept this delivery without an invoice.

By the time I'd snapped out of the personal hellscape of my sleep-deprived mind, the delivery driver had already unpacked the last barrel and gone on about his day. The warehouse smelled like bourbon now, oaky and strong, reminding me way too much of my father for me to tolerate it any longer.

I could handle it another time.

Or... never.

I turned and moved in the opposite direction, dodging conversation with... everybody. I couldn't think of a single person close to me who hadn't insisted it was too soon to return to work, that I should at least take some time until after the funeral.

They didn't fucking get it though.

It wasn't that they hadn't suffered a loss too, and I didn't want to take that from them – didn't want to diminish what they were feeling. But from the lost babies, to my brother, and now my father... I had too many goddamn ghosts in my head for idle time to be healthy.

They didn't understand the way all this shit... *haunted* me.

I accepted that there was nothing more Emil or I could've done about the pregnancy losses. We'd exhausted our finances, followed instructions to the absolute letter, with no success. Of course, I wasn't happy with the end results, but I was satisfied with our *effort*.

We did *everything* we could.

I couldn't say the same when it came to Phoenix, and to my father.

Depression and anxiety had always plagued my brother, from a young age. To my parents' credit, they'd sought real treatment for him – therapy, medication, holistic medicine, prayer, institutionalization... they *tried*. None of it seemed to hit quite the right note.

Eventually, as an adult, he shifted to self-medicating, with drugs and alcohol.

Frankly... it was the healthiest he'd ever seemed.

But of course, we knew that could only last so long.

I could hear the decline in his voice, see the addiction eating away at him. Gently, I urged rehab, but he refused. Things got worse, and I urged harder.

He overdosed, and I insisted – signed the paperwork myself for him to go, and had the bills sent to me. But I had a wife, and a business – I couldn't stay.

Neither did he.

The people who ran the rehab, they talked to me about how you couldn't force someone to do something when they weren't ready. They'd had many patients who would complete the program, just to appease their loved ones. And then as soon as they left... they went right back to those vices.

Addiction was a mean sonofabitch, with long, sharp claws.

So, I stopped trying to force it and just... talked to him.

We talked all the time, and I made sure he was talking to Lark too, and having dinners with our parents, and keeping up with the cousins.

And he was *good*.

I wasn't naïve enough to believe he was *sober*, but the connection with his family was keeping him from the clutches of the worst of it.

And then he came to me in a dream.

That shit had never happened before. He'd said he was sorry, and not to try saving him, and I got my ass on a plane, since he wasn't answering his phone. I didn't alert my parents there in Louisiana, because it was getting late, and I didn't want to worry them over a damn *dream*.

I knew he was gone when I got to the door.

I knew I was too late, I just... I couldn't accept that. No last words? No fucking explanation?

No.

If I got him to the hospital... they could save him.

I *knew* better, but it was like I had to try anyway.

He told me, in the dream, not to try to save him, and I almost died defying his words.

That was the first and last time I took one of those dreams lightly.

Way down deep, in the rarely-accessed recesses of my mind, I knew I'd failed him. Sure, on a surface level I could remind myself of the counselor's words about not forcing it, could tell myself Phoenix was a grown man, one I wasn't responsible for. And I could live with that. Could live with myself.

I should have imposed it though.

Should have argued and fought, should have dragged his ass to rehab or the doctor or the church or the bayou or wherever the fuck, should have laid him at the feet of anybody who could help, and *stayed there*.

Maybe it still wouldn't have worked.

Maybe the eventual outcome would've been the exact same.

But... at least I would've done all I could.

Maybe that would've counted for something, and I wouldn't have ended up failing my father in the same damned way. Sure, Henry Kimble was a stubborn motherfucker, but maybe if I'd just pressed him a *little* harder.

Maybe he'd still be here today.

Okay.

So, that wasn't exactly it, and I knew it. With a little time, we'd gotten answers for my father's sudden demise, and I understood that the tumor growing in his brain was something no one could have done anything about.

But if we'd just *known* earlier, at the very least, we could've maximized his time.

I'd known something was wrong with him, and instead of insisting that he get seen, I let weeks go by – weeks we could have spent like they were the last we'd have. Instead, he'd spent his last days in a mashup of confusion and anger, bracketed by moments of clarity where he was probably terrified, knowing something was wrong.

Too prideful to say anything to any of us.

"Get some rest, old man."

Not the worst last words, but definitely not what I would've preferred. There were things I still needed to say, things I still needed him to say to *me*. About life, and love, and family, and all the elements of business I had yet to learn.

And now he was gone.

So... yeah.

I needed to work.

Needed to keep my mind occupied, or I'd burrow too deep into the guilt and regret, and never get free of their hold.

Back up in the office suite, I made sure the office door across from mine was closed before I made the trek down the little hall, closing and locking my office door behind me once I was inside.

"You've been avoiding me."

Fuck.

I took a deep breath as I turned away from my door to find Keris sitting at my desk, arms crossed. She was right – I *had* been avoiding her, which made her unexpected presence even more potent.

"What can I do for you Ms. Bradford?" I asked, heading for the other side of the desk.

"You can cut whatever this bullshit is," she quipped, following me and blocking my access to my chair. "Don't shut me out."

"I don't have time for this. I can't deal with it."

She frowned, not budging. "Can't deal with what? With *me?*"

"Yes," I snapped, nostrils flared. "I have work to do, and so do you."

Instead of backing down, she nodded. "Oh – so, it's as I expected.

You were grieving your brother, so you shut Emil out, buried yourself in work. Destroyed your marriage. Now you're grieving your father, so you want to shut *me* out, and bury yourself in this business again. But I'm not about to let you do that."

"Keris... get out of my way."

Her eyes were full of fire as she stared up at me, propping her hands on her hips. "*Make me.*"

I grabbed her by the arms, firmly moving her aside, only to have her plant her ass on my desk once she wasn't blocking my chair anymore. Now I couldn't access my laptop or keyboard.

"Stop fucking around with me," I told her. "I've got shit to do. *Move.*"

"No."

"*Goddamnit*, Keris!" I bellowed at her, fully pissed now. "Do I have to pick you up and toss your ass out of here?!"

"*Do it*," she taunted, not shrinking. "Toss me out, yell, curse, whatever the fuck you have to, but you *won't scare me off*. You're not capable of that. I'm just gonna stay right here, in your face, annoying the fuck outta you until you stop trying."

"*Why* are you doing this?!" I growled. "My father died three days ago, and this is the bullshit you think I need?!"

"If you'd let me give you what you *need*, I wouldn't have to *do this bullshit!*" she countered, standing to get back in my face. "The very first time we met, you asked if I believed in kismet, or... *destiny*. You asked me that, because you believed I was *it* for you."

"What the fuck does that have to do with anything right now?!"

"*Everything*." Her voice cracked over her words, making a whole different pain erupt in my chest. "You made me believe in you. I bought into the hype, even though I didn't want to. You said it yourself – there was a shift. And I don't believe the timing was a coincidence."

I shook my head. "Please get to your point, before I really do toss your ass outta here."

"*You need me*," she quipped, jabbing a finger into my chest.

"That's why we met when we did, why this has gone like it has – *you need me*. You need a reason to *not* bury yourself in work, to not drown in your guilt, and get suffocated by your grief. I'm the reason, Laken. I would've been fine, but you inserted yourself into my life, and made me *believe you!*" she shouted, shoving at me this time. "So, you don't get to just... walk away. Not without a fight."

This was why I couldn't sleep.

Because I knew she was right, and I didn't want to hear it from Phoenix. I'd drank myself into the only slumber I'd had since my father passed, ensuring I wouldn't have to hear his insistence that I hold tight to this woman, letting her be my "reason".

I didn't want a reason.

I wanted to lose myself.

She didn't understand what she was asking of me.

"You know what? Nevermind," Keris spoke again, already backing towards the door, hands raised. "I'm being ridiculous. *You* just lost your father, and *I*... am supposed to be heeding red flags when I see them. So, if this is what you want to do, how you want to grieve... it's really not up to me to try to change it. I'm sorry for bothering you," she said, with tears in her eyes, sounding so... defeated.

She didn't even wait for me to respond before she opened the door, taking off down the hall, and I had no idea what to say, or even *why*, but... I followed her.

"Keris..."

"I had a dream." She stopped in her tracks, turning halfway in my direction as she wiped her face. "You're all I've been able to think about for days, wondering if you were okay, how I could help, wanting to be there for you even though you wouldn't talk to me. So... of course I had a dream, right? But... your brother was there." She waved her hands in front of her. "Trust me, I know how *insane* that sounds, because I've never met him. Never seen him. But... it's so vivid in my mind. He begged me to come to you, to not back down, to make you understand, and I... *God* I just realized how fucking stupid and desperate that must've sounded, and how... completely inappropriate it was, when you're.... I'm sorry," she stammered, then rushed the rest of the distance to her office, closing her door behind her.

"*Shit*," I muttered, hurrying after her, but when I tried the door handle, it was locked. "Keris!" I called, accompanying with a persistent knock that went – unsurprisingly – unanswered.

What the fuck am I supposed to do now?

I knocked again, and when I still didn't get an answer, went back down to my office, pissed off and confused. There was a bottle of bourbon in my desk, typically reserved for special occasions – I'd been dipping into it a lot over the last few days.

Today, apparently, was no different.

I poured myself a few fingers and sat down, not even bothering to open my laptop.

I was done for the day.

The sound of the door woke me up.

I hadn't even intended to dose off, but obviously I had, and now the sun had faded, leaving my office bathed in darkness.

I quickly realized it wasn't my own door, and the only other person who'd been up here today was Keris, so... it had to be her.

I sprung from my seat to look out, dismayed when I didn't see her in the hall. I rushed to the elevator bank, calling her name as the doors slid closed.

She looked me right in the face, but made no move to catch the doors.

Fuck.

I sprinted for the stairwell, almost busting my ass in an attempt to catch her before she made it out into the bar. I burst through the door just as she was stepping off the elevator. She gave me nothing more than a quick glance before she turned to head out.

"*Keris.*"

She stopped walking, adjusting the strap of her laptop bag on her shoulder as she turned, looking in my direction without meeting my gaze. "What can I do for you, Mr. Kimble?"

I sighed. "O-kay. I... guess I deserve that."

"You don't." she shook her head, lifting her eyes to mine. Hers were red and glossy, the surrounding skin puffy like she'd been crying. "I'm just trying to... not be personal, right now, since you've made it clear that's what you'd prefer. Can I help you?"

"That's not what I'd prefer," I corrected her, even though... I wasn't even sure about the correction, actually. "I just... have no idea what the fuck I'm doing right now."

"You're hurting, Laken. It's hard to know what to do, when you're hurting."

"But I don't want to hurt you."

She blinked, then turned away from me, not moving fast enough for me to not see the fresh tear that escaped down her cheek as she shook her head. "You shouldn't be concerned with that right now. You're grieving, and you're busy. You have enough going on, without worrying about me. I'll be fine. Goodnight."

"I don't want you to be fine. I want you to be happy."

She turned, giving me a heart-rending smile. "And I want you to grieve in whatever manner you feel is necessary. You're the one who suffered a loss."

"I am. But I *don't* want to hurt you. I just need some time to... keep my head down."

"You should take all the time you need."

My eyebrows went up. "You would be good with that? With waiting?"

"No. But you should still take all the time you need."

"*How can you say that?*" I asked, tossing my hands up in frustration. "Up in my office, you were trying to tell me I needed you, but now you're saying you won't wait?"

Keris nodded, finally turning fully in my direction. "Yes, that's exactly what I'm saying, Laken. You can grieve however you want to, and I won't begrudge you that. We do what we can to be okay. But you *cannot*, after selling me some dream of being your soulmate, set me aside while you bury yourself in work to avoid your feelings, and expect me to be there waiting to be dusted off. I won't do it. Because that goes against what *I* need."

"So you're telling me I can either be with you, or grieve my father?"

She scoffed. "You know *goddamn* well I'm not."

"I don't know shit, Keris. How about you make it plain."

"Fine. You can grieve by isolating yourself, and alienating the people who care about you, while this business keeps you warm at night. *Or...* you can let them – let *me* – be there for you. You can tell me what you need, without pushing me away and pretending I don't exist. You can talk to somebody, instead of being eroded by regrets. You can use the resources around you to process in a healthy way," she suggested, shrugging. "You won't get any further argument from me about either option. But only one of those options will have me sticking around as anything more than your creative director. You should choose whichever option speaks to you."

She turned around, walking away from me again – I was sorely tempted to let her go, and tell her not to come back. I recognized the self-sabotage though, had gotten intimately familiar with it in the last weeks and months before Emil started the divorce process.

I hadn't *wanted* her to leave, but I hadn't done anything to stop it, either.

I couldn't make that mistake twice.

I didn't call out to her this time – I *went* to her, wrapping my arms around her from behind, before she could open the door leading to the bar.

"Come to Louisiana with me," I said, dropping my mouth to her ear.

She shook her head.

"You don't have to do that," she said, turning in my arms to face me. "I don't need to be in your face, connected to your hip. If you need time alone to process, I'm *not* trying to impede on that. I just want you to be okay. And to not shut me – or anybody – out."

"I know," I told her, using my thumb to wipe the tears from her face. "But you threatened to walk away, and I can't let that happen, cause you're... mine, Keris." I cupped her chin in my hand. "This is fucking with me. And I'm not handling it well, and I'm... not fucking okay. I probably won't be, for a minute, but... you're *mine*," I repeated, lifting my other hand to bury fingers in her hair. "You won't let me push you away... fine. I won't try to anymore. But your ass is gonna be *right* beside me while I figure out how to get through this a different way."

"Okay." She nodded, as she tried to blink back a fresh round of tears.

"Stop crying."

"I'm trying to," she half laughed, half complained, letting her laptop bag drop from her shoulder before she circled her arms around my waist, reinforcing our embrace.

I pressed my lips to her forehead, breathing her in. God knows I'd missed her over the last few days, but she... she made me *feel* too damned much. Maybe that was the point though – I couldn't shut myself down to avoid my grief and have her too. I couldn't have it both ways.

I could feel nothing or feel everything.

But I didn't have to be alone with it.

"Y ou wanna ride somewhere with me?"

Keris looked up from the suitcase she'd packed and unpacked at least four times, her eyebrows bunched. "Right now? Our flight is in a few hours..."

"Like *eight* hours," I countered, shaking my head. "Don't tell me you're one of *those* people about flying."

She frowned, zipping the suitcase closed before she gave me her full attention. "*What* people? Responsible ones, who don't want to miss their flights?"

"Anal ones, who need to be there three hours early."

She wrinkled her nose, but didn't respond, prompting me to laugh.

"Oh, *shit*. You *are*, aren't you?"

"Is this supposed to make me want to "ride somewhere with you?","," she asked, the laughter in her eyes contradicting her stern expression.

I shook my head, taking a seat on the bed beside her suitcase. "Not really, probably. But I hope you'll come anyway."

Thirty minutes later, we were flying down the highway, with no music, and the windows down. It was one of the last few "warm" days of fall, and we were taking full advantage of the open road leading to our destination. Away from the noise pollution, air pollution, light pollution of the city, it was peaceful. The further you got, the quieter it was, to the point that we seemed to be the only ones on the road for miles.

From the highway, I pulled off onto a side road that would lead to a farmhouse and barn if I drove far enough, but I didn't need to. I parked on the makeshift shoulder, so my SUV was out of the way if anyone needed to pass, and turned the car off.

Keris looked around, taking in our surroundings before she turned to me, confused.

"Um... why the hell are we here?" she asked, and I grinned.

"Get out of the car, Ms. Bradford. Come find out."

Without waiting for her response, I exited myself, coming around to her side to open her door. As I helped her out, she lifted her nose in the air, taking a deep inhale before she looked to me for confirmation of what she likely easily guessed, after working at *Night Shift* for even this short time.

"*Hops*," she whispered, as her mouth spread into a smile.

The sun was already starting to go down, so we were working

with limited daylight as we approached on the tall, corkscrewed hop bines. It was past time for harvest, so most of them had already been plucked, but there were still a few of the fragrant cones left behind.

"If I'd waited until after we got back, it wouldn't be here anymore. Not like this. They're going to burn it next week," I told her, as she reached to pluck one off, crushing it between her fingers.

She looked up, alarmed. "Why? Is something wrong?"

"No. Just to... kill off any possible disease, harden off the soil, and... it just feels..."

"Like rebirth," Keris finished for me, nodding. "Burn it all down and start over."

"Yeah."

Keris raised her fingers to her nose, inhaling the scent of the hops.

"You're going to get on the plane smelling like a lush," I teased, coming behind her to hook an arm around her waist. "That aroma is hard to wash off."

"Ah, damn," she laughed. She turned in my arms, her eyelids drooping low. "So... why did you want to bring me here?"

I cast my gaze over her head, out to the rows and rows of hops that comprised the farm. Sixty acres, purchased from an older Black farmer who was struggling to keep up the crops, and keep the land out of the grasp of vultures who wanted it for some corporation or another.

We'd worked it out that he and his family got to stay on his land, and he learned to grow a new crop.

Hops.

"I was supposed to bring Pops out here," I told her, looking up at the sky as it grew steadily darker. "I never told him about this – it was supposed to be this surprise. Supposed to remind him of the rye, wheat, and corn farms he grew up around. He was always talking about how he didn't understand why I'd want to fool with beer – like I'd forgotten all my roots. This was going to show him that... making bourbon and making beer aren't really that different. He would've loved it."

For a long moment, Keris was silent. Then she reached out, struggling to pull off a chunk from one of the sturdy bines. "You think they'll let us bring this on the plane?" she asked, turning to me once she had it her hands.

I frowned. "Why?"

"So instead of the flowers everybody is going to toss on the casket, at the burial... you can show him this."

My eyebrows went up, as I took the section of the plant from her hands. "You... might be onto something."

"I have good ideas sometimes. But... I'll look it up on my phone on the way back to the city, just in case. So I don't have to curse anybody out at the airport."

I shook my head as I grabbed her hand, leading her back to my SUV. "You're *that* kinda flyer too?"

"Only when I have to be," she countered, turning to me as I opened the door for her. "Mostly because I despise flying. So everything is just... a hassle."

I frowned. "You don't like flying? Why are you just now saying something?"

"Because it doesn't matter. You asked me to go, so... I'm going."

Damn.

When I thought about it now, I could barely believe I'd wanted to not have her around during this time. Her presence, obviously, didn't make the loss of my father hurt any less, but having her near had definitely accomplished something I'd been missing in those first few days, after I pushed her away.

She reminded me I was human.

That it was okay to feel shit, and that *not* feeling shit didn't actually... work?

I was just burying it all, to get unpacked at some inevitable later date, and fucking up my relationships in the meantime.

It was counterproductive, and I wouldn't have realized it if she hadn't... spazzed.

Her word, not mine.

I tossed the hops somewhere in the vehicle, using my free hands to grab her hips, pulling her into me and pressing her against the SUV at the same time. Immediately, her arms went up, circling my neck to pull me in for what I really just intended to be a quick kiss, but... I couldn't seem to stop.

Keris moaned against my lips as I kissed her harder, opening for me gladly when I flicked my tongue against the seam of her mouth. My hands drifted lower, cupping handfuls of her ass as I tried to pull her, impossibly, closer.

She unhooked her arms from my neck and went for my belt.

I didn't stop her.

The sun was gone completely now, our only illumination coming from the stars. I slipped my hands underneath her sweater dress, hiking it up around her thighs, pushing her panties aside as she freed me from my boxers.

A low, guttural groan eased from my throat as I buried myself inside her, for the first time since before... the launch.

She was hot, and wet, and... just fucking perfect.

Like *home*.

Her booted legs hooked tight around my waist, I started moving, settling into a slow tempo. She grabbed my face in her hands, pulling my mouth to hers for another connection between us.

I couldn't keep it slow for long.

Even with where my head had been over the last days, I'd missed the hell out of her, and apparently the feeling was mutual. She rocked her hips into me as best she could, an unspoken urging for me to go faster, harder.

So I did.

I put a hand between us to find her clit, using the fabric of her panties as a barrier from the hop powder on my hands. I played with her as I stroked, knowing exactly how quickly it would get her where she needed to go.

She came hard, thighs shaking, screaming into the dark. I was right behind her, not even bothering to pull out, just remaining buried as deep as I could get, relishing the feeling of her pussy contracting around me as I let out some animalistic sounds of my own.

When we finally got ourselves disconnected from each other, and seated and buckled into the vehicle, Keris turned to me with a grin. "You planned that, didn't you? Was that a bucket list item? *Get booty in the hops field at least once.*"

"You came on to me," I reminded her, as I turned the SUV around and navigated back to the road. "So maybe it was *your* fantasy."

She stuck her lip out as she thought about it. "Oh... I guess I did start that, huh?"

I laughed as we turned back onto the highway, to head back to the city. It had cooled off some now, so no more windows down – but it was very cozy with the music turned low, and the heat on.

I reached for Keris' hand with the one I wasn't using to navigate, squeezing when she interlocked her fingers with mine.

We'd never talked about it again, but it struck me then what she'd told me in the elevator bay, two days ago.

I had a dream.

If I hadn't believed before that she was meant for me, that would've been the moment I could no longer deny it. I'd cut myself off from dreaming so I wouldn't see my brother's chastisement... but he'd still gotten the message across.

I lifted her hand to my mouth, kissing the back of it. Glad as *hell* that I hadn't let her walk away from me.

I *did* need her.

I heard the message loud and clear.

FIFTEEN

KERIS

Perhaps...
        I think...
    Maybe...
    I may have made a mistake?

I'd been so gung-ho to keep Laken from slipping into old, unhealthy habits, that I really hadn't considered the fact that people – especially *stranger* people – were... not quite my thing.

But I was the one who'd – *bafflingly* – pushed for this.

I just *had* to open my mouth, instead of letting it ride.

So, instead of uttering a single word of complaint, I was going to give Laken what he said he needed from me, which was to be by his side for this funeral. And I was going to do it with grace.

The Kimble family made it really, *really* easy though.

They were in mourning, of course, but they tackled it with a glass of bourbon in hand and smiles on their faces. The only funerals I'd ever been to before were fairly somber occasions, so that's what I had in mind – what I expected.

This family didn't do it like that though.

They went all out - *flowers, doves, food, family, liquor.*

That seemed to be the theme.

The actual homegoing service was the closest thing to a "normal" funeral, and it was pretty low key. But then it was followed, immediately, by a trip to the French Quarter to join a second line parade that was pretty much the polar opposite.

I didn't say it out loud to anyone else, because I was positive it was a completely inappropriate reaction but... I had a *blast*.

Spectators lined the streets as the Kimble family marched, danced, and sang, to celebrate Henry Kimble's life. To send him off in style. I got spun around and plied with drinks by a few of the younger cousins, and even Laken's mother at one point, dancing with complete and utter joy that contradicted her tear-filled eyes.

It was *impossible* not to get swept up in the infectious energy of the raucous music. Horns and keyboards, drums and guitars, blues and zydeco and jazz. Even Laken pulled me into him more than once to dance, somewhat hindered by his old leg injury from the accident with Phoenix, but he still had some moves.

It was... pretty amazing.

Afterward, the family all met back up at Laken's parents' house, a big, beautiful historic home in the heart of New Orleans. I listened to story after story about their family ancestors and history, from slavery to prohibition, all the way up to them having to evacuate because of Hurricane Katrina, and offering refuge in their Kentucky properties for other residents who'd had to leave their homes.

I was completely fascinated, by all of it.

This level of family history, this ritual I'd been invited to be a part of, with Laken's mother, in her grief, passing down stories that had been relayed to her. Some of which were *Kimble* family stories, the family she'd been brought into because of Henry.

It was beautiful.

And it was a completely foreign concept to me.

I never knew my birth parents, and my adoptive parents were taken away from me so young that I'd never gotten anything like this. I was privileged to have a good enough childhood, but the hell I suffered at the hands of my grandmother blocked my access to most of those memories. I had to get through those first, and I wasn't interested in reliving them. Not when I could focus on what was ahead of me instead.

"Here," Lark said, sliding onto the settee next to me and putting a drink in my hand. Marlene had gotten tired, and was helped up to her room by the family great-aunts, so the crowd was starting to drift away. People were heading back to the dining room for food, or other areas of the house. Laken had disappeared nearly an hour ago, with some of the cousins.

"Do I look like I need this?" I asked, laughing as I accepted what appeared to be a lemon drop - the same drink Lark had in her hand.

She grinned at me and shook her head. "Nope. I need it," she said. "And I just didn't want to drink alone."

"Well, in that case... to Henry," I said, gently tapping my glass against hers before I raised it to my lips to drain half of what was, indeed, a lemon drop, down my throat.

"Whatever you did, or said, with Laken?" Lark mused, relaxing back into the lush fabric of the couch where she'd joined me. "Thank you. I really thought we were about to lose him again, and so did Mama. With everything else... that really would have broken her."

"Yeah."

That was the part I hadn't yet mentioned to Laken. For one, I didn't know how to bring it up to him, and for two... I didn't know if it was even necessary. But in those days where he was virtually ignoring me, not even responding to any of my "*Are you okay, just one word, just let me know*" texts, I was scared for him. In desperation, I said something to Cal, who confirmed my suspicions and reached out to Lark, who had already gone back to Louisiana with their mother.

She called me later that day, because she was worried about him too and shared Marlene's concerns.

I didn't know what the hell to do.

The very *last* thing I wanted was to be a bother to Laken while he was hurting. But then I had that damn dream, likely sparked by an overactive imagination and the intensity of my concerns about him. And I... completely forgot all my resolve to just let this thing go how it was going to go, to not try to force anything either way.

It was like I had to... *save* him.

I cared about Laken.

A lot more than I even knew, a lot deeper then I realized. If I could help it, I *couldn't* let him slip back into what even he described as unhealthy, unsustainable, and undesirable.

I still wasn't sure I'd done the right thing, but he seemed okay with it now - even *grateful* – and Lark and Marlene were relieved.

I expected Lark to say something else, but when I looked in her direction, her head was tipped back on the settee, and she was passed out asleep. The day had been full of celebration, for sure, but it'd still been a long one. And even with all the joy, there was no avoiding the underlying grief.

Both were exhausting.

I took the glass from Lark's hand and put it along with mine on a coffee table nearby. Gently, I woke her up just enough to be able to lead her back to her room, where I dropped her off and then went in search of Laken.

I didn't have to look very far.

Off the study, downstairs there was a closed door, and I could hear voices behind it as I walked. After a moment of hesitation, I knocked.

"Come in," a male voice that wasn't Laken's called, but I opened it anyway, thinking maybe they at least might know where he was.

"Oh, *sorry*," I said, backing out almost as soon as I stepped in. I'd definitely found Laken and the cousins, but they were down here with drinks and cigars, the kind of socializing I didn't want to interrupt.

"Hold up," Laken called, and I stopped in the open doorway as he stood. "I think that's my cue, guys," he said starting the exit process.

"No," I shook my head. "I don't want to interrupt. Just tell me where to go."

"I need to call it a night anyway," he said, coming to wrap a possessive arm around my waist. I had already met these guys earlier so there no need for an introduction now. We said our goodbyes, and then Laken led me upstairs, to a room not far from where I'd taken Lark.

Because we'd arrived so late the first night, we stayed in a hotel near the airport – this was the first night I'd spend in the house.

In Laken's bedroom.

"You're definitely the finest girl I've ever had in my room," he teased, pulling both of our bags from the closet – we'd brought them with us this morning, but I hadn't seen them since we got to the house.

"*This* house, or before it was rebuilt?" I asked, looking around at the jerseys that decorated the walls, music posters, trophy case. "This isn't the same room you had as a kid, is it?"

"We were lucky enough that the water didn't come up here too much – the first level is what really got ravaged. All our pictures, posters and stuff like that, were able to be saved."

"Oh, that's a relief," I said, taking a seat on the end of his bed. "It would have been a real crime against humanity if you'd lost all your *Dragon Ball Z* posters," I teased, pointing to an anime poster hanging on the closet door.

Laken shrugged as he opened his suitcase. "Hey now, you're not gone shame me for what I was into as a kid."

"Really, it's not even shaming because I was into *exactly* the same things. Ohhh, my grandmother *hated* it," I said. "Just completely didn't get it. Especially when I would watch the ones that were still in Japanese, just with the English subtitles? Whew, she would get so mad at me."

He turned to me, eyebrows furrowed. "Mad? Why?"

"Who knows. I swear she just needed a reason. One of my favorite ones though, I wasn't even a kid anymore when it came out – I was definitely in college... maybe. You ever watch *Fullmetal Alchemist?*" I asked.

Laken shot me a look like I was crazy. "I was probably too old to still be into all that, but... I can't front. The Elric brothers were my homies. Went through a *wide* range of emotions with those kids."

"Yeah," I agreed. "You know what's funny? A few years ago, I watched it again, and I feel like there were so many things that I just really didn't even pick up on, when I was so much younger. Like that whole principle that the show centered around, right? Equivalent exchange. If you want something... you have to give something else up."

"They learned that lesson a pretty hard way," Laken replied.

In the show, *the law of equivalent exchange* was something magic users were bound by. Ed, the main character, was an alchemist, able to use rune-like symbols to create certain effects. He and his younger brother, Al, were grieving the loss of their mother, and attempted to use alchemy to bring her back from the dead. Their attempt failed, and cost them... a lot, physically.

If you wanted something... you had to be willing to give up something else.

"You know what it makes me think about?" Laken spoke up. "The things we've had to give up... maybe good, maybe bad to make this thing between us work. I wanted to withdraw from everything. Losing Pops... it just felt like there wasn't shit else that really mattered. But you... you wouldn't let me do it. In the moment, I was so *pissed*. But I think about it now... how good this has been, being around my people. Celebrating Pops." He was quiet for a moment, then shook his head. "I wasn't going to come," he admitted. "I was going to just... shut down and try my best to not fucking feel anything. Just keep working, you know? Because I thought that was better than... facing it. It was what I did before – it was what I *knew*. But I couldn't do that, if I wanted you."

I nodded, thinking about my therapist's words, and *equal, opposite reactions*. "I could see that," I agreed.

He stopped whatever he was doing in his suitcase, to take the empty space next to me. "And you...you were not into this, at all," Laken laughed. "And you damn well made sure I knew – you weren't going for it, you didn't believe in this destiny shit, your best friend owns a gun she ain't afraid to use it, you were really on one."

I laughed. "You're right, I was."

"Look at us now though. You let that go... that fear, and reluctance that maybe seemed easier to you. Made you feel safer to wrap up in. But... you gave this a chance, and because you did, you were able to give me the push I needed, to give up what I needed to give up too. And I'd like to believe we're both better for it."

I smiled, intertwining my fingers with his as I let my head rest on his shoulder. "Yeah. I think we are."

"You tired?" he asked, as my eyes were closing.

"*Completely.*" I looked up, to meet his gaze. "And you must be too. Physically *and* emotionally."

He nodded, then completely defied those words by scooping me into his arms, carrying me across the floor to the bathroom. "Let's take a shower."

"Together?" I asked, scowling as he put me down, and started taking off his clothes.

"Yeah. Get naked, woman," he demanded with a wink, and I... got naked.

I couldn't front – it felt amazing to be under the hot shower spray after being out all day, but even better to do so in Laken's arms. We *did* actually clean ourselves too, but a bulk of our time was spent caressing and touching, teasing and kissing, but not actually taking it all the way *there*.

We could wait for that.

Back in his room, I dressed in one of his oversized tee-shirts from high school, because in all my packing preparations, I'd still forgotten pajamas. We nestled together in the queen-sized bed that had been brought in for visits as an adult, and Laken was asleep damn near as soon as his head the pillow.

I laid there a while though, awake.

Just watching him, barely believing this was my life. A month ago, I'd felt so completely broken, so utterly *lost*, and now... everything seemed so right.

Well... not everything.

Not for *him*.

Fresh tears sprang to my eyes as I thought about what he'd lost – the depth of which I couldn't even imagine. Not even just his father, but that big moment of pride he didn't get to have with the launch. The anniversary date, for a while at least, would likely haunt him.

It made my chest ache, just thinking about it.

How the hell was he supposed to recover from that?

Logically, I knew "love" wasn't the answer, not really. And I still felt bad for spazzing on him to keep him from burrowing into *Night Shift*, even though I knew *that* wasn't the answer either.

And... it scared me a little, that I even cared.

As callous as it would sound to say aloud, I couldn't imagine feeling something this profound for Walter. Not even in the early years, when I actually *liked* him still. Actually... he *had* lost a parent, his mother, about a year before that ugly night up in the mountains.

I sent him flowers.

The difference was striking.

And terrifying.

"*Go to sleep, Keris,*" Laken grumbled in my ear. "You're thinking loud as hell."

I giggled, pushing my ass back against him. "Thinking doesn't make a sound, sir."

"When normal people do it, no. Your *overthinking* ass sounds like a dial-up modem."

"*Woww.* This is such an unnecessary dragging."

I smiled as he re-anchored his arm around my waist, tucking me in closer to his chest. "It wouldn't be happening... if you were asleep. Trust me – you're going to want to get some rest for tomorrow."

My eyes popped open, wide. "Why? What's happening tomorrow."

The deep rumble of Laken's chuckle vibrated the whole bed.

"My aunts are happening tomorrow."

There were flowers on my doorstep when I finally made it back "home".

No card.

There was only one person with any business sending me flowers, and modesty wasn't one of Laken's qualities. If they were from him, they'd say so.

They didn't, so I left them right where they were.

In a few weeks, I'd be in my new place – new furniture, new neighbors, new *energy*.

Really, I didn't feel like the time could pass fast enough.

The things I'd taken from storage were already packed, back in the boxes I'd never gotten around to not living out of. Being here only temporarily had always been the plan, and I was *so glad* to have seen it through.

I couldn't *wait* to get out of here.

I put my suitcase down and settled at my kitchen counter to go through the mail I'd stopped to grab from my box. There was a card there from Keisha, some kind of wedding reminder thing now that the big day was almost here, the usual junk mail, a couple of bills, and.., something from Walter's lawyer, making me roll my eyes as soon as I saw the name printed on the envelope.

Here we go with some bullshit, again.

Against my better judgment, I opened the certified letter and skimmed the contents – some bullshit about the amount I'd been sent when he finally released the money from the shared accounts to me.

A *two-hundred-dollar discrepancy,* when the total amount was tens of thousands.

Pettiness, pure and simple?

And for *what?*

For the life of me, even when I got deep-down honest with myself about my own mistakes, the things I'd done over the years that might've hurt, I couldn't see a reason for the way he was carrying on. It was *ridiculous.* I could admit to being reticent, to being cynical, maybe we weren't having sex often enough. I didn't care to paint a picture of myself as some perfect little long-term girlfriend, because I was sure I *hadn't* been.

But *all this?*

This was something else.

He'd violated me, gaslighted me about it, until it was impossible to do so anymore. And then, when he found out about the failed pregnancy resulting from his *crime,* he decided that hitting me in the face was the best path forward.

And now, instead of just letting the toxic shit go, it seemed like he insisted on punishing me for *daring* to refuse to be a part of it anymore. For the audacity of leaving.

I crumpled the letter, tossing it into the recycling bin with the rest of the junk mail.

I wasn't letting that bastard occupy my headspace a *single* moment longer.

My phone chimed with a new message, and I pulled it from the pocket of my soft wool hoodie to look at the screen.

"Remind me again why I thought work was the answer to my problems? I just want to dive face first in your titties and SLEEP. – Laken"

I must have missed the first notification sound, because the timestamp was from several minutes ago – enough that I wasn't surprised at all when a knock sounded at my door before I could even type out a reply.

Shaking my head, I went to the door, pulling it open with a smile. "I'm *not* a pillow service, for your– *Walter*!?"

My face dropped into a frown as I realized it was *not* Laken showing up at my front door unannounced. As usual, Walter was nicely dressed, and he was honestly a handsome man – both things that shouldn't have made it an issue to simply... be with someone else.

Instead, he was... *here*.

I didn't even care to ask what he wanted – I started to close the door, but he stuck his foot in the jamb, stopping me.

"It's about time you stop this nonsense, and *talk to me*, Keris!" he demanded. "What is it going to take for me to get through to you?"

I shook my head. "It's not going to take anything, because there's nothing for us to discuss. We were dating, and now we're not. Is something about that confusing?"

"The fact that you can throw away ten years of *both* our lives so suddenly, over a misunderstanding – *that's* what is confusing to me." His light brown skin flushed red as he spoke. "You were *pregnant*, Keris! And I had to find out in passing from the doctor who *stripped your fertility without you saying a goddamn thing to me!* Can you even imagine how that felt?! Having her ask me how your recovery had gone, how you were handling it, emotionally – when I thought you were getting a goddamn *cyst* removed?!"

"You have *lost* your fucking mind!" I snapped. "Can I imagine how *you* felt? Me, the woman you almost *killed* because you stuck that completely unexceptional dick of yours in me without my permission, and then tried to make me think I was *crazy*. That I imagined it!"

"*Permission?!* Keris, we'd been together for a decade, I didn't think I needed a notarized invitation for sex!"

"*Bullshit!*" I screamed, right in his face, trying my best to hold back tears of rage. "You damn well know better, Walter, and you will not stand in my fucking face and act like you don't. But you know something? *It doesn't fucking matter.* This, between us, is *over.* Consider this the "talking about it" you say you needed and leave me the fuck alone. Move your foot."

He narrowed his eyes at me. "Keris..."

"*Move. Your. Foot.*"

"We are *not* finished."

The hell we weren't.

Since he wouldn't move it on his own, I pulled the door open wide and then slammed it, hard, right on his unwelcome foot. I'd never been so appreciative of the soft leather boat shoes he was so enamored with – they offered *no* protection against the force of the steel door.

He let out a completely satisfying screech of pain and hopped back – goal accomplished. I slammed and locked the door, ignoring it when, a few moments later, he started beating on my door.

Well... at *first,* I could ignore it.

But he didn't go away – he just got louder, screaming at me to *open the goddamn door.* I'd pulled my phone back out, fingers poised to just call the police on his ass and get it over with, when he suddenly stopped.

I frowned as I crept back up to the door, putting my eye to the peephole to look out.

"*Oh my God!*" I gasped, when the little lens revealed Walter sprawled on the floor in front of the door, twitching like he was in pain. I unlocked and flung the door open, concerned I'd given the man a heart attack.

That was when I saw the wires.

I followed them up to where Natalie was standing a few feet away, holding the taser the wires had come from.

"What the *fuck* is going on?" she asked, not taking her eyes off Walter, who'd started whimpering. "Did he put his hands on you again? Should I turn this thing all the way up and put this shit to rest?"

"*No!*" I hissed, dialing the number that had been the original plan anyway. "Get it off of him, before you get in trouble!"

"I got people in the police department, I'll be fine. You got some onions in there? Help me drum up some tears real quick."

"*Stop it.*"

"I'm sick of him, Keris," Nat snapped. "I came over here to hear about beignets and shit, not kill anybody, but I can just turn this dial real quick and—"

"Yes, *hello,*" I said, responding to whoever had answered the phone at BPD. "*Hush!*" I shushed Natalie. "I... need to report a disturbance, I guess."

Natalie rolled her eyes at me as I gave the information over the phone, then took the taser from her hands. "What good, exactly, do you think this is going to do?"

"None, probably," I admitted. "But we can't keep shocking him forever, and I want him away from me. Maybe the police will get him to leave me the hell alone."

It didn't take them very long to arrive, with medical treatment for Walter, who started hollering about pressing charges. To their credit, the officers immediately shot that down, as soon as one of my neighbors came out to confirm my report that he'd been screaming and beating on the door.

"Listen, Ms. Bradford," one of them, the male officer, said, coming to me after spending several minutes listening to Walter rant. "I'm not going to lie to you – he didn't put his hands on you, so there's not a whole lot we can do. I can book him on a disturbance, but it's unlikely to go anywhere. You can file a restraining order, but... I probably don't have to explain the limitations of that."

"You mean, that it doesn't mean shit or help shit?" Natalie chimed in. "No, you don't."

I shot her a glare, then turned back to the cop. "Okay. So what are you telling me then?"

He let out a heavy sigh, shaking his head. "Look – that guy is a complete asshole, I get it. You don't want anything else to do with him. He claims he just has something he wants to say to you, and then he's done – he'll leave you alone. Let this sonofabitch do his little whining, so he can get it out and move on. I think it's probably the best path forward, without anybody going to jail."

"Fuck that, take his ass to jail!" Natalie shot back, and I was inclined to agree.

"Why should I have to hear anything from him? He's harassing me – showing up at my job, showing up here. I'm surprised I haven't caught him following me at any stores. It's ridiculous! And no, I won't play into it. There has to be another way."

Again, the officer sighed. "I get that – and trust me, I don't like it either. I'm just telling you what I've seen. I got no problem booking him – it's clear cut. But he's *not* going to leave you alone until he's ready, and if a conversation is all it takes to speed that along… just get it over with."

"What guarantee do I have that a conversation is all it's gonna take?"

He shook his head. "None, honestly. But it's probably worth a shot."

My gaze shifted to Natalie, seeking her feedback.

"*Fuck. Him.*" were her only words.

I closed my eyes to steel myself, propping my hands on my hips.

"Fine," I said, as ready as possible for this whole ordeal to just be *over*. "I don't have shit to say to him, but whatever – with the police here, I'll listen. He's got three minutes, and then if he bothers me again, I'm going to consider it a threat against my life and act accordingly."

The officer nodded.

"Self-defense is self-defense."

When he walked off to go get Walter, Natalie rounded on me, braids swinging. "Have you lost your mind?! You're seriously going to talk to him?!"

"I'm *tired* of this, Nat. I'm ready to be done. Do you have a better suggestion?"

She sucked her teeth. "Yeah – I'm about to invite his ass on a hunting trip. Big game."

"*Please*," I hissed at her, as the two officers and Walter approached.

Walter was wearing an ugly sneer, likely the result of whatever he was feeling when he came to my door, exacerbated by me slamming his foot and Natalie electrocuting him.

All things he'd brought on himself.

"Say whatever is you need to say," I snapped at him, when he didn't immediately start talking.

Somehow, the scowl on his face deepened.

"I hope you're happy," he grumbled. "You *wasted* ten years of my life, trying to please your stuck-up ass. You think you're so much better than me, don't you? Too good for me? *You're not*," he spat. "You're just a barren, aging, mid-rate designer, using your body to keep a job. How long you think this one will last, huh? You'll be too old and used up for it to work again, won't you?"

The female officer snatched him by the collar. "Okay, that's eno—"

"No," I interrupted, inhaling a deep breath through my nose. "Let him get it all out."

"You know that's the only reason he wants you, right?" Walter continued. "You're just a piece of ass to him. *Another* piece, probably. But you don't care, right? You just latch onto someone who you think can do something for you, and *suck the life out them*, like you did to me. Soulless bitch. What happened to you, Keris? Your grandmother beat the heart out of you? That's how you can just throw me away? *Fuck you. Fuck you!*"

I ran my tongue over my dry lips. "Are you done?"

"*Fuck you!*"

"*Are. You. Finished?!*" I snapped, stepping in closer – enough that the officer raised a hand to tell me to keep my distance.

"Yes, I'm done. *Completely.* Your loss. Sterile bitch."

Again, I sucked in a deep breath, every nasty thing I could say in response to the ugliness he'd hurled at me right on the tip of my tongue.

I smiled.

"Make sure you *stay* done."

Then I turned and walked away, back into my building, ignoring the tantrum Walter launched in response to my refusal to engage. From when we were together, I knew exactly how much it enraged him, which made it so much sweeter than *anything* I could say.

"Hey Natalie," I said, turning to her in my apartment as I pulled out my phone to finally text Laken back, and see if he was coming this way. Because if not... "I think I want to go to the gun range."

She raised an eyebrow at me. "Seriously?"

"Yup," I nodded. "He said his little bullshit piece, trying to hurt me, I guess. But the things he believes... either aren't true or is shit that doesn't even – *can't* even – bother me at all. That's supposed to be it – supposed to be the end. But in case it isn't... I want to be prepared to handle this bastard."

Natalie stared at me a moment, then threw her arms around me for a hug.

"Oh sweetie. I thought you'd never ask!"

SIXTEEN

LAKEN.

My father would've *hated* this suit.

He would've complained about the one I wore to his funeral too, but he would've downright *hated* this one.

Why does it fit so close?

What's wrong with basic colors?

Where is your damn tie?

Yeah.

The subtle houndstooth pattern of the charcoal gray suit I'd chosen for this occasion would drive him fucking *nuts.*

*"A grown ass man in yellow. Where the hell you learn **that**?"*

Nevermind that the "yellow" was only an accent color – mustard-toned threads woven through the impeccably tailored suit. He would fixate on it, and pick the shit apart, and in return I would clown him for whatever sweater vest and blazer combo, or khakis and polo, or whatever my mother had dressed him in.

Damn I missed that man.

Weeks had gone by now, and my chest still ached when I talked about him. Not that I thought I would be "over it" – I had it on good authority that wasn't really... something that happened.

Time would dull the ache, but the ache never left.

I guess I just... buried the shit so deeply right off the bat with Phoenix that I never went through this phase. Not that I didn't mourn him, I just numbed myself to the reality of it in the immediate aftermath, barely even letting myself think about him.

In the long run... I think it made it hurt even worse when I finally let myself feel it.

With this loss... I guess I was spreading it out a little more.

It would be good to have some distraction now though.

I rang the bell at Keris' new place, looking around as I waited for her to come to the door. I *much* preferred this over the other spot, and not just because of the lack of traumatic memories associated with it.

This building had real security, which lowered my chances of ending up in prison if Walter Edwards knocked on her fucking door again.

I couldn't even describe the anger I felt when I heard about his visit that resulted in the damn *police* getting called. Definitely on a level I'd never experienced before. I'd been made to promise I wouldn't say shit to him at this wedding, if he even showed.

I reluctantly agreed to not *saying* anything, but that didn't mean I wasn't looking for any and every possible opportunity to trip his ass.

When the door opened and I saw Keris, for the first time in a few days, after a trip to check on my mother, my eyes went wide in surprise.

"*Goddamn,*" I muttered, stepping in and closing the door behind me as I took in her appearance.

Keris ran her hands over hips, nervously smoothing the fabric of her dress. "Do you... like it?"

She wasn't blonde anymore.

The summery tone had been replaced with an incredibly flattering dark copper, the strands straightened and cut into a short bob. It was sexy as hell, honestly, and with her in this emerald green wrap dress that perfectly hugged her curves, and lips painted an even darker copper than her hair...

"Keris... I don't know if we're going to make it to this wedding."

"*Laken, stop!*" she squealed, dodging my hands as I tried to grab her waist.

I dropped to my knees in front of her, catching her hands to keep her in place. "Baby, it's been a long time."

"It's been literal *days*."

I moved my hands to her knees, to slide under her dress, up to her thighs. "Just let me... can I just look at it?"

"Laken!"

"*Please*," I teased her, pushing the dress up her legs. For all her protesting, she didn't move as I hiked the fabric up past her hips, to pull the skimpy panties she was wearing aside. She was freshly waxed, which meant her pretty pussy was on full display, and I aimed right for it, planting my nose at the crest of her thighs to inhale.

"You said let you *look at it*," she reminded me, her hand on my head to push me back.

I hooked an arm under her thigh, easily hiking it over my shoulder to open her up to me. "The *smell it* and *taste it* were silent."

Her knees buckled as I covered her with my mouth, forcing her to catch herself on the edge of the couch behind her. She gripped it for dear life, gasping as I forced her panties further aside to make sure there was no barrier between me and her pussy.

I wanted *every* bit of what was mine.

"*Fuuuuuck!*" she groaned, as her hips rocked involuntarily, reacting to my mouth on her clit. She was so damned sweet, so damned perfect, soaking wet as I gripped handfuls of her ass to keep her where I needed her. I spread her cheeks open, tasting everything, slurping up every drop of her arousal, licking and kissing and devouring her until her thighs were vibrating against my head as she cried out my name.

I let her high-heeled feet back to the ground after she came, and she watched, panting, as I unbuckled and unzipped, freeing my dick. I thought I was pushing it, thought I'd have to beg, but she pushed herself onto the back ledge of the couch and untied her dress, showing the rest of the skimpy ass lingerie she had underneath.

Hell yes.

With no hesitation, I accepted the access she was granting, burying myself to the hilt as she hooked her legs around my hips. Her mouth fell open in a gasp, and *fuck* if I didn't feel the same way. I wasted no time starting a steady stroke, both of us watching, enthralled with the erotica visual of me plunging into her.

Fucking *art.*

I pushed in closer, closing the gap between our bodies and using one hand to tug one of her nipples. I couldn't see the jewelry through the lace but I could feel it, using it like my own personal plucking tool to drive her crazy.

Messing up her makeup would have pissed her off, so I put my mouth to her neck instead, sucking and biting as I drove into her. The neckline of the dress would cover whatever mark I left.

She felt so damned *good* – too damned good – *so damned good* that much too soon I could feel myself approaching the edge. I slipped a hand between us, pinching her clit between my forefinger and thumb with the same pressure I was giving her pierced nipple.

She came so hard, screamed so loud there was no way the whole building didn't hear her.

Fuck I wanted to stay in her all day.

Obviously though, I knew I couldn't.

I pulled out when I came so she wouldn't be leaking uncomfortably for the length of this damn wedding, then reluctantly went to clean up. She joined me in the bathroom to put herself back together, looking so good I wanted to do it all again.

But I knew this was important to her.

So instead of switching up on her, I pulled out my phone as we checked ourselves in the full-length mirror in her room. I drew her close to me, my arm draped possessively around her shoulders as I snapped a picture.

"Okay," I said, once I had it. "Now, we're ready to go."

D*amn she looks good.*
We hadn't talked yet about what had sparked Keris to make a somewhat drastic appearance change, but it certainly suited her. I didn't know if it was *just* that, or because I'd spent a few days away and just missed her, but I couldn't stop looking at her.

Couldn't stop *touching* her.

"Exactly how long do we have to stick around?" I murmured in her ear, making her giggle as my lips purposely skimmed her neck. We'd already sat through the actual ceremony and were at the reception now.

I'd much rather be eating *her* than some catered... whatever the fuck they were serving.

"At least until the first dance," she told me, in a distinctly scolding tone, even though her eyes were just as lust-filled as I felt. "Then... I'll properly welcome you back to the city."

Then she flicked her tongue at me.

Shit.

Just the thought of Keris' mouth had my dick getting hard, so I tried to focus on something else.

"Keris Bradford!" I heard, and Keris and I both turned in the direction of that annoyingly shrill voice in time to be greeted by a woman who I assumed was a former coworker. "Well, aren't you just glowing," the woman gushed, hugging Keris and giving her that fake air kiss thing that women who didn't really like each other did.

"Sheila, hey," Keris greeted enthusiastically, offering just enough energy to not be overtly rude.

Sheila, apparently, looked between me and Keris expectantly, and when Keris didn't say anything, she sucked her teeth. "Well, aren't you going to introduce me to your new man? I won't lie – I've heard a little gossip, that apparently you have a thing for your bosses," she laughed, as if a joke like that would be remotely funny to Keris.

"Spoken like a woman who couldn't bag a boss if she tried," I chuckled, offering Sheila my hand. "Laken Kimble, owner of *Night Shift*."

I laughed, again, as Sheila didn't accept my offered hand, instead letting out a huff as she scurried away, offended.

"You didn't have to do her like that," Keris scolded, playfully, as she slipped her arm through mine.

I shook my head. "The hell I didn't. Let's go dance."

We did exactly that, peppered with more socializing with Keris' former peers – much more pleasant interactions than the one with Sheila had been. When we were alone, Keris explained that Sheila had been something like a rival, but not really, because Sheila never quite managed to live up to anything Keris did.

It didn't escape my notice that Sheila had blonde hair, in damn near the same style and color as what Keris had recently left.

The catered food actually wasn't bad, and the bride and groom were cool. The groom actually owned a nightclub across town that had placed a big order with *Night Shift* – he was already low on stock, and preparing to place another, larger order, which was good as hell to hear.

I *never* got tired of good feedback, as hard as we'd worked to pull it all off.

Because I hadn't been there for the launch, this was the type of reaction I had to rely on, versus getting anything in person from that night. I still hadn't been able to bring myself to watch the footage or anything, but I was hearing nothing but good things, which made all the sacrifices over the years feel worth it.

All in all, it was a decent enough time, but all I *really* wanted to do was get the hell out of there and get back inside my woman.

"I need to use the ladies' room," she whispered to me, as soon as the toasts were over.

"You need some help? Need me to come with you?" I asked, grabbing her hand to keep her from getting away.

"Behave yourself, please."

I groaned as she slipped away, then sat back in my chair to look around.

As far as I knew, Walter's bitch ass was supposed to be in attendance, but I hadn't spotted him yet. Maybe he'd decided not to show?

No sooner than that thought slid across my mind, my gaze landed on that Sheila chick again.

Walter had his arm around her.

These are some weird motherfuckers.

I found something else to look at – started watching the bride do her customary dance with her father.

It made me a bit verklempt, honestly, but even that was better than the feelings Walter inspired – feelings I really didn't want to lean into at this wedding. Unfortunately for me though, I must have caught *his* attention. I felt eyes burning into the side of my head, and when I looked up, *of course* it was him.

I tipped my glass of champagne in his direction.

I was really, *really* trying to be cool.

But the more I thought about it, the more annoyed I got – I'd told his ass to stay the fuck away from Keris. I got up, and pushed my seat in, straightening my cuffs as I headed purposefully in his direction, fully intending to ruin his night.

"I wasn't taking too long, was I?"

Suddenly, Keris was in front of me, smiling, her eyes bright and happy. She was still buzzing from what we did before we came – I could see it in her face. And... she was having a good time.

If I fucked with Walter... I wouldn't be ruining just *his* night.

"Not at all – you ready to dance again, or are we heading out?"

Before Keris could answer, one of the bridesmaids rushed up, taking her by the arm.

"*All the unmarried ladies to the floooooor,*" the DJ called, and there was nothing I could do to save Keris from the – based on her expression – dreaded bouquet toss.

She made sure to stay as far on the margins as she could get.

Unfortunately for her... that was exactly where Keisha's toss landed.

Keris only barely actually "caught" the bouquet – it was more like an interception, before it knocked her upside the head. All the women squealed like it was the most exciting thing in the world, but Keris looked like she wanted to sink into the floor – a fact I teased her about as soon as she came back to me, with the bouquet in her hand.

"Is this a hint I should be taking, Ms. Bradford? Keris Kimble *does* sound pretty good."

She rolled her eyes. "Do *not* push your luck. I haven't run screaming in the other direction yet – that's gonna have to be good enough for now."

Laughing, I pulled her into my side as we headed for the exit – passing directly by Walter, who couldn't stop staring at us as we approached.

I *really* did intend to just walk past his ass and go about my own business, but as soon as we were in earshot, he started muttering shit.

I was gonna be cool, but then I heard the word *"slut"*.

I stopped, looking him dead in his face. "What was that, Walt? Do you have something you need to say?" I asked, stepping in front of Keris to make sure I was between them. "You don't have to lower your voice – you can say what you need to say out loud."

"This is a civilized event," he said. "Not the place for the kind of *discussions* you like to have."

"Then keep your fucking mouth shut when I walk past, and there won't be a problem, will there?"

I said that and then kept it moving at Keris' urging.

"Can't believe the desperate slut brought that brute in here."

This time when I stopped, I took a moment to glance at Keris, who gave me a barely perceptible nod.

Or maybe I imagined that.

Either way, I turned around and socked Walter right in his fucking mouth, then shrugged at the security that came rushing my way.

Completely worth it.

"I really should be mad at your ass, you know?" Keris said. Despite those harsh words, her mannerisms were completely gentle as she pressed an ice-cold bottle of beer to my sore knuckles and slid another in front of me on the bar.

"You'll never convince me to not defend your honor," I told her. "Not when he decided to pull that shit right in my face."

"You could've gone to jail."

I scoffed. "Those rent-a-cops weren't gonna do anything."

"If the *real* cops had come."

"But they didn't."

"They *could've*," she insisted, cupping my chin in her hand, her delicate fingers burrowing into my facial hair. "But... you did get him pretty good. And he totally deserved it," she admitted, letting a smile slip onto that pretty ass face. The darker hair made her features even more striking, especially now that her wedding makeup was gone, and she was fresh-faced. Her velvety soft lips pouted as her fingers brushed my hand. "I still don't like it though."

I shrugged. "You're nobler than me. When motherfuckers go low, I'm getting right down there with their asses. You stay up here on the high road to patch me up when I'm done."

She laughed, shaking her head as she turned her gaze around the bar. It was a Saturday night, loud and crowded – exactly the way I liked it.

"You know I thought this was gonna be like... a dive bar? When I first decided I was coming here. I wasn't expecting like, a whole experience."

I chuckled. "Baby, that is probably the understatement of your life."

"That... is very accurate. Who knew the bartender I intended to screw and never see again would end up being... my wedding date tonight?"

"Damn, that's all I get?" I asked, finally picking up the beer she'd given me and taking a long swig.

She looked back at me with a wicked gleam in her eyes, and a sexy grin. "What would you prefer to be called?"

"Your man," I countered immediately, grabbing her thigh and squeezing against the thin fabric of her leggings. "You're my woman, so it's only appropriate, no?"

Her head tipped to the side. "I *am* your woman? Says who?"

"Says me." I leaned into her, growling the words in her ear. "You got a problem with it?"

She pulled her bottom lip between her teeth, trying to suppress a smile as she shook her head. "Nah. Not at all."

"That's what I thought."

She did a whole lot of giggling and squirming, but didn't move away as I kissed her neck.

"Well this is just *insanely* cozy, isn't it?"

The sound of Natalie's – Keris' best friend, and the only event planner *Night Shift* would ever use for any damn thing moving forward – voice made me pull back on my public display of affection, but just a little.

"Tell her how good we look together, Natalie," I urged, nudging Keris' shoulder.

"Oh y'all are adorable," she immediately gushed. "That picture of you two on the *Night Shift* Instagram account, with that caption?" she kissed her fingers. "Literal perfection."

"Wait, what picture?" Keris asked, eyes wide as she went into the pocket of her sweatshirt for her phone.

Natalie and I exchanged a look while we waited for her reaction.

I chuckled when Natalie mimed a choking gesture as she mouthed, *"she's gonna kill you."*

A moment later, Keris looked up, completely unamused as she pinned me with a disapproving gaze. *"The (second) First Lady of Night Shift looks good as hell, doesn't she? May be time to craft a new brew. She has me feeling very... inspired,"* she read aloud. "Seriously, Laken?"

"It's *sweet*, Keris!" Natalie argued on my behalf. "Hashtag, Team Laken."

Keris sucked her teeth. "You're not supposed to be on his side, heifer! What are you doing here anyway?"

Natalie beamed, tossing a handful of her waist-length braids across her shoulder. "Well... a certain handsome bartender asked me to come have a drink, and I have decided to take him up on the offer," she told us, with a pointed look at Cal behind the bar.

He looked up from fixing drinks, noticing that she was there and breaking into a big ass grin himself. "Natalie, you came!"

"Hopefully you'll be having the same revelation again later tonight too," Natalie quipped, winking at Cal, whose eyes got big as fuck before he stammered something unintelligible and went off to make more drinks.

"Oh, I am going to have *such fun* with this one," Natalie laughed, until Keris poked her in the shoulder.

"Nat, he is a *baby*," Keris insisted.

"Calvin is twenty-eight years old," I spoke up, coming to Natalie's aid... since she was *hashtag, Team Laken* and all.

"See?" Natalie asked. "And I'm thirty-seven. Meaning everybody involved is old enough for you to mind your business, and *no*, I do not care to be reminded about my hypocritical commentary on any age gaps for relationships you might have had in the past," she added, prompting an eye roll from Keris.

"*Only* because I know you're going to give that boy the time of his life do I not have any further complaints," Keris said, and Natalie grinned.

"*Thaaanks* friend. Oh my *God*," she shrieked, suddenly. "Laken, what happened to your hand?!"

"He thinks he's Princeton Lattimore is what happened to his hand," Keris answered, before I could speak up. "He *punched* Walter. A civil suit is probably coming."

Natalie turned to me with a grin. "*My man*," she said, raising her hand for me to slap with mine as I laughed. "Keris always wants to be on this *higher ground* shit, and I keep trying to tell her violence is the only answer with some folks."

"See – I *knew* you were my kinda people," I told her, and Keris blew out a big sigh.

"Don't you have some young dick to ride?" she asked Natalie, who nodded.

"As a matter of fact, I do. Let me have him get me drunk for free first though. You didn't hear that," she told me.

"Hear what?" I asked, shaking my head as she shot finger guns in my direction before she headed to the end of the bar where Cal had retreated. "Natalie is... very different from you," I observed, out loud. "Not bad, at all – just different."

Keris grinned. "I *adore* her. We met in college, and she has just been... a beam of light for me ever since. Made me believe in humanity again. Probably saved my life, honestly. She actually found my therapist for me."

"Well, if she did all that for you, she's forever good in my book too then," I told her, dropping a hand to squeeze her thigh again. "You ready to get out of here?"

"You haven't even finished your beer."

"I'll take it with me."

She laughed. "Wow, why are you suddenly in such a hurry to leave?" she asked.

I leaned in, putting my mouth right up to her ear. "Because... fuck this beer. I miss the taste of *you* in my mouth, *First Lady*."

She bit her lip again, turning to me with lowered eyelids. "In that case... come on upstairs, *Mr. President*. Cause the feeling is mutual."

SEVENTEEN

KERIS

"Do you realize you haven't stopped smiling since you sat down?"

I raised an eyebrow at Dr. Alexander's assessment, immediately schooling my features into... anything else.

"Really?" I asked, and she laughed at me, which was... well deserved.

I was being ridiculous.

"Yes, *really*," she answered, with a deep, contented sigh. "Don't get me wrong, I *do* think you should continue a healthy dialogue with a therapist, whether it's me or someone else. It's an excellent way to take care of yourself. But with that said... you are a *remarkably* different woman from the one I first met all those years ago. Hell... you're different from even two months ago. And based on that smile, I bet I can guess why."

My eyes widened. "Am I *really* just out here cheesing without realizing?"

"*Cheesing*, no. It's subtle. Written all over your face, and in your eyes. You're *happy*, Keris. And it really is okay to be that."

I shook my head. "I know, it's just... would you be terribly disappointed if I admitted I was still a little scared? Like... way in the back of my mind?"

"I would be very confused if you weren't," she countered. "Yes, I've been preaching to you about living in the moment, and embracing the positive, but it's not a destination. You haven't *arrived*. This is a journey you will be on constantly. Sometimes you may have to stop and fuel up. And... it's very common to be afraid of getting lost or blowing out a tire. These bad things, these hindrances... they're very possible. But they aren't *probable*, and they certainly aren't inevitable."

"I hear you," I told her, with a deep breath of my own. "I just never would've imagined this as my life. You just said it a minute ago, so I *know* you remember what I was struggling with when I first came to you."

She nodded. "I do. Punishment. An unexpected pregnancy, and sudden, traumatic loss. You thought God was punishing you, because your grandmother had conditioned you into believing sex was something to castigate."

"Right. You asked me, "*How are you so sure it's punishment, versus a lesson in compassion, or spiritual maturation, or character development?*" and I swear I don't think I slept for days."

She laughed. "Well, I'm sorry for making you lose sleep, but I stand by those words. If you're a believer, you believe it's all in His hands, that He knows and guides your path. Why on earth would you decide *you* understand or know His motives, without even attempting to ask? And when you *do* ask, are you really speaking to God if you're – ultimately - met with anything other than grace?"

"In *one* conversation... you blew all my Grandmother's bullshit right out of the water. I made myself unlearn everything," I mused.

"And how are you doing with that?" Dr. Alexander asked.

"Really well, I think. Being back in that apartment, sometimes it did trigger things for me, but I feel like everything else that was going on kept me from drifting too deep back into all that. There were definite vestiges of the trauma, but now that I'm in my new place... I'm good. And I don't feel like anybody is frowning down on me after sex."

"That's how you felt in her home?"

I nodded. "Yes. Like... residual guilt, or something, even though I'm a grown-ass woman, who is *not* ashamed that I *love* sex... with the right person."

Her head tipped to the side. "We'll come back to *the right person*, but I'm thrilled to hear you've been able to enjoy your healthy sexual appetite. It's not an easy thing to move past the sort of conditioned guilt you had stamped on you."

"Well... as crazy as this might sound, I think the years with Walter may have helped with that. Spending years and years having... very mediocre sex, it was just kinda like... well there's no way I'm supposed to feel guilty for *that*," I laughed. "But then it was like, well, if it's not good enough to feel bad about after, why exactly am I even doing it? So, *all* of it sort of faded to the background, for me. But then it all culminated in this non-consensual encounter that was just so shrouded in its own bullshit that I don't think there was room for the other stuff. I never found myself feeling like it was punishment for my actions. More like punishment for my *inaction*. It never would've happened if I hadn't been complacent and had already ended the relationship."

Dr. Alexander had her hand propped on her chin as she listened to me. "That's fair," she conceded. "But also, not something to dwell on, I wouldn't think."

"I absolutely agree. But going from *that* encounter I didn't want, to months and months later having this experience I was willing to forget all my scruples for... it's just a transition I'm really glad I managed to make."

"Because you don't think you and Laken would be together, if you hadn't agreed to sex that night?"

"I think Laken and I were always going to end up together, one way or another."

Dr. Alexander raised an eyebrow. "That's a marked difference from declaring that all his *fate* and *kismet* talk was ridiculous."

"Oh, I still think it's ridiculous," I laughed. "I just also think... life is a little ridiculous sometimes. I feel like a whole year's worth of it has happened in the last few months. New relationship, new job, new place, new *hair*. Everything is different."

"And how does it feel?"

I closed my eyes, considering the question. "It... feels great. My own space that I chose and decorated myself, in a neighborhood I love. My job... I used to always say, *I'm not a marketing girl, I just make stuff look good.* But at *Night Shift*, I *am* a marketing girl, and I love it. If it had just ended up being graphics, I'd be bored by now, but because I was really accepted into the culture of the company, and considered part of the *team*, I've been able to cultivate my role, and provide value in a way that contributes to *Night Shift*, yes, but it also gives me a whole new experience – and title – I can take with me if I ever leave. Which I... can't even imagine at this point."

"So you're fully integrated?"

"I feel like I am."

"Into a... family?"

I pushed out a deep sigh and laughed. "I had not really thought about it that way, but... yes. I feel like I'm part of a family, and not just with *Night Shift* either. The Kimbles have really embraced me. But you know... that's really a catch-22."

"How so?"

"Well, I *love* that they so obviously care for me, but... I've ended up caring for *them*, too. And it's a weird space to be in, *caring* for all these people, after... only really caring about Natalie, for so long. You remember I was so proud of myself, for not being jealous of Laken's ex-wife, of her presence, her continued connection to Laken, all that?"

Dr. Alexander nodded. "Yes, I'm proud of you for that too."

I scoffed. "Wait until you hear this though – I may not be jealous of Emil when it comes to *him*, but when it comes to his *mother?* It's an ache like I've never felt before."

"Does his mother not like you?"

I shook my head. "No, it's not that at all – I think his mother *adores* me. She just... she still adores Emil too, and Emil... is having a baby. What would've been her first grandbaby, if Emil and Laken were still together. I've personally accepted my infertility, and it's not something that's an issue for Laken either, but I can tell it bothers her."

"Which is... selfish. You understand that, right?"

"I do," I agreed. "But I also get it. Especially with her having lost her husband, you know. She just wants family."

"And you have a real soft spot for that, because of your history."

"True."

She leaned toward me in her chair. "Empathy is a great quality to have, Keris. But I want to caution you not to let it interfere with healthy boundaries. It's okay to not have those conversations with her, if they leave you feeling inadequate, or like you're being compared to someone who isn't even part of the family picture any longer. Yes, you're right – it's completely understandable that she desires grandchildren, that she still likes her son's ex-wife, all that. It's *not* okay to make *you* feel bad about those things though. Okay?"

"Okay," I nodded, knowing she was right.

"Good. Now, let's go back to this *right person*," she declared, smiling. "We've talked about the new job, the new place. You're fitting into the family well, and the new hair is *amazing*. Now... let's talk about Laken."

Instantly, I could feel a smile creeping across my lips, despite my attempts to suppress it.

"Laken is great," I said, brushing my hair back from my face. "He is... hardworking, and sexy, and insanely thoughtful, and amazing in bed, and... arrogant, and bossy, and stubborn, and I... love it. I love *all* of it. I love *him*," I admitted for the first time, even to myself.

"You *love* him?"

"I do."

"And the feeling is mutual?"

I smiled. "Yes. Neither of us has said it, but... isn't that honestly the *least* of ways to express something like that?"

Dr. Alexander nodded. "I agree. Love is so much more than those... insufficient words. But the words are important too. Why haven't you said it?"

"I think I might have *just* realized it," I laughed. "Like just then, when I said it to you. I mean... I have put my entire self on the line to make sure he's okay, and help make him happy, because he does so much, for so many people, and he works so hard. I just... I'm in awe, of him. And as for why *he* hasn't said it.... My best guess is that he probably thinks *I* think it's too soon, and he doesn't want to scare me away."

"Are you giving him a reason to believe he should be afraid of scaring you off?"

"I don't think I have, not lately. But in the beginning, I... was skittish. I don't blame him. But I don't need to hear the words yet - I feel it from him, in everything. Even when I'm pissing him off. *Especially* when I'm pissing him off. The lines he won't cross, the things he *won't* say to me in anger."

"Ahhh," Dr. Alexander sighed. "A partner who knows how to govern themselves, even in anger, is a beautiful thing, isn't it? A lot of times we make these exceptions for comments and actions that are borne out of emotion. Sometimes, it's warranted. But we cannot simply do and say whatever we want because of our feelings. There are lines that simply should not ever be crossed, within the bounds of interpersonal relationships. I'm glad to hear you have them, and respect them."

I laughed. "Well it's only been like four months since I *met* him, so I'm not going to pat either of us on the back quite yet. We're still... honeymooning. But I see it, and I appreciate the hell out of him for it."

"*Good*," Dr. Alexander mused, smiling again as she nodded. "I am *very* proud of you, Keris. You're not done growing, not finished learning yourself, but you're figuring it out. Keep being gentle with yourself, and keep on enjoying that good man, and that good sex, and that good job, and this great hair."

I grinned. "Yeah. I really think I will."

Once I left Dr. Alexander's office, I headed straight for *Night Shift*.

Laken was back from another trip to Louisiana, and we were supposed to be meeting for lunch. However, as soon as I walked into the bar, I noticed a face I hadn't expected.

Marlene.

"Keris, sweetheart," she gushed, extending her arms to pull me into a hug I gladly accepted. Despite what I talked about with Dr. Alexander, I really did like Marlene, and believed the feeling was mutual.

"I brought Kenny back to you," she said, gesturing at Laken, who was right behind her, seeking an embrace of his own.

"Really mama?" he scolded, still hating the little nickname I personally thought was adorable. His arms were as warm and comfortable as always, but in his face, I could see that the trip had worn on him.

It always went one way or the other – either some needed time around his family, or an unwelcome reminder of his father's absence. As far as I knew, Marlene wasn't supposed to be returning with him, so that had probably been an impromptu decision. So instead of him having the trip back to decompress and be alone with his thoughts, he'd likely spent that time comforting his mother.

"Why don't you and I go have lunch?" I asked Marlene, purposely leaving Laken out of the equation. I wasn't looking at him, but I could practically feel the relief emanating from him when Marlene gave an enthusiastic *yes* to my invitation.

He gave me an appreciative smile over his mother's head, and I shot him a wink before she and I headed out. If he needed a break, I was more than willing to give it.

Maybe a little selfishly.

Something I'd forgotten to bring up with Dr. Alexander was my concern that once he reached a period of more diluted grief, Laken would get frustrated with how much time I enjoyed spending alone. As much as I enjoyed him, enjoyed Marlene, enjoyed Lark, enjoyed the whole *Night Shift* team, it was still my natural inclination to be alone. I *enjoyed* spending time with myself.

For now it worked out, because there were times when Laken just wanted to be by himself – in those moments when he was just... deeply feeling the loss of his father.

I created space for him to be comfortable telling me so, and part of what made that easy was because I liked being alone anyway. It made our moments together even better.

I just hoped I'd be able to get the same space when the time came where *he* didn't need it as much anymore.

Of course, there was also the chance that by the time he didn't need it as much, *I* wouldn't even want it.

Already, so much about me had changed, so many things I'd accepted as truths simply didn't exist anymore. The way my life had gone, especially the events just before Laken and I met, had forced me to build these walls around myself. And seemingly without much effort... Laken had simply knocked them right down.

———

"Hello?" I muttered groggily into my cell phone, eyes still closed. When the ringing woke me up, I'd just fumbled for it in the dark, my thumb naturally, knowingly moving into the right position to swipe the screen and connect the call.

"You weren't asleep were you?" Laken's voice rumbled over the line.

"Yeah, actually."

"It's only like ten at night."

"Yeah, and your mother had me drinking pitchers of margaritas at lunch like it was water. That lady has some kinda liquor tolerance."

"Oh damn," he laughed. "I should have warned you."

"Yes, you should've. What's up?" I asked, finally sitting up in the dark. "I called after I dropped Marlene at the hotel."

"I was occupied, sweetheart. My bad," he apologized, unnecessarily. "Come open your front door."

I groaned, wishing I'd already gotten over myself enough to just give him a damn key, so I wouldn't have to drag myself out of bed. I got up though, opening the door to an obviously exhausted Laken.

"Why do you smell like a distillery?" I asked, covering my nose. "Have you been drinking?"

He chuckled, pulling me into a hug. "Nah, I wish. Once you left with Mama, I finally made myself get those bourbon barrels cleaned and ready for use. They should be good to go in a few days."

"Did you come straight here?" I asked, wiggling out of his hold.

"I actually showered first, but the smell was pretty strong. I was tempted to put on a mask," he told me, from my kitchen, where he was undoubtedly grabbing himself a *No Angel*, the brew I always kept in stock for myself.

When he reappeared, I raised an eyebrow at him. "Can I get back in bed now?"

Instead of answering, he walked back to the door to kick off his shoes, then approached me, wrapping an arm around my waist to pull me against him.

"Thank you, for earlier," he murmured, then pressed his lips to mine, wasting no time in taking it further by slipping his tongue into my mouth. It was a welcomed invasion, sweet and spicy thanks to the beer, and just... the taste of *him*.

"You're welcome," I told him, when he finally pulled back. "Did it help?"

"Yes."

"Good."

He finished off the beer as we walked through my bedroom door. He left the empty bottle on the nightstand so he could strip down to his boxers before he pulled me into the bed with him.

I didn't think we'd go very far.

He kept me close to him, with deep, slow kisses that had me ready to rip his boxers off, but I contained myself. I almost cried with relief when his hand crept between us, under the waistband of my panties and between my legs, teasing and flicking and caressing, but refusing to make me cum.

I was on the verge of screaming at him in frustration until he rolled over onto his back, pushing his boxers down. When his dick sprang free, I didn't need a single word of instruction.

My mouth was already on him.

The spicy-clean scent of his body wash clung to his skin, blending with his natural aroma to act like some kind of aphrodisiac, spurring me along. I tried my damndest to swallow him whole, ignoring the urge to gag. I took all of him in, relishing the feeling of him in my throat, and his reaction to it all. His big hands dug into my hair underneath my silk bonnet, gently guiding me up and down as I sucked, keeping my curls out of the way so he could see my face.

He always wanted to see everything, so I wanted that too, making a big production of it until his hands started gripping harder, his hips bucking forward to get deeper. And when he came, I made sure he saw himself on my lips and tongue before I swallowed it.

Then I rid myself of the nightgown and climbed on top of him. Got rid of the bonnet too – on the nightstand, so I wouldn't have to search for it later.

Laken's hands went to my hips, pulling me onto his dick hard enough to make me gasp, and keeping me there, stretching and throbbing until he finally set me free to start moving.

God, he felt good.

He always did, but it was still a revelation every time, and it seemed as if the feeling were mutual for him. Laken wasn't shy about moaning with me, grunting and groaning and grimacing, whatever. He *wanted* me to know it was good for him.

I whimpered when his hands moved from my hips to my breasts, to pull at the rings piercing my nipples. Tiny platinum hoops with his name micro-engraved in them, a possessive ass gift I'd spent all night "thanking" him for.

I hadn't known until that exact moment, that I *loved* shit like that.

And I loved when he pulled at them, tugging until he got a whine of pain mingled with pleasure out me. The harder he tugged, the harder I rode, our sweat-dampened skin slapping together, merging with our utterances of pleasure to fill the silence in the room.

I shifted my position to put my knees a little further back so I could grind on him, creating friction against my clit. He released one of my nipples, grabbing the back of my neck to pull my face down to his, damn near suffocating me with a kiss as I came.

My whole body shook as he took over the work of pumping into me, creating wave after wave of aftershocks until his fingers dug hard into my hips, keeping himself buried deep as he released.

Then, we breathed.

"Would it be weird if I named it after him?"

Laken and I were up on the viewing platform, using the height as a perfect vantage point to watch as the BBC distributed the latest batch of *Rebirth* into the bourbon barrels, instead of the usual kegs – or bottles.

They, and Laken, had explained to me in painstaking detail both times, how barrel-aging the beer wasn't new, but was still unconventional, and could be hit or miss. If it went like they wanted it to go, all the great qualities that made *Rebirth* a crowd favorite would remain, while also picking up the subtle sweetness of the bourbon, an oaky aroma from the barrels, and a deep verbena flavor, if they were patient.

Laken was.

I'd heard the long-rolling argument, about cracking one open after a month or so, just to see how it was going, but Laken refused – maybe a holdover from his roots in bourbon-making. The process took time, and confidence, and a willingness to fuck up and learn from the mistake, all of which Laken had.

So, they would wait.

"*No guts, no glory,*" he'd said.

"I think that would be a beautiful tribute to your father," I answered, still watching the barreling process. "The beer you created for your brother, aged into something entirely new, for your father. You tell me the exact name, and I'll start working on the label," I told him, turning to meet his gaze.

Only, he wasn't there anymore.

Not at just above my eye level, like usual.

He was... lower.

Down on one knee.

"Laken, *please* don't—"

"*Hush*, woman," he demanded, pulling a ring from his pocket – a ring that made me laugh, as tears filled my eyes.

A diamond-encrusted hop.

"Just listen to me, okay?"

I nodded. "Okay."

"I *love* you, Keris. I don't give a shit if you think that's... whatever you might think it is."

I shook my head. "I don't. I love you too."

"You're not supposed to be talking," he scolded, grabbing my hand. His eyes were glossy too, but he started laughing as people in the brewhouse noticed what was happening and started playfully heckling us. He raised my hand to his mouth, kissing the backs of my fingers. "But that is... relieving to hear."

"He gone cry in the car if you don't say yes!" Ellis yelled.

"Shut the fuck up!" Laken yelled back, grinning as he turned back to me. "This ring is... a gift, okay? Beer requires hops, and I... require you, Keris. That's what this represents," he said, slipping it onto my finger. "That's all, for now. But in a year – when we open those barrels, that have taken so much faith, and patience, and dedication... I'm gonna ask you a different question. Offer you a different ring. I'm telling you now, so you'll have time to process."

"Yes."

Laken's eyebrows went up. "Wait, what?"

I shook my head. "Laken... the only reason you aren't asking your real question now, is because you think I'm afraid. And I am, for sure. But you know what?" I asked, blinking back tears. "No guts... no glory, right? So how about you ask me your *real* question, I say yes, and... we serve... *Henry's Renaissance* at our wedding?"

Laken was on his feet before I could even react, grabbing my face. Applause erupted around the brewhouse as he kissed me, then pulled back to murmur against my lips. "I love you, Keris Bradford. Will you marry me?"

"Yes," I told him, again, blinking back tears. "And I look forward to whatever happens while we wait."

the end.

ABOUT THE AUTHOR

Christina C. Jones is a modern romance novelist who has penned many love stories. She has earned a reputation as a storyteller who seamlessly weaves the complexities of modern life into captivating tales of black romance.

ALSO BY CHRISTINA C JONES

Wonder (Post-Apocalyptic)

Love and Other Things

Haunted (paranormal)

Coveted

Mine Tonight (erotica)

The Love Sisters

I Think I Might Love You

I Think I Might Need You

I Think I Might Want You

Sugar Valley

The Culmination Of Everything

Equilibrium

Love Notes

Grow Something

In Tandem

Five Start Enterprises

Anonymous Acts

More Than a Hashtag

Relationship Goals

High Stakes

Ante Up

King of Hearts

Deuces Wild

Sweet Heat

Hints of Spice (Highlight Reel spinoff)

A Dash of Heat

A Touch of Sugar

Truth, Lies, and Consequences

The Truth – His Side, Her Side, And the Truth About Falling In Love

The Lies – The Lies We Tell About Life, Love, and Everything in Between

Friends & Lovers:

Finding Forever

Chasing Commitment

Strictly Professional:

Strictly Professional

Unfinished Business

Serendipitous Love:

A Crazy Little Thing Called Love

Didn't Mean To Love You

Fall In Love Again

The Way Love Goes

Love You Forever

Something Like Love

Trouble:

The Trouble With Love

The Trouble With Us

The Right Kind Of Trouble

If You Can (Romantic Suspense):

Catch Me If You Can

Release Me If You Can

Save Me If You Can

Inevitable Love:

Inevitable Conclusions

Inevitable Seductions

Inevitable Addiction

The Wright Brothers:

Getting Schooled – Jason & Reese

Pulling Doubles – Joseph & Devyn

Bending The Rules – Justin & Toni

Connecticut Kings:

CK #1 Love in the Red Zone – Love Belvin

CK #2 Love on the Highlight Reel

CK #3 – Determining Possession

CK #4 – End Zone Love – Love Belvin

CK#5 – Love's Ineligible Receiver – Love Belvin

CK # 6 - Pass Interference

CPSIA information can be obtained
at www.ICGtesting.com
Printed in the USA
LVHW100606170522
718911LV00005B/243

9 781698 567969